Crosscurrents / Modern Critiques Third Series

Edited by Jerome Klinkowitz

Robert A. Morace

The Dialogic Novels of Malcolm Bradbury and David Lodge

Southern Illinois University Press
CARBONDALE AND EDWARDSVILLE

Printed in the United States of America
Edited by Mara Lou Hawse
Designed by Design for Publishing, Inc.
Production supervised by Linda Jorgensen-Buhman

92 91 90 89   4 3 2 1

Library of Congress Cataloging-in-Publication Data

Morace, Robert A.
  The dialogic novels of Malcolm Bradbury and David Lodge / Robert
A. Morace.
      p. cm.—(Crosscurrents/modern critiques. Third series)
  Bibliography: p.
  Includes index.
  ISBN 0-8093-1519-X
  1. English fiction—20th century—History and criticism.
2. Dialogue. 3. Bradbury, Malcolm, 1932– —Fictional works.
4. Lodge, David, 1935– —Fictional works. I. Title. II. Series.
PR888.D49M67 1989
823'.914'0926—dc19   88-29339
                                                                 CIP

The paper used in this publication meets the minimum requirements of
American National Standard for Information Sciences—Permanence of
Paper for Printed Library Materials, ANSI Z39.48-1984. ♾

for Neela

The truth is never pure and simple. Modern life would be very tedious if it were either, and modern literature would be a complete impossibility.

Oscar Wilde, *The Importance of Being Earnest*

It must not be forgotten, I sometimes forget, that all is a question of voices.

Samuel Beckett, *The Unnamable*

Contents

x
Contents

Crosscurrents/
Modern Critiques
Third Series

IN THE EARLY 1960s, when the Crosscurrents/Modern Critiques series was developed by Harry T. Moore, the contemporary period was still a controversial one for scholarship. Even today the elusive sense of the present dares critics to rise above mere impressionalism and to approach their subject with the same rigors of discipline expected in more traditional areas of study. As the first two series of Crosscurrents books demonstrated, critiquing contemporary culture often means that the writer must be historian, philosopher, sociologist, and bibliographer as well as literary critic, for in many cases these essential preliminary tasks are yet undone.

To the challenges that faced the initial Crosscurrents project have been added those unique to the past two decades: the disruption of conventional techniques by the great surge in innovative writing in the American 1960s just when social and political conditions were being radically transformed, the new worldwide interest in the Magic Realism of South American novelists, the startling experiments of textual and aural poetry from Europe, the emergence of Third World authors, the rising cause of feminism in life and literature, and, most dramatically, the introduction of Continental theory into the previously staid world of Anglo-American literary scholarship. These transformations demand that many traditional treatments be rethought, and part of the new responsibility for Crosscurrents will be to provide such studies.

Contributions to Crosscurrents/Modern Critiques/Third Series will be distinguished by their fresh approaches to established topics and by their opening up of new territories for discourse. When a single author is studied, we hope to present the first book on his or her work or to explore a previously untreated aspect based on new research. Writers who have been critiqued well elsewhere will be studied in comparison with lesser-known figures, sometimes from other cultures, in an effort to broaden our base of understanding. Critical and theoretical works by leading novelists, poets, and dramatists will have a home in Crosscurrents/Modern Critiques/Third Series, as will sampler-introductions to the best in new Americanist criticism written abroad.

The excitement of contemporary studies is that all of its critical practitioners and most of their subjects are alive and working at the same time. One work influences another, bringing to the field a spirit of competition and cooperation that reaches an intensity rarely found in other disciplines. Above all, this third series of Crosscurrents/Modern Critiques will be collegial—a mutual interest in the present moment that can be shared by writer, subject, and reader alike.

Jerome Klinkowitz

Preface

HOW FAR CAN the contemporary novelist go in a small world in which the rate of exchange is no longer fixed, a world in which narrative verities have turned into narrative possibilities? I take this question, which in a world of folio volumes I might also take as my title, from five works—three of fiction, two of criticism—by Malcolm Bradbury and David Lodge. The conflation is significant for the simple reason that their works are themselves conflations—or more accurately dialogues—involving various and often conflicting views, styles, and forms which when taken together form a map of the contemporary novel and, more importantly, an alternative to the balkanization that has characterized the critical study of contemporary fiction during the past decade. Beginning as realists, as novelists of manners, as writers of campus novels, Bradbury and Lodge soon began to explore, both in their fiction and in their criticism, the possibilities as well as the limitations of realistic writing. They discovered in their situation as novelists working simultaneously within and against the English literary tradition a situation analogous to that of the postwar liberal humanist who had previously served as the focus of the Anglo-liberal novel.

As novelists of manners, Bradbury and Lodge deal with the same general literary types: educated middle- or lower middle-class characters stumbling through the postwar period of change and uncertainty and stress. More specifically, Bradbury deals with the lives of befuddled academics caught midway between two worlds: old England and new, home and abroad. Lodge places his characters, many of whom are also academics, in a double bind, for they are also Catholics living through or immediately before or after the liberating yet nonetheless disconcerting upheavals of Vatican II. The conflicts these characters face are the stuff of realist fiction and could easily find their way into novels by Forster or Amis or Greene. Bradbury and Lodge, however, are not only the heirs of the English literary tradition; they are as well literary critics who have demonstrated a keen interest in (and a certain skepticism about) recent critical theories. This interest and, equally important, the debate carried on by and between Bradbury and Lodge over the nature and purpose of both fiction and criticism have found their way into the novels—novels which, even as they have become increasingly innovative and postmodern in form and technique, have remained rooted, precariously and self-consciously, in the realist tradition. As a result, they have proven to be more accessible than the more overtly and more rigorously programmatic academic fictions of such (largely unread) innovators as Walter Abish, Raymond Federman, and Ronald Sukenick (who, of course, have not had the benefit of working within an already established tradition of academic fiction—in England, the popular "campus novel" subgenre). In Bradbury and Lodge, the realistic conflicts between civilian and military, English and American, pre- and post-Vatican II gradually give way to an exploration of the semiotics behind such conflicts. As one character in Lodge's *How Far Can You Go?* says, without fully understanding what his words imply, " 'I think you could say that the crisis in the Church today is a crisis of language.' "

However, for Bradbury and Lodge the world, both in and out of the novel, is not merely a playing field of arbitrary and ultimately meaningless signifiers. The point for the Catholic Lodge and for the liberal humanist Bradbury is not to go as far as one can but, rather, to pose the question of how far one can, or should, go so as not to overstep no longer clearly identifiable bounds that are as much ethical and moral in import as they are semiotic in structure. Their most distinctly innovative works—Bradbury's *The History Man* and *Rates of Exchange*; Lodge's *Changing Places, How Far Can You Go?*, and *Small World*—are best approached not simply as departures from the realism of the earlier novels but as variations on and extensions of the authors' central narrative and cultural concerns. Even as their later fictions have exhibited a greater degree of what Jerome Klinkowitz has called self-apparency, even as they have increasingly undermined naive realism and the political and philosophical assumptions upon which such realism rests, these works have also tended, cautiously and with reservations, to validate certain of these same assumptions. Far from resulting in literary conservatism (the usual charge leveled against postwar English fiction), this unwillingness to abandon realism altogether, coupled with the "clerkly skepticism" (Frank Kermode's phrase) fostered by their work as literary critics, has caused Bradbury and Lodge to write novels that are not only more accessible but, more importantly, far more open-ended than the doggedly indeterminate fictions of many contemporary writers.

It is this nonprogrammatic open-endedness that has led me to approach the fiction of Bradbury and Lodge through Mikhail Bakhtin's theory of dialogism. I do not intend to use the novels in order to illustrate, or prove, the viability of Bakhtin's theory or to apply it rigorously, which is to say reductively. Dialogism is not a method but a tendency vital to the development of the novel in general and to the novels of Bradbury and Lodge in particular. As Bakhtin has convincingly demonstrated, the history of the novel is the history "of the deepening of its dialogic essence." More specifically, his theory sensitizes us to what I believe is a necessary ambivalence, or openness, in Bradbury's and Lodge's work. It is an ambivalence which manifests itself in their desire to maintain the Anglo-liberal tradition (other than as an anachronism, that is) in the face of and, paradoxically, in conjunction with the postliberal and (by the 1970s) the postmodern challenges to that tradition and all it implies about art and man. Dialogism helps us to better understand the precise character of Bradbury's and Lodge's efforts to "renegotiate" the terms upon which the Anglo-liberal aesthetic can be strengthened by the very forces which threaten it. Admittedly, I find Bakhtin's theory appropriate for still another reason. Dialogism leads, as if inevitably, to that postmodern self-apparency of language to which the careers of Bradbury and Lodge also, as if inevitably, tend. Yet in Bakhtin's theory as in Bradbury's and Lodge's novels, this tendency exists only in dialogic tension with another and equally strong force, the belief that language is, as Bakhtin's biographers have noted, "important only because of its capacity to express values . . . to mean something" (Clark and Holquist 187). My plan is to approach Bradbury and Lodge via Bakhtin in order to identify certain of the ways in which language and values simultaneously compete with and support one another. My hope is that this effort will generate additional interest in their fiction and lead future critics to discuss it using other, equally valid approaches.

According to Bakhtin, novelistic dialogism is opposed not only to monologic dogma but to literary relativism as well. Dialogue involves a play of voices, no one of which emerges as final or superior; the play is serious, however, for its goal is a truth which, although elusive, even unattainable, does exist. In the dialogic novel, not even the narrator/author enjoys privileged status; he too takes part in the dialogic interplay, the ultimately open-ended give and take of voices and views.

Freed of monologic, or univocal, meaning, the dialogic novel inevitably leads to the extreme of deconstructionist intertextuality (Julia Kristeva's synonym for Bakhtin's dialogism). In theory, intertextuality leads to the infinite and uncontrollable play of meanings; in practice, as Jonathan Culler has pointed out, it often degenerates into the study of specific, identifiable sources. I propose to approach Bradbury and Lodge in dialogic fashion, adapting Bakhtin's theory of the dialogic imagination rather than mechanically applying it and, concerning intertextuality, to steer a middle course, to limit pragmatically—rather than to multiply deconstructively—the boundaries of intertextual play. My primary concern will be with the play of voices—character's, author-narrator's, etc.—within a text. However, each of these novelists is also a critic, and as critics each has taken the other to task; as novelists, critics, and close friends (even collaborators), they have responded to and often directed the other's literary efforts in certain directions; and, as well, each is engaged in an overt dialogue with the literary tradition and with the current "situation of the novel." Given all these matters and, too, the fact that each has found America and its literature, particularly its postmodern fiction, especially attractive, it is necessary to consider the dialogic nature of their fiction in broader terms. For the writings of Bradbury and Lodge not only raise the questions of how far the characters can go and how far the novelist can go, they also raise the question of how far the critic can go as he attempts to negotiate between, on the one hand, the didactic earnestness of Anglo-American practical criticism, with its emphasis on close readings and aesthetic wholeness, and, on the other hand, the free and sophisticated but often narcissistic play of intertextuality.

Acknowledgments

AMONG THE MANY people who have had a hand—or a Bakhtinian voice—in the writing of this book, I especially wish to thank Jerry Klinkowitz, Sam Coale, Peter Siedlecki, Kay Sullivan, Richard Long, Jacqueline Lyew, Laurie Craven, Mara Lou Hawse, Piotr Parlej, Renata and Piotr Maksymowicz, Albert and Divina Rosetti, the Daemen College Faculty Research Committee, President Robert S. Marshall and the Trustees of Daemen College, the students in my magister seminars at Warsaw University (Zosia Lesinska, Basia Sciborowska, Hanka Michalska, Krystyna Mazur, and Magda Zaborowska in particular), and especially and always my parents, my son, Jason, and my wife, Neela, to whom this work is dedicated.

1

Critical Assumptions

" 'DO YOU KNOW also a campus writer Brodge ... who writes *Changing Westward?*' " asks a character in Malcolm Bradbury's most recent novel, *Rates of Exchange*. " 'I think he is very funny but sometimes his ideological position is not clear' " (268–269). The speaker's confusion is as understandable as her conflation of authors and titles is funny. It is as funny, in fact (or fiction), as Lodge's own attempt to clear the matter up in his most recent novel, *Small World*, in which two writers, one of them looking suspiciously like the real Bradbury and the other like the real Lodge, divide the world (of fiction) between them while having a drink at a half-factive, half-fictual meeting of the Modern Language Association. This open acknowledgment by each writer of the other's "presence" in his work points to the important symbiotic relationship that has existed between them since the early 1960s, when they were faculty members together at the University of Birmingham. Since that time they have not only appeared, in typically postmodernist fashion, in one another's works, they have collaborated in the writing of satirical revues for the English stage, have reviewed each other's books, and have acknowledged their indebtedness to one another in dedications and prefaces. More importantly, Bradbury and Lodge have carried on a long-term debate on the aims and methods of literary criticism that is of considerable interest in and of itself and, of at least equal importance, for the ways in which this debate has affected their work as writers of fiction. I am, however, less concerned with Bradbury's direct influence on Lodge's criticism, or with Lodge's direct influence on Bradbury's, than with the dialogical nature of their novels, of which their direct, identifiable influence on one another is but *a* manifestation, and not necessarily the most important or the most interesting.

Before turning to the novels, a number of preliminary tasks need to be addressed. One is to define, for the purposes of this study, Mikhail Bakhtin's theory of narrative dialogism, or, more specifically, of the dialogic novel, a theory that is, happily, becoming better and more widely known among Anglo-American critics. A second task is to identify the main currents in the criticism written by Bradbury and Lodge—the points of agreement and contention. The voices heard in their debate will be heard in their novels and therefore in the chapters which follow, often, however, in curiously angled ways. The voice of Bradbury or Lodge the critic is not necessarily (perhaps not ever) the voice of Bradbury or Lodge the novelist or that of the authorial narrator in any one of their works. It is, however, *a* voice, one which *will* be heard, with varying degrees of distinctness. And the third task to be addressed is to identify the main currents in the criticism written about Bradbury and Lodge and to attempt to situate their work as novelists in the double context of the postwar British novel and contemporary (including postmodern) fiction. As for the first of these, the discussion of Bakhtin, it is not intended as an introduction to Bakhtin's theory but instead as a selective discussion of those aspects of the theory upon which I have drawn for my discussion of that literary hydra, the "push-me-pull-you" of contemporary British fiction, Brodge, author of *Changing Westward*.

I do not exaggerate when I say that Bakhtin devoted himself to the study of the novel—to its sources, form, importance, essential character, and, above all, to its being the only truly revolutionary genre: open, fluid, formless, incomplete, protean, anti-canonic, "the genre of becoming" (*Dialogic* 22). Especially important to Bakhtin's theory and to this study of Bradbury and Lodge is Bakhtin's tracing the history of the novel back to its source in the popular laughter of folklore in general and the carnival in particular. During the carnival time, Bakhtin explains, the static and serious world of order and authority gives way, temporarily, to a chaotic but comic babble, to liberation from all rules, to lawless proliferation and renewal. Authority and orthodoxy lose their privileged places in a society suddenly given over to pluralism, leveling, and "joyful relativity" (*Problems* 107–108). The eternal dissolves, becoming the multiplicity of the present, a distinctly physical moment marked by the abandonment of authoritarian reason and the triumph of the multi-voiced and the heterodox. In literary terms, dominant style gives way to a profusion of styles, no one of which can claim authority over any of the others. The carnivalesque atmosphere that is so clearly evident in the works of Rabelais lives on in all the seriocomic genres, including and especially the English comic novel. What all the seriocomic genres have in common is (to varying degrees) the self-consciousness entirely absent from the serious genres, which tend to promote stasis and orthodoxy. This self-consciousness, which is of course one of the hallmarks of much contemporary fiction, forms the basis of Bakhtin's theory of the dialogical novel, which according to Bakhtin is at once representational and self-referential. As he explains, in the seriocomic genres, "alongside the representing word there appears the *represented* word" (*Problems* 108). In the English comic novels of Fielding, Smollett, Sterne, and Dickens, cited by Bakhtin, as well as in the more recent comic fictions of Amis, Greene, Waugh, Bradbury, and Lodge, this self-consciousness evidences itself as parody, that is to say in the author's distancing himself from the common language that he otherwise seems to be using so transparently. Such works, Bakhtin explains, have no "style" as such but instead possess a profusion of self-consciously employed styles, a paradoxical style based upon the absence of *"a normative shared language"* (*Dialogic* 308). The point here is not that some novels are wholly or partly parodic while others are not. For Bakhtin, the novel is essentially parodic; it is itself a parody of other genres as genres, a carnivalesque literary form that exposes and therefore undermines both their formal and their linguistic conventionality, as well as what that seriousness implies: authority, orthodoxy, stasis. Parody, Bakhtin contends, creates "a decrowning double" (*Problems* 127); it puts language in quotation marks and in so doing calls attention to the fact that in the novel, as in the world, "a particular language . . . is always a particular way of viewing the world" (*Dialogic* 333). Given what literary and cultural critics such as John Gardner, Gerald Graff, and Christopher Lasch have said and written during the past decade about the limitations inherent in the parodic mode, I need to add that, for Bakhtin, to parody does not mean simply to debunk. (Recall Gardner's complaint about that arch-parodist, Donald Barthelme, that his only message is better to be disillusioned than deluded.) Parody, as Bakhtin defines it, liberates, freeing language from myth and reality from language. A second, related, point needs to be made here. Bakhtin's interest in, or obsession with, linguistic dialogue was shared by most of the Russian formalists, with whom Bakhtin was for a time associated. What sets Bakhtin apart, however, is (in Michael Holquist's words) his "extraordinary sensitivity to the immense plurality of experience" (xx). Only the essentially carnivalesque and parodic novel can expose and represent this immense plurality, Dostoevsky's novels in particular. In them

Bakhtin discovered "a plurality of independent and unmerged voices and consciousnesses, a genuine polyphony of fully valid voices," as well as a fictional world as "profoundly pluralistic" as Bakhtin's conception of human life (*Problems* 6, 26).

Not surprisingly, Bakhtin believed that (as Todorov has explained) the novel has flourished chiefly during "periods of weakening central power" (Todorov 58) and that to follow the history of the novel is to trace the "deepening of its dialogic essence": "Fewer and fewer neutral, hard elements ('rock bottom truths') remain that are not drawn into dialogue. Dialogue moves into the deepest molecular and, ultimately, subatomic levels" (*Dialogic* 300). That is to say, dialogism extends not only out, drawing more and more elements into the dialogic configuration, but down as well, so that in addition to the dialogic play of voice against voice, language against language, the reader begins to discern voices within voices, languages within languages. In these "microdialogues," "all words . . . are double-voiced, and in each of them a conflict of voices takes place" (*Problems* 74). Thus we find dialogue everywhere and at all levels. There is not only the dialogic interaction between characters, of course, and between utterances, but also between words, between styles, between languages, between a character and his words and thoughts, between character(s) and author, between novel and reader, between the author and his other works, between the text and the intertext. Obviously, certain of these dialogues will be explicit in the novel, others implicit. Either way, the result is the same: "an Einsteinian universe" of "multi-voicedness," a "polyphonic novel" in which the dialogic pluralism is not a means but an end, not "the threshold to action" but "the action itself" (*Problems* 16). For Bakhtin, the dialogic novel is revolutionary and liberating, not in its overt dogmatic message but in its covert destabilizing structure. For Bakhtin, there is no appropriate ("poetic") language for the novel, no dominant voice, mood, or tone, no wholeness of character, no narrative closure, and above all no ultimate authority. Nor can there be, for as Bakhtin explains:

> Irony has entered into all the languages of modern times . . . ; it has introduced itself in all the words and all the forms. . . . Man in modern times does not declaim but he speaks, that is, he speaks within restrictions. Declamatory genres are essentially preserved as parodic or semi-parodic ingredients of the novel. . . . The uttering subjects of high declamatory genres—priests, prophets, preachers, judges, leaders, fathers-patriarchs, etc.—have left life. They have been replaced by the writer, the simple writer, who inherited their styles. . . . The author's search for a discourse that would be his own basically is part of the search for genre and style, for the position of the author. That is now the most acute problem of contemporary literature, that has led many authors to give up the genre of the novel and to replace it by montage of documents, by the description of objects; it ultimately leads them to concrete literature and, in some measure, to literature of the absurd. All of this could be defined, in a sense, as different forms of silence. These searches have led Dostoevsky to the creation of the polyphonic novel. Dostoevsky was not able to find a discourse for the monologic novel. (quoted in Todorov 102)

Bakhtin's dialogic novel is a more inclusive term for what Umberto Eco has termed the "open work" or "work in movement" that began to "emerge at the same time as the physicists' principle of complementarity." Modern art, like modern physics, is therefore doomed to incompleteness, to discontinuity, indeterminacy, and internal contradiction. Invoking Werner Heisenberg and Nils Bohr, Eco contends that the open work is ultimately relativistic (*Role* 47–66). Bakhtin, on the other hand, emphatically denies that dialogism and relativism are in any way synonymous: "both relativism and dogmatism equally exclude all argumentation, all authentic dialogue, by making it either unnecessary (relativism) or impossible (dogmatism). Polyphony as an *artistic* method lies in an entirely different plane" (*Problems* 69). Where Eco, following Peirce, finds "endless semiosis" and where Derrida, in his critique of logocentrism and the metaphysics of presence, finds (in Vincent Leitch's words) nonexistent "structural necessities" and "floating signifiers at play" (Leitch 35–36), Bakhtin posits the very real presence of an author who, although he does not manifest himself in any one of the novel's languages, does nonetheless exist "at the center of organization where all levels intersect" (*Dialogic* 49).

The dialogic novel is characterized less by deconstruction's "warring forces of signification" (Barbara Johnson's phrase) than by the less bellicose and certainly less nihilistic view that languages intersect in various ways, as in Dostoevsky's novels, where "almost no word is without its intense sideward glance at someone else's word" (*Problems* 203). When Bakhtin writes that "there are no 'neutral' words and forms" and that "contextual overtones . . . are inevitable in the word" (*Dialogic* 293), he is laying the groundwork for the problematic concept of intertextuality, as Julia Kristeva has dubbed it in her seminal essay on Bakhtin (64–91). Intertextuality is the essence of dialogism, as dialogism is the essence of that omnivorous "supergenre," the novel (Holquist xxix). And, like dialogism, intertextuality moves in two directions simultaneously: down into the text and out into the world (or worlds: social, cultural, historical, biographical, etc.). Further, intertextuality exists on two planes as well; one plane involves what is actually present in the specific work and the other what is physically absent from the text but, nonetheless, contextually present. Thus, the problematic nature of intertextuality—for as Jonathan Culler has pointed out, it is a slippery term which seems to encompass both the narcissistic wordplay of Derrida and the more or less scholarly source studies of critics, including (surprisingly) Kristeva (104–106). In his *Deconstructive Criticism: An Advanced Introduction*, Leitch distinguishes between context, which he associates with setting limits to a literary work, and intertextuality, which he claims involves the overrunning, or abolishing, of such limits (160). But this overrunning of borders is not in fact what Bakhtin had in mind when he defined the novel "as a diversity of social speech types . . . and a diversity of individual voices, artistically organized" (*Dialogic* 262–63). Bakhtin was concerned, as Wayne Booth has noted, not only with the novel's "'centrifugal' force dispersing us . . . outward into a seeming chaos," but as well with the "various 'centripetal' forces preserving us from overwhelming fluidity and variety" (Booth xxi–xxii). It is this same tension—or ambivalence—which Tony Tanner in *City of Words* (1971) has also found at the heart of the postwar American novel that characterizes the fiction of Bradbury and Lodge, writers who both as novelists and as critics have sought to extend the boundaries of contemporary British fiction while at the same time searching out ways in which the novel *as novel* (not as *text* or *ficcione*) may continue as a viable literary form.

Although reviewers and critics often seem to assume just the opposite, there is no "novel" as such, no Platonic form or Aristotelian definition capable of containing literature's most protean genre. And there is no Brodge, of course, no author of *Changing Westward*, other than as a dialogic image, the product of the reader's intertextual imagination. Similarly, there is no "Bradbury" or "Lodge" either, not in any simple sense, for these are novelists who are also critics, or alternately (the distinction is by no means trivial), critics who are also novelists. Academic fictionists, one is tempted to say, but academic fictionists with a difference, if by the term we mean writers who are generally thought to write for the academy (Barth, Pynchon, Gass, the Joyce of *Ulysses* and *Finnegans Wake*) rather than merely about the academy (Mary McCarthy's *The Groves of Academe*, Amis's *Lucky Jim*, Gardner's *Mickelsson's Ghosts*). Although as critics they have demonstrated a sympathetic interest in contemporary literary theory, and as novelists they have often made this interest a vital part of (or voice in) their novels, their work (both critical and imaginative) has remained entirely free of the hermeticism that characterizes much academic writing (again both critical and imaginative)—so much so that Lodge's most academic fiction, *Small World*, has proven to be his most popular novel as well. In sum, I think it can be said that Bradbury and Lodge, both as novelists and as critics, have been at once sympathetic towards and skeptical about both the critical and literary traditions from which they have emerged and the critical and literary situations in which they now find themselves. Moreover, as critics and novelists they have demonstrated their awareness of both the benefits and the dangers inherent in such a close, indeed virtually incestuous, relationship, and they have made amply clear that—contra Barthes, Derrida, et al.—fiction and criticism are by no means equal, that the latter plays a decidedly subordinate role. That is what they as critics say, and that is what their critical practice implies. Their fiction on the other hand strongly suggests that the relationship between criticism and imaginative writing may be far more problematic, as I will go on to explain in subsequent chapters. Here, I wish only to make a number of preliminary points, as it were, about Bradbury and Lodge as critics.

Bradbury's criticism is marked, above all, by a Jamesian expansiveness, that "openness of sympathy which Bradbury has said is the only real justification for criticism's existence" (*Possibilities* 27) and which he also associates with the novel as a genre and with liberalism as both a sociopolitical and, more especially, a literary phenomenon. Instead of emphasizing (as he says Lodge does) the novel as a "completed whole," Bradbury stresses its "imaginative growth," the "organic development" of "the evolving tale" (*What* 57; *Possibilities* 56). There is, Bradbury claims, a logic behind the writing of a novel, but it is one "for which both writer and reader are searching." Thus, for Bradbury, the novel is less a clearly definable literary form than a vista of "possibilities" (the title of his 1973 collection, subtitled "Essays on the State of the Novel"). However, in order to complete his liberal-humanist definition of the novel, Bradbury posits against these possibilities the dialogic counter-voice of authorial "obligations," "commitments," and "responsibilities." As he explains in *Possibilities*:

My point is that, while there is no single dynamic generically charac-teristic of novels, its main structural characteristics arise from its scale, narrative character, and compositional obligations; that this must be seen as a structure or action, one which involves persons and events in a closed, authorially conditioned world, in which inhere the princi-ples, values, and attitudes by which they may be ordered, judged. (291–292)

The expansiveness of Bradbury's definition of the novel (what some might object to as its looseness), like his Jamesian ap-proach to criticism, accounts in large measure for his objection to Lodge's critical practice and theory, which he judges at once "incomplete" and "too monolithic," too much preoccupied with fiction's verbal texture, too little with its evolving structure and inherent referentiality ("Language" 130). Eschewing the assumed narrowness of Lodge's linguistic analysis, or for that matter any critical method that focuses on any single feature, Bradbury calls for a "synthesizing action." He demands a criti-cism as expansive as the novel itself, which for Bradbury is of course the literary manifestation of the liberal-humanist self: unique and uncoerced, open to "contingency" rather than molded by the dictates of either an aesthetic or a political formalism (*Possibilities* 289). The novelist, Bradbury claims, is under "a double obligation": to his art and to his world, to what Bradbury (borrowing his terms from Iris Murdoch) dis-tinguishes as "form" and "contingency" (*What* 13). The diffi-culty in combining these two opposing forces is the dilemma faced by modern man in general and by the contemporary writer in particular, as Bradbury neatly summarizes in his description (or self-description?) of the main character in Bel-low's first novel, *Dangling Man*. Joseph, Bradbury writes, is "a clerkly intelligent man of humanist aspirations, struggling between outward history and inner freedom and finding that there are no adequate laws for their connection—that essential anxiety of contemporary fiction" (*Saul Bellow* 37).

To understand and to attempt to mediate between these opposing forces and ideas typifies not only Bradbury's literary theory (though theory may be too pretentious a word to use here) but his critical approach as well: his tendency towards the "comparative" and the "interdisciplinary," his desire to "relate and reconcile," his calling for an "eclectic" approach and "plural methods." It is evident, too, in his many collaborative projects, in books such as *The Social Context of Modern English Literature*, and in his evenhanded editing of *The Novel Today: Contemporary Writers on Modern Fiction* (1977), in which, during a time of noisy polemics on surfiction, moral fiction, and the like, Bradbury reprints a wide variety of opinions, a dialogue of voices: Iris Murdoch, Philip Roth, Michel Butor, Saul Bellow, John Barth, David Lodge, Frank Kermode, Graham Greene, Angus Wilson, Ivy Compton-Burnett, C. P. Snow, John Wain, Muriel Spark, John Fowles, B. S. Johnson, Philip Stevick, Gerald Graff. Although Bradbury often writes of the need for a "synthesis" of critical approaches, it is not so much a synthesis that he himself provides as "a stimulating anthology of distinct but mutually reinforcing accounts" (to borrow his description of the *Modernism* volume he edited with James McFarlane for the Pelican Guides to European Literature series, 1976). Open, sympathetic, and fair-minded, Bradbury is an eminently stimulating anthologist. That is his major strength as a critic, and, too, his major weakness, leading him to merely catenate facts, alternatives, possibilities, etc., or to generalize rather than to analyze, to assert earnestly rather than to prove analytically. (To say, as Bradbury does, that the novel's "organic development . . . is natural and instinctive as well as severely deliberate" is, as one of the dwarfs in Barthelme's *Snow White* would claim, to say nothing at all [*Possibili-*

ties 56].) This shortcoming may derive from the fact that Bradbury the critic often writes in his capacity as Bradbury the
teacher: *What Is a Novel* (1969), for example, grew out of an
undergraduate course he taught at the University of Birmingham, and *The Modern American Novel* is not (and does not
pretend to be) a critical study of its subject but, instead, a useful
introduction to it. Even more, I suspect that this shortcoming
derives from the liberal tradition that has largely shaped Bradbury's thinking, and that in his fiction he both espouses and
questions. His fiction deals with characters who must struggle,
as Bradbury himself does, with opposing desires, cultures,
values, sign systems, etc., in an effort—invariably unsuccessful—to arrive at an equable rate of exchange. In this fashion,
the weakness of Bradbury's criticism becomes, as we shall
shortly see, a major strength of his novels. In them he tests, as
well as preserves in modified form, the liberal-realist aesthetic.

Not surprisingly, Bradbury has been attracted to writers in
whom he discerns a similar interest (and ambivalence). He
judges Saul Bellow, for example, a "formally and philosophically conservative writer" whose importance stems from his
bringing "new meaning to contingency" as he attempts to
salvage the liberal self and the form of the liberal novel (*Saul
Bellow* 11–12). And he sees E. M. Forster as neither a Victorian
nor a modernist, but as a writer who "held the centre," "explor-
ing it, for its moderating virtue, with a complex mixture of
commitment and scepticism" while other writers "risked themselves at the extremes" (*Possibilities* 91; *Forster* 3–4). For a writer
who has described himself as "cautious" (Interview with
Todd), the wording here is significant, but no more so than
his praising Forster's work as "a fiction of incompleteness
rather than solutions," having more in common with the "revealed plots" of much modernist and contemporary (or post-
contemporary) fiction than with the "resolved plots" of the
"totalizing novels" of the nineteenth century. In the novels of
Murdoch and Fowles, and even in the more daring innovative

fictions of the past few decades, Bradbury detects a desire "to make realism and fictiveness co-exist," "to preserve as much humanism for the novel as can be got," and, most importantly, "to maintain the idea of character against the swamping text" (*Possibilities* 229; *Novel Today* 19). The "retextualizing of realism" ("Foreword") that Bradbury espouses involves considerably more than a few token gestures towards postmodernist self-consciousness on the part of the otherwise conventional writer, for what is at stake is not merely a literary style but a mode of seeing and a mode of being as well. Bradbury elaborates on the problem in a two-part essay entitled "A Dog Engulfed by Sand" (1977–78; reprinted in revised form as "Putting in the Person: Character and Abstraction in Current Writing and Painting" 1979), which begins in Bradbury's characteristically personal mode.

I want here to offer some thoughts on the way a novelist writing now . . . might feel under pressure to diverge from the spirit of realism in the novel, to have problems in the representation of character and the supposedly substantive world, and so incline in the direction of what we might conveniently call "abstraction." . . . And I write as a novelist who began writing in the postwar season of realism, with a decided attachment to that empirical, moral, liberal tendency, but who has since felt . . . that the mode of realism is filled with implicit understandings and assumptions that it grows harder to accept. ("Person" 181)

It is much harder, I might add, given Bradbury's definition of the liberal novel as a work in which "there is some community of need between self and society, where the individual may reach out into the world of exterior relationships . . . where the possibility of moral enlargement and discovery resides" (*Saul Bellow* 29). Unable to continue writing conventional realism in an unconventional and seemingly unrealistic age and unwilling to accept cheerfully "the dehumanization of art"— the triumph of aesthetic form over the human subject—Bradbury finds himself "much concerned with the question of how to create and pose a human figure in a world that can no longer be regarded as comfortably 'realistic' " ("Dog" 51). What is needed, Bradbury feels, is the "retextualizing of realism," a hoped-for but elusive synthesis—or better, a "stimulating anthology"—of the traditional and the innovative, of the human and the formal. As a novelist who is also a critic who has written approvingly of Gilbert Sorrentino's distinctly postmodernist pastiche, *Mulligan Stew* (1979), and of such decidedly anti-postmodernist critiques as Christopher Lasch's *The Culture of Narcissism* (1978) and Gerald Graff's *Literature Against Itself* (1979) ("Age"), he wants to "renegotiate" the terms upon which the liberal novel can be made viable in a postliberal age. As we will now go on to see, a similar ambivalence animates Lodge's work, compounded (as in Bradbury's case) by precisely the same dualism of critic/novelist.

"The novel supremely among literary forms has satisfied our hunger for the meaningful ordering of experience *without* denying our empirical observation of its randomness and particularity" (*Novelist* 4). Lodge's definition of the novel clearly echoes Murdoch's and Bradbury's discussions of necessity and contingency, as well as Frank Kermode's provocative comments in *The Sense of an Ending* on fiction as a successful combination of credulity and "clerkly skepticism." Of course, when Lodge speaks here of the novel, he is in fact referring to the form as Ian Watt has defined it, in which (in Lodge's words) "the dominant mode, the synthesizing element, is realism" (*Novelist* 4). We can, however, be a bit more precise, for Lodge's realistic novel is the liberal novel as well; "the aesthetics of compromise go naturally with the ideology of compromise" (*Novelist* 33). And for this reason, Lodge, like Bradbury, is concerned with realism's definable past and its uncertain future, though his reasons for questioning its continuing viability are not precisely Bradbury's. What troubles Lodge is less Bradbury's fears concerning the growing dehumanization of art in the twentieth century than "the difficulty of being committed to aesthetic, philosophical, and moral principles which seem more reliable but drabber than the principles upon which most great 'modern' art was based" (*Language* 267). Although he rejects Robert Scholes's claim that film has made "literary realism redundant" (*Novelist* 17), he does acknowledge that British writers may be overly committed to realism and resistant to non-realistic literary modes. More importantly, he realizes that the postmodern age is indeed a time of crisis for the novelist, who suddenly finds himself standing at a crossroads where the novelistic tradition appears to diverge in two quite different directions. One road looks towards the fabulation of Barth, Vonnegut, and others which Scholes has espoused, and the other towards those "empirical narratives"—Capote's *In Cold Blood*, for example, and Mailer's *The Executioner's Song*—which seem less novelistic than journalistic in technique as well as in effect. Instead of following one path or the other, contemporary writers should, Lodge counsels, adopt a third course of action and "*build their hesitation into the novel itself*" (*Novelist* 22). The result will be what Lodge terms "the problematic novel," a work in which the writer can remain loyal both to reality and to fiction (contingency and necessity, skepticism and credulity) without nostalgically thinking he can any longer reconcile them. Following the example of Sterne in *Tristram Shandy*, the writer of problematic novels makes "the difficulty of his task . . . his subject" and "invites the reader to participate in the aesthetic and philosophical problems that the writing of fiction presents" (*Novelist* 23–24). Problematic novels do not signal the exhaustion of the novel as a genre but, instead, its continuing dialogization and replenishment. (Recall here not only Barth's two well known essays but, as well, the ending of his aptly titled novel, *Sabbatical*.) The problematic novel represents a way to continue the development of the genre rather than either breaking with it altogether or maintaining the realist/liberal tradition as a literary anachronism. A "comedy about the causes of postmodernism" (as Bradbury has described it ["Dangerous Pilgrimages" 65]), Lodge's *Changing Places* is a problematic novel which clearly implies that as the "synthesis" which realism once made possible becomes more difficult— perhaps impossible—to achieve, the novelist can turn to the construction, or compilation, of works in the form of "stimulating anthologies," variations, that is, on the collage technique that Barthelme has perfected in his short stories. Concerning another, and earlier, problematic novel, Doris Lessing's *The Golden Notebook*, Lodge has noted that the author "seems to be using the conventions of realistic fiction while being aware of their limitations and building this awareness into the novel itself, so that [Lodge contends] you have a very interesting, fruitful tension between the novelistic commit- ment to rendering experience through traditional forms and yet an inquiring, adventurous, very candid questioning of those conventions, ultimately raising all kinds of questions about art and reality. I'm interested in the art and reality novel, but I distrust the cheap victories, that come by throwing reality overboard altogether" ("David Lodge Interviewed" 116).

On the one hand, then, Lodge wants to maintain the realist tradition against the "easy victories" of certain experimental writers such as William Burroughs. On the other, he is just as critical of those writers and critics who embrace realism unthinkingly as he is of those who reject it out of hand. He has steadfastly maintained that in discussions of the novel, it is far too easy for the critic to appeal to reality as the arbiter of literary worth, especially in the case of "the realistic novel, which works by concealing the art by which it is produced, and invites discussion in terms of content rather than form, ethics and thematics rather than poetics and aesthetics" (*Modes* 52). What Lodge seeks to establish, not merely to assert, is that realism is indeed a form of literary art, aesthetically every bit as interesting in its metonymic way as modernism is in its essentially metaphoric manner. It is, of course, Lodge's interest in the English realists of the nineteenth and twentieth centuries and, too, the writing of his own early realistic fiction that have led him to fashion his largely successful apologia in defense of an aesthetic that has, during the past half-century, been much maligned and, if Lodge is right, largely misunderstood. But it is the abiding power of the modernist aesthetic and of the critical approaches that have come in the wake of *The Waste Land* and the *Wake* that have caused him to approach realism on modernism's own terms. Beginning with his New Critical close reading of the *Language of Fiction*, Lodge has sought to prove that realism succeeds, not on the basis of fidelity to "real life" but instead on the basis of the writer's ability to create aesthetically the experience that the reader naively assumes has merely been reproduced. Lodge's position is, given his commitment to realism, surprisingly similar to Barthes' in, for example, his "Structural Analysis of Narrative": "What takes place in a narrative is from the referential (reality) point of view literally nothing; 'what happens' is language alone, the adventure of language, the unceasing celebration of its coming" (295). And from Lodge's early "axiom" that "the novelist's medium is language; whatever he does qua novelist he does through language," it is only a small (but significant) jump to William Gass's well-known (and, to John Gardner, infamous) remark,

It seems a country-headed thing to say: that literature is language, that stories and the places and the people in them are merely made of words as chairs are made of smoothed sticks and sometimes of cloth or metal tubes. Still, we cannot be too simple at the start, since the obvious is often the unobserved. . . . It seems incredible, the ease with which we sink through books quite out of sight, pass clamorous pages into soundless dreams. That novels should be made of words, and merely words, is shocking, really. It's as though you had discovered that your wife were made of rubber: the bliss of all those years, the fears . . . from sponge. (27)

Not that Lodge goes nearly as far in his celebration of the language of fiction or, as Gass does, in taking such delight listening to the hum of his own valvèd voice. It might, in fact, be more accurate to say that Lodge *cannot* go quite so far given the import of his critical comments and critical method; he possesses a distinctly contemporary but not at all pessimistic sense of the limitations (rather than Bradburyan "possibilities") inherent in all human activities, including the writing and interpreting of imaginative literature. In their debate on criticism and fiction, Lodge has faulted Bradbury for espousing a poetics of the novel that is too inclusive (and, I might add, at times too vague) to be practicable. In fact, Lodge maintains that "no single method or approach can hope to explain adequately a literary work." Although his efforts are doomed to incompleteness, Lodge's critic can enter into that "continual stream of human conversation . . . in which works of literature have their meaning, and their very existence" (*20th Century* xvii). What he describes is an implicitly dialogic criticism which, although prone to specialization and hermeticism, has nonetheless become, in Lodge's judgment, "an increasingly cosmopolitan and collaborative enterprise" (*Novelist* 286). Lodge makes a similar point about contemporary fiction. He finds in it an "amazingly wide spectrum of modes and genres, *none of which can be considered dominant*" (*Novelist* ix), and all of which (as he explains in *Modes of Modern Writing*) operate within a literary continuum bounded by metaphor at one end and metonymy at the other. "The metaphor/metonymy distinction explains why at the deepest level there is a cyclical rhythm to literary history, for there is nowhere else for discourse to go except between these two poles" (220).

Working within the framework of such inherent limitations—the residue, I suspect, of his Catholic upbringing—Lodge has, since the publication of *Language of Fiction* in 1966, steadily, though cautiously, modified his critical approach as well as his definition of language, making them less restrictive, more structuralist, but by no means expansive. From the New Critical analysis of verbal patterns and surface texture, he has moved to the study of the deeper structures and narrative grammars and has recently taken a special interest in Bakhtin's theory of the dialogical novel.[1] Even as he has praised Barthes' tour de force, *S/Z*, Lodge has been far more deeply influenced by both the theories and practice of Gerard Genette, whom Robert Scholes has approvingly described as a "low structuralist" who, unlike Barthes et al., has refused to relinquish the openness of the individual text to the abstractions of structuralist theory (159). Under Genette's influence, Lodge has become increasingly concerned with novelistic form, which for Lodge includes "all the means of literary presentation from the largest to the smallest in scope; the design of the plot, the point of view of the narration, symbolic action, figurative language, right down to the construction of the simplest sentences" (*Working* 108). Of Genette's influence on Lodge, Bradbury has spoken approvingly (Interview with Todd), as well he should given his own mild interest in structuralist theories and, more significantly, his own emphasis, in his debate with Lodge, on the importance of novelistic form.

This is not to say that Lodge has finally come to accept what Bradbury has known all along. Rather, their debate has in fact taken the form of a dialogue, another of Lodge's "fruitful tensions" and Bradbury's "stimulating anthologies." In it, there has occurred a decided shift in critical emphasis, a merging, or, better, a mingling of voices that never were quite so monologically opposed as these writers' uncharacteristic polemics at times made them seem. Among the most important of the sources to which these voices can be traced is Mark Schorer's seminal essay, "Technique as Discovery" (1946). Not that they read Schorer in quite the same way. Bradbury

1. See, for example, Lodge's "Mimesis and Diegesis in Modern Literature" and his review of John Updike's novel, *Roger's Version*.

stressed Schorer's interest in the way the adoption of a certain style or technique leads the writer to discover and to explore his subject. Lodge, on the other hand, emphasized Schorer's demystification (or, to use Bakhtin's word, "decrowning") of the literary work's ostensible subject and the author's discovery of technique *as* subject rather than as a merely subordinate means to a higher thematic end. The development of Bradbury's and Lodge's careers as critics and (more especially and more interestingly) as novelists implies a (not necessarily conscious) rethinking of "Technique as Discovery" in the context of the general cultural and critical climate and, more particularly, in the context of one another's works—both interpretive and imaginative—as well as their own evolving novelistic practice. We need to realize that even as Bradbury, as critic, has emphasized the formal and referential dimensions of the novel, he has, as novelist, become increasingly preoccupied with verbal texture, with the language of fiction, though not as an alternative to liberal-humanist art or as a sign of his surrender to dehumanization. And Lodge has followed a similar, though in a sense opposite, course, moving from the analysis of the language of fiction and the writing of a fiction of language to a growing awareness of and preoccupation with the form of the novel and the problem of referentiality. It is tempting to speak here of the parallel development of two writers who have been colleagues and who continue to be friends, of novelists who are also critics. But I believe that what we have here are not parallels, strictly speaking, but points of intersection that form the necessary background for the discussions of the novels that follow. In these novels Bradbury and Lodge continue to search out ways to satisfy their own and their readers' hunger for the meaningful ordering of experience, without denying their own and their readers' empirical observation of its randomness and particularity.

The importance of these novels, both as contemporary fictions and as postwar British novels, is considerable; yet, the academic response to them has thus far been surprisingly slight, especially from American critics. One reason for this neglect is that Bradbury and Lodge continue to be thought of as critics first and fiction writers second. The other reason is that their novels are neither as securely realistic as the overwhelming majority of British fictions nor as insistently innovative as certain others. Hard to classify, their work becomes easy to passively disregard if not quite actively dismiss. The little academic criticism that has appeared thus far has been of a decidedly introductory nature or has been published in such out-of-the-way journals as *Revista Canaria de Estudios Ingleses*; or critics have sought to domesticate even Bradbury's and Lodge's most disruptive and disturbing novels by reading them within an unnecessarily narrow "British" context. Even one of the best of these, Patricia Waugh's discussion of *The History Man* and *How Far Can You Go?*, in her *Metafiction: The Theory and Practice of Self-Conscious Fiction*, illustrates this tendency all too well. Waugh's conclusion, that British metafictional texts "manifest the symptoms of formal and ontological insecurity but allow their deconstructions to be finally recontextualized or 'naturalized' and given a total interpretation" (19), may accurately describe the novels of Murdoch, Spark, Barnes, and others, but not those of Bradbury and Lodge, whose dialogical openness resists all efforts to impose any such "total interpretation." This includes the happy ending which Robert S. Burton has more recently imposed on Bradbury's *Rates of Exchange*. Like the novel's protagonist, its author (Burton confidently claims) is finally "able to read the signs clearly and ultimately find his way back to a home rooted in a stable domestic and literary tradition, from which standpoint he writes conventionally moral fictions mixed with stylistic ingenuity" (Burton 105). Praise such as this condemns Bradbury's narrative technique to marginal status, subordinating its dialogic thrust to the critic's demand for the resolved plot of conventional fiction. Even as they downplay, to varying degrees, discourse in favor of dogma, Waugh and Burton at least recognize that discourse does play a role in Bradbury's and Lodge's novels. Other critics have proven less generous, or more obtuse, and have assumed what Bradbury and Lodge clearly do not: that unless it declares itself otherwise fiction is realistic, naively so, and therefore best approached with equal naivete on the part of the critic. Walter Evans, for example, discusses Bradbury's collection of short stories, *Who Do You Think You Are*, under the heading, "Focusing on Personal Crisis," where he faults the author for his failure to "more powerfully, more freely evoke his characters' emotional depth" (145).[2] What apparently failed to cross the critic's mind is the possibility that the personal crisis in these stories may be as much the writer's as the characters' and the absence of emotional depth a narrative strategy rather than an aesthetic mistake.

Admittedly, putting Bradbury and Lodge in the perspective of innovative fiction is a tricky business. They are not included in *Postmodern Fiction: A Bio-Bibliographical Guide*, edited by Larry McCaffery (1986). Then again few English writers are, but whether this fact suggests the continued conventionality of recent British fiction or the general ignorance of—or resistance to—that fiction on the part of postmodernism's critics, many of them American, remains un-

2. Compare J. R. Banks's complaint that in *Small World* Lodge fails to create "fully naturalistic characters" (81). Randall Stevenson proves similarly obtuse in his comprehensive *The British Novel Since the Thirties:* "Though some of Bradbury's novels include self-conscious modernist techniques, these appear fairly modestly and intermittently: like Lodge's, it is mostly to the realist tradition that his work belongs. His best-known novel, *The History Man* (1975), for example, is a satire whose only substantial departure from conventional narrative technique is its extended use of the present tense" (191–192).

clear. Waugh, a British critic, includes a surprising number of British writers in her *Metafiction*, and in *The Survival of the Novel: British Fiction in the Later Twentieth Century* (1981), Neil McEwan contends that postwar British fiction is considerably less conservative than American critics believe. It is, McEwan states, "in dialogue with the Victorian tradition and the innovative present."[3] Unfortunately, McEwan's "dialogue" comes to look suspiciously like monologue when he asserts that recent British fiction is "technically adaptable even though stubbornly realist" (3). If, as A. S. Byatt has pointed out, "the difficulty of 'realism' combined with a strong moral attachment to its values" has been a major problem and challenge for the postwar British writer, then perhaps the problem and challenge for the critic of this postwar British fiction is to define as precisely as possible the ways in which certain of these writers have met the postmodern challenge and managed to open up a dialogue between realism and self-apparency without "stubbornly" resolving the tension between the two.

One critic who has faced this challenge is Peter Widdowson. His "The Anti-History Men: Malcolm Bradbury and David Lodge" merits special attention for being the most comprehensive, the most fully argued, certainly the most provocative, and perhaps the most perverse piece as yet to appear. Unlike the majority of their critics, Widdowson

3. McEwan's "argument is that, well within the literary world of fabulation and nouveau roman, writers in Britain have achieved a creative relationship with the traditional novel. As a result they have managed to keep their work close enough to common experience to make their experiments and to ensure the novel's continuing life" (ix). McEwan devotes individual chapters to Fowles, Murdoch, Wilson, Powell, Hartley, and Golding. He cites Bradbury's and Lodge's criticism approvingly but does not discuss their fiction despite its appropriateness to his rather general thesis. He does, however, discuss the importance of Bakhtin's theory of *menippea* to the study of contemporary fiction (14–19).

neither overlooks their postmodern techniques nor dismisses them out of hand; neither does he alternately praise them, only to downplay them, in order to glibly situate Bradbury and Lodge within the "the realist tradition." Instead he calls special attention to the presence of these techniques in their novels and to Bradbury's and Lodge's approving comments on recent trends in literary theory. But he does so only in order to unmask them. "Beneath the 'progressive' surface sophistication and brilliance of their work are ideological implications of considerable reactionary force; or, at least, of a cleverly disguised neutralisation of the potentially disruptive developments which they themselves purport to deploy" (Widdowson 6). Appearances to the contrary, Widdowson is not indicting Bradbury and Lodge for their failure to be sufficiently postmodernist, but for their being "anti-history." Their professed interest in postmodern techniques and recent critical theory are merely a smokescreen, an attempt to disguise the true purpose of their work which, as Widdowson defines it, is to defend English bourgeois culture against the tide of history (as Widdowson, again, defines it). Their fiction is essentially and covertly realistic in form and in its implications; its values are those of Arnold and Leavis and, therefore, of bourgeois capitalism. The postmodern "surface" of their novels "belies" the deep meaning which Widdowson alone accurately discerns. In effect, Widdowson resolves the discrepancy between overt form and covert message by privileging the latter, just as many other critics, less Marxist in their approach, have, with similar aplomb, privileged the former in order to find in Bradbury and Lodge the comforting assurances they themselves crave: the bourgeois liberalism that Widdowson finds so distasteful.

What Widdowson fails to consider as he goes about his father Karl's business of unmasking bourgeois liberalism in even its most postmodern disguise is that the tension needs to be discerned but not necessarily resolved. This, however, is precisely what Widdowson cannot do without himself committing the sin of omission of which he accuses Bradbury and Lodge: that lack of commitment to "history" which evidences itself in the nostalgic, generally unthinking, and entirely anti-historical acceptance of the bourgeois values that their novels and criticism covertly encourage. "Conservatism, quietism and defeatism," as well as "the specious liberal freedom of having it both ways" (24, 27), characterize their work. Their novels, as Widdowson reads them, prove to be nothing more than " 'conservative' comic realism masquerading as an open, non-deterministic post-modernism" (27). To arrive at such a conclusion, Widdowson must impose his own closure, itself determined by his Marxist approach, upon the novels in general and on their endings in particular.[4] But to resolve, or close, the novels in this manner entails disregarding the aesthetic reality of the works themselves. Their novels typify the English comic novel, not as Widdowson but as Bakhtin has defined it, and so have more to do with carnival than conservatism. Standing within the comic novel tradition which they at once exemplify and extend, Bradbury's and Lodge's works prove stubbornly resistant to all forms of closure, including Widdowson's and, it is hoped, the one adopted in these and the following pages. Widdowson sees Bradbury and Lodge affirming the bourgeois-liberal-realist tradition, even as they pretend to do just the opposite: that is, even as they pretend to be postmodern. I, on the other hand, see Bradbury and Lodge as wishing quite openly to preserve the tradition that Widdowson claims to have unmasked; but even as they seek to preserve this

4. Widdowson's readings of the endings of the novels is bewilderingly reductive. Far better are the essays by Theo D'haen and Jean-Michel Rabate in which parallels are drawn between Lodge's endings, his criticism, and the novels of John Fowles.

tradition, they find themselves increasingly unable to do so. Far from disguising their liberal values and aesthetic, they put them under increasing and inevitable postliberal pressure in an effort to discover whether any of the tradition can and should be maintained. In this sense, Bradbury's and Lodge's work as critics has kept them honest, has helped keep them free of that naivete, or bad faith, that characterizes so much Anglo-American fiction and criticism: a willed ignorance of the fact that it is both novelist *and* critic who are at the crossroads. To preserve and to openly question (and so to transform) is their aim; closure is for others.

The question that has only recently begun to trouble postmodern writers in the United States and on the Continent (as well as their most approving critics), is how, in McCaffery's words, the writer is to use "experimental strategies to discover new methods of reconnecting with the world outside the page, outside of language" (xxvi). This question is one that a number of postwar British writers have been struggling with for quite some time. Bradbury and Lodge appear to have faced it somewhat earlier, and certainly a good deal more directly, than did many of their English colleagues. As critics and as novelists they have put their Anglo-liberal aesthetic under increasing postmodern pressure, and as a result they have been able "to break out of the straitjacket of genre and conventionalised narrative that has limited so much of modern British writing" (Bradbury, *No, Not Bloomsbury* 359). The reason they could do so is, in large part, the result of their mutual interest in and attraction to America in general and to contemporary American fiction in particular. This is a rather large claim but one the importance of which ought not to be overlooked. Writing about Iris Murdoch's failure to gain entry to the United States in the late 1940s, John Fletcher, one of Bradbury's colleagues at the University of East Anglia, has commented that "one can only speculate how different her literary career may have been if, at this very formative stage of her life, she had been exposed to American culture" (549). In the case of Bradbury and Lodge, we can do considerably more than speculate. They have spoken and written about their American experiences and have even set a number of their stories and novels in the United States. However, although Bradbury's *Stepping Westward* and Lodge's *Changing Places* are clearly their most American fictions in terms of setting and subject, two later works—Bradbury's *Rates of Exchange*, set chiefly in eastern Europe, and Lodge's *How Far Can You Go?*, set almost entirely in England, may be their most American and their most postmodern in terms of treatment. (Significantly, Bradbury completed *Rates of Exchange* while working on his study of *The Modern American Novel*, and Lodge wrote *How Far Can You Go?* shortly after completing his analysis of postmodern American fiction for his *The Modes of Modern Writing*.)

I do not mean to imply that "American" and "postmodern" are synonymous, only that an important connection does exist, as Lodge, McCaffery, and others have been quick to point out. Nor do I mean to suggest that "postmodern" and "contemporary" are equivalent terms, only that for a work of the seventies or eighties to be considered truly contemporary it must evidence an awareness, perhaps even a grudging acceptance, of postmodern assumptions, though not necessarily of postmodern techniques. Exhaustive checklists of these techniques are readily available (see, for example, Lodge's *The Modes of Modern Writing*, Bradbury's *The Modern American Novel*, and McCaffrey's "Introduction" to *Postmodern Fiction*). As used in this study, however, the term postmodernism signifies not a particular literary mode but, instead, a general tendency whose origin and nature Allen Thiher has defined especially well. "Thought and language have changed our expectations about literature" and have "made problematic our belief in the primacy of the visual" and in "the iconicity of language" (3). The crises of referentiality and representation evident in postmodern writing give it the appearance of being entirely new and disruptive. The irony here is that postmodernism's break with the past is not nearly as apocalyptic as many would like to believe. "A true postmodernist," John Barth has explained, attempting to correct certain apocalyptic misconceptions about his "Literature of Exhaustion" essay, "keeps one foot always in the narrative past . . . and one foot in, one might say, the Parisian structuralist present" ("Literature of Replenishment" 70). Lodge is even more emphatic about this relationship: "Postmodernism cannot rely upon the historical memory of modernist and antimodernist [i.e., realist] writing for its background, because it is essentially a rule-breaking kind of art, and unless people are still trying to keep the rules there is no point in breaking them, and no interest in seeing them broken" (*Modes* 245). The relationships between past and present and between the conventions of the Anglo-liberal tradition (which Bradbury and Lodge have inherited, as well as largely accepted) and the postmodern techniques and assumptions (to which they have been increasingly attracted) are necessarily dialogic.

That there should be a close relationship between dialogism and postmodernism should hardly come as a surprise, for Bakhtin's checklist for the dialogic novel, drawn up in the 1920s, reads like the Borgesian precursor of postmodern fiction: carnival impiety, multiple styles and languages, linguistic uncertainty (the "*auto-criticism of discourse* is one of the primary distinguishing features of the novel as a genre" [*Dialogic* 412]). And, above all, there is the fact that the dialogic novel "parodies other genres (precisely in their role as genres) . . . [in order to expose] the conventionality of their forms and their language" and to insert "indeterminacy" and "semantic openness" into these otherwise closed forms (*Dialogic* 5, 7). As Bakhtin has noted, the history of the novel is the history "of the deepening of [its] dialogic essence" (*Dialogic* 300). It is a history which leads, perhaps inevitably, to the kind of writing labeled postmodern and, more particularly, to the decidedly dialogical novels of Malcolm Bradbury and David Lodge. Their novels are truly "double-voiced," or, to use a word from Lodge's *Changing Places*, "duplex," which in telegraphic jargon refers to the sending of two messages simultaneously in different directions along the same line. In their novels, one detects the same use of "decrowning doubles" and "sideward glances" that Bakhtin noted in Dostoevsky's fiction, where "everything . . . lives on the very border of its opposite" (*Problems* 176). Theirs is a fiction of structural, thematic, semantic, and inter-textual doublings, echoes, and mirror reflections: a fiction which simultaneously undermines and endorses; a fiction at once academic and accessible, referential and self-reflexive, British and American, Anglo-liberal and postrealist; a fiction tentative about its commitments yet increasingly committed to its own tentativeness. My purpose in the chapters which follow is to make the openness of their fiction more apparent: to identify the play of dialogically intersecting voices not in order to subordinate some to others, and in this way to resolve the dialogical tension, but in order that the voices may be heard in all their confusion and complexity. Approaching Brad-bury's and Lodge's novels in this manner, we will come to better appreciate the fact that their works stand neither for tradition nor against it but, rather, both together, and at once.

2

Eating People Is Wrong:
Yes or No?

WRITTEN LARGELY WHILE the author was still a student
and published when he was just twenty-seven years old, *Eating
People Is Wrong* is clearly an apprentice work composed and, just
as importantly, read and reviewed in the shadow of Kingsley
Amis's *Lucky Jim*. Amis's novel undoubtedly influenced Bradbury: how could it not have? But one can make either too much
or too little of the influence, transforming an author just beginning his career as narrative ventriloquist into either a mere par-
rot or an English original. Bradbury is neither. Although he
may not have intended *Eating People Is Wrong* as a campus novel
("Introduction" 1), a campus novel is indeed what it is, at least
in part: one of the last of the fifties' academic fictions, a subgenre
that includes Mary McCarthy's *The Groves of Academe* and Lionel
Trilling's "Of This Time, Of That Place" as well as *Lucky Jim*.[1]

1. Concerning the relationship between *Lucky Jim* and *Eating People
   Is Wrong*, James Gindin has noted, "In spite of all the critical
   comparisons and interlocking references, Bradbury's satire is different from Amis's, Bradbury always more concerned with issues,
   less implicitly committed to pragmatic success in the world or to
   mocking contemporary forms of incompetence" ("Bradbury" 91).

Angus Wilson's 1952 novel *Hemlock and After* exerted a less obvious but perhaps more "potent" influence. Its appeal for Bradbury was double. It was, as Bradbury read it, "a latter-day liberal novel, concerned, as E. M. Forster was, both to realize liberal humanism as a potential, but also to see its historical conditions, determinants, and limits." Also, however, *Hemlock and After* involves a "teasing out of the possibilities of the traditional novel" that, while certainly muted in Bradbury's first two novels, nonetheless plays a significant role in his aesthetic ("Coming Out" 186). Although Bradbury's comments on Wilson, written in the 1980s, reflect his most recent interests, they nonetheless help to foreground the important but by no means obvious link between his thematic concerns in *Eating People Is Wrong* and his own teasing out of the possibilities of the liberal novel. His comments play upon what Lodge has subsequently and punningly called "the importance of being Amis," and the difficulty or perhaps the impossibility or at least the inadvisability of being Amis any longer. *Eating People Is Wrong* and *Hemlock and After* are examples of "moral realism," which, as Trilling has explained, "entails not only the awareness of morality itself but of the contradictions, paradoxes and dangers of living the moral life." Trilling's comments, taken from his book on Forster, are quoted by Bradbury in his 1975 essay on Trilling ("Lionel Trilling" 619) and echoed in his comments on Wilson and in his discussions of Forster's novels. It is not some tenuous thread I am trying to trace (or fabricate) here but one of Bradbury's major preoccupations, his concern with the "most basic question" raised in Forster's novels: "how, in the face of contingency, one structures meaning" (*Possibilities* 112). It is precisely the same question that Bradbury finds at the heart of Jewish-American fiction, the novels of Saul Bellow in particular, and that the reader finds in Bradbury's own work, especially his most Bellow-like novel, *Eating People Is Wrong*, in which "past and present don't quite mesh" and, consequently, "it is hard to know quite where to get one's values from" ("Introduction" 6).

This is the problem faced by the novel's withdrawn hero. Stuart Treece, or simply Treece as he is most often and most minimally called, is a man who has risen from humble beginnings to the now equally humble heights of department head and nominal specialist in eighteenth century literature at a provincial university in an "anywhere" city, a university that looks like a railway station and that originally served as an asylum for the insane. With his degree from London University (rather than Oxford or Cambridge) and his wartime service in the London Fire Brigade, Treece is at best a marginal man, professionally, socially, politically, historically, and morally. Although still young (in his late thirties), he already seems old; the liberal/socialist of two decades earlier has become in the 1950s something of a reactionary. " 'Once, I can't help remembering,' " his colleague Jenkins explains to the generally inept and decidedly unheroic Treece, " 'we used to think people like us were important. Now we're just a little group of disordered citizens with no social role in the society we live in' " (23). The question for the reader is whether Treece (as well as the liberal tradition he represents) has been unfairly dispossessed or whether he is himself responsible for his (perhaps deserved) diminishment.

Like a Bellow protagonist, Treece ponders but cannot bring himself to act or even to make a decisive choice. Driven by "self-discipline and moral scruple" (46), he seems a caricature of the liberal self. Pushing himself to be entirely fair-minded and ethically upright, he succeeds only in being indefatigably indecisive. "[Scrupulous] in the face of action" (83) is the way he explains himself to Emma Fielding, who for Treece is alternately a student, a friend, an assistant, a nursemaid, a confidante, a lover, a mother, and the mirror image of his own liberal soul. But Emma understands that, noble sentiment aside, Treece isn't "really saying anything" (83), for his scruples may in fact be merely a poor substitute for selfless moral action, a way, that is, to avoid taking any risks. As Jenkins, a sociologist, explains, " 'You prefer a good honest Western *doubt*—with all the personal ineffectiveness and depression that that entails. You presumably think that your position is actually superior . . .' " (178). Treece does believe that his position is superior, but even about this he remains, paradoxically but in a sense consistently, indecisive; even about doubt he remains dialogically confused rather than monologically certain.

Doubt is the essence of his character, the residue of a once vital liberalism. It is also, however, the vital center of Bradbury's narrative method. The reader accepts Jenkins' judgment of Treece as correct, but the fact that Jenkins, a specialist in group dynamics, is so adept at role-playing suggests that he may also be oblivious to those deeper, perhaps anachronistic, values which Treece in his own fumbling way wishes to preserve. The reader will certainly agree with another of Treece's colleagues, Viola Masefield, that Treece fits Simone Weil's definition of the religious man all too well: "Morality will not let him breathe" (101). But Treece's situation is at once existential and comical. Just as he begins to succumb to Viola's seductive charms, Treece imagines that "the room began to boom with moral reverberations" (103)—and the sound of narrative laughter. Nonetheless, Bradbury's comedy remains essentially serious. Like Jenkins, Viola may be right about Treece, yet the reader cannot quite bring himself to trust entirely someone whose flat is described as "a showpiece of the unendurably modern. . . . When you went there, you always discussed things as they discussed things in *Vogue:* What does one do with dustbins to make them look interesting" (86). Viola's desire to be in vogue accentuates her absurdity (which is the opposite of Treece's) and thus undermines her credibility, but not to the point that the reader can quite reject her judgment of Treece. In dealing with Viola, as in dealing with virtually all of the novel's characters, Bradbury plays view against view, voice against voice, both within characters and between them.

The Vice Chancellor's blueprint for the university as an entirely practical, financially sound institution, for example, is played against Treece's worthy but nebulous idea of the university as a haven in a heartless world. (It is, incidentally, a haven which Treece is unable to effect even on the micro-level of his own personal/professional dealings with students.) The ideal and the real, the traditional and the contemporary, the necessary and the contingent are never left in isolation but always brought into conflict. Each intersects with and continuously redefines the other.

Tonally the novel resembles Treece, "a person without a firm, a solid centre" (47). Instead of a dominant tone, the novel consists of a number of alternating ones, each challenging and modifying the others. In one chapter, for example, Emma tells Treece that their rejection of a particularly unlikeable but perhaps brilliant student, Louis Bates, has brought all "their civilized pretensions" (170) crashing down around them. In the very next chapter, such moral concern becomes comically ludicrous moral hyperbole when Treece claims to discern in the theft of a journal article from the departmental reading room clear evidence that his fellow academics "were chipping steadily away at [his world's] hard, round moral core" (170). The juxtaposition of the two passages calls attention not only to Treece's inability to distinguish significant from trivial matters of moral concern but, as well, to the less obvious but no less significant streak of moral hyperbolism in Emma's thinking. In other words, the tonal distinction that exists between the two passages exists within each passage as well. *Eating People Is Wrong* would undoubtedly disappoint its main character, for it lacks the "hard, round moral core" that he requires. Rather, like Forster's *A Passage to India*, though of course on a much smaller scale, Bradbury's novel concerns the "confusion and muddle" that result when two different value systems meet (*Possibilities* 112). Thus, the primary issue in *Eating People Is Wrong* is, as Martin Tucker has pointed out, the very commitment that Treece himself lacks. "He is the eternal questioner: everyone listens to his questions, but no one tries to answer them, including himself. His questions are never meant to be answered: that is his tragedy" (19–20). But in this "sad comedy" ("Introduction" 7), Treece is only partly a tragic figure, and about him Bradbury expresses a necessary ambivalence. Bradbury agrees with Treece's Anglo-liberal desire to leave his character undefined but knows too how such a desire can easily degenerate into moral evasion.

Like Emma, the reader cannot help but admire Treece's scrupulous honesty. Critical of the shortcomings of his fellow men, he is self-critical as well, aware (even hyperaware) of his own failings, deficiencies, and inconsistencies. It is true that his habitual pose is one of withdrawal, especially at parties, where Treece prefers reading to mingling. And it is also true that he is at times given to offering sententiously to others advice that is at least just as pertinent to himself. " 'The point is this,' " he tells a foreign student whose megalomania and depressive withdrawals make him a fit caricature of Treece's own personality; " 'life here may be difficult, but you can't go on retiring into lavatories indefinitely' " (28). What is more characteristic of Treece's character and of Bradbury's novel in general, however, is some of that same quality that Bradbury has found in the fiction of Aldous Huxley, whose novels, Bradbury has pointed out, "are largely novels of inaction, for his scrupulous, devastating analysis usually produces in the central character a masochistic withdrawal from action" (*Possibilities* 140–166). In *Eating People Is Wrong*, it is Treece's withdrawal into endless (though not entirely fruitless) self-analysis that is masochistic, comically so. "The trouble with me," thinks the everthinking Treece, "is . . . that I'm a liberal humanist who believes in original sin. I think of man as a noble creature who has only to extend himself to the full range of his powers to be civilized and good; yet his performance by and large has been intrinsically evil and could be more so as the extension continues" (12). Or, to put the same matter more in the form of a nervous, befuddled stand-up comic's one-liner: "It is well I am a liberal, and can love all men, thought Treece; for if I were not, I doubt if I could" (29). Such self-reflexive and certainly self-deprecating irony characterizes Treece's thinking, which almost invariably takes the form of an internalized dialogue. Treece's speech on the other hand tends towards monologic uniformity and, often, pomposity as well. It sounds at times weirdly misplaced, wildly inappropriate, as in his absurdly formal comment to Emma, " 'And the question remains: is it right to stay in the protected corner, where things are controllable, or should one venture out, and start again in a new world, where things are strenuous, and reclaim something else from the wild?' " (56). All of this is much ado about very little, not whether Treece should be or not be, do or not do, but whether he should, as scheduled, take a road test in order to secure a license to drive a motorscooter—a test he takes and of course fails several times. Endless examination of conscience leads Treece to accuse himself of being a "parasite," specifically because he can offer other people (Emma in particular) only his own desperate need. But Treece is linguistically a parasite as well, as his choice of the word "parasite" itself suggests. He draws his moral superiority—or, alternately and masochistically, his moral inferiority—from an antiquated rhetoric divorced from both the speech and the facts of contemporary life. He can speak of responsibility, but he cannot act responsibly or, for the most part, even make his moral imperatives sound convincing to others. Similarly, he can speak of the importance of human relationships, but he cannot actually, either physically or emotionally, enter into any except abstractly, through and in language alone.

Although Emma admires Treece for his honesty, she is also made uneasy by him (as perhaps the reader is too), for his justified self-doubts give voice to her own feelings of being similarly marginal and inconsequential. Emma has good reason to worry and to hear herself in Treece's plaintive voice. At twenty-six, she is still trying to complete her thesis on fish imagery in Shakespeare's tragedies. More importantly and less comically, she is, if not a parasite like Treece, then a Fowlesian collector. "Emma," we learn, "collected people" (105), including Treece, of course, but also the elderly Bishops in whose fastidiously middle-class Georgian home she rents a room. Like Treece, she takes refuge from the contingencies of post-Georgian reality. Treece keeps his possessions to a minimum, thinking in this way to keep his character free. Emma on the other hand is drawn to antiques (not only the harmonium she longs to possess but human antiques as well: Treece and the Bishops). Their methods are different but their purpose is the same: to recoil from the contemporary. " 'Oh, you expect too much from life,' " Treece tells her; " 'You're just like me' " (37). This would be merely self-congratulatory sentiment were it not for Emma's (like Treece's) habit of carrying on internal dialogues, questioning her beliefs and assumptions, not so much to undermine or discredit them as to keep the moral search alive. She seeks to balance, however precariously, the abstract "liberal self" that she and Treece like to invoke as if it were some kind of magical charm and that sense of being "just people" (as one of the novel's foreign characters puts it) that might represent either the fulfillment of the liberal dream or its defeat by democratic levelling (225).

The test of the liberalism that Emma and Treece espouse is Louis Bates, a "fragmentary . . . splendidly irreconcilable" character who seems to have stumbled out of a John Braine novel or a John Osborne play via Kingsley Amis into a fictive world where his "anger" appears even more comically inappropriate than Treece's moral musing (17). It is through Treece's eyes and liberal biases that we first see the "fragmentary" Bates as "a curious mixture of the promising and the absurd," "a kind of hideous juxtaposition of taste and vulgarity," "his tone . . . a mixture of dejection and . . . could it be pride," a buffoon who cannot be taken seriously but who nonetheless possesses "good sense and taste" (13, 17–18). It is not so much that Bates is an ambiguous character as a composite caricature. Like Emma, he is twenty-six years old and therefore (especially as an undergraduate) older than the other students. And like Treece, he comes from a working-class background, is earnest, is prone to taking pratfalls, and is, as Treece once was, rebellious and visionary. (Henry Treece, it is worth noting, was one of the romantic writers against whom the Angry Young Men revolted.) Not surprisingly, Bates is drawn to both Emma and Treece, who, earnest liberals that they are, feel obliged to like Bates even as they recoil from him. Bates is for Treece an obligation, but he is as well (as not only the reader but Treece too understands) a grotesque version of what Treece himself is. Bates is Treece's comically decrowning double who boldly and cartoonishly speaks what the timorous Treece allows himself only to think. This aspect of their narrative relationship is made especially, and perhaps too insistently, clear in "The Adult Education Class," originally part of the manuscript version of the novel which Bradbury (wisely I believe) excised and subsequently published as a self-contained short story (in *Who Do You Think You Are?*). In it, Treece, while lecturing to his adult education students (plus the marginal Bates, who is neither entirely an undergraduate nor entirely an adult), suddenly realizes that none of his students shares his assumptions and beliefs about literature, and it is at this prosaically climactic moment that "from the far end of the table a voice suddenly spoke." Treece soon recognizes the voice as that of Bates, who, moved by Treece's words, castigates the others for their ignorance and their ingratitude. Bates's speech causes Treece to feel "shame in his apologist" and, immediately after, "shame for being ashamed of his apologist" (*Who Do You* 63), who is, as well, "his own half-self" (67) from whom he will never be free. In the novel, such similarities are generally left implicit, suggested as parallels and, especially, heard as echoes. The reader hears, for example, in Bates's comment, " 'I always enjoy *myself*. . . . But I'm not so sure I enjoy other people' " (131), something of Treece's mental remark, quoted earlier, "it is well I am a liberal, and can love all men . . . for if I were not, I doubt if I could." What the reader doesn't hear in Bates's comment is, however, equally important: the absence in Bates's speech of that self-deprecating but saving irony that characterizes Treece at his most self-aware moments. The reader notices the same pattern of similarity and difference when Bates, out rowing with Emma, fails to protect her from the swans that begin to crowd around their boat. Contemplating this typically Treece-like act, Bates adopts a typically Treece-like tone of romantic plaintiveness, expressing himself, again like Treece, though in an even more exaggerated way, in the form of a mental speech: "He wished he was a man of action; he wished he could do things. I suppose, he thought, Hamlet was just like me" (229).

Bates is so comic a figure precisely because he takes himself and his world so seriously, so monologically. Unlike Treece, or Treece's Chaplinesque precursor, Prufrock, he cannot perceive, much less understand, even glancingly, his own absurdity. Almost totally devoid of any self-awareness whatsoever, Bates appears simplistic and comically dogmatic: " 'I just want a straight answer, yes or no . . . is this a bounded, or boundless, universe?' " (21). Everything about Bates is monologic, including his love letters to Emma, which "had been so pompous and ill considered in tone, and so unrelated to effective action, that it was impossible for Emma to think of them without either annoyance or amusement" (82). He compares himself to Keats, accepts William Blake's marriage as an appropriate model for his own, and with the same lack of self-awareness or ironic detachment, can shout rhetorically and "apoplectically, 'Damn, damn, damn. . . . What's wrong with me? I'm the plaything of gods. The buffoon, the whipping-boy, the scapegoat' " (115). His remark only serves to remind the reader that Lear and Ahab cut one kind of figure and Bates quite another. A walking *Bartlett's*, he speaks not in tongues but in quotations, serenely unaware of the quotation marks that ironize his words, or if aware, only minimally so. Wanting to start a conversation with a girl at a party, for example, he first has to remember his Dale Carnegie. When present in a scene, he monopolizes all conversation, and when absent often serves as the topic of conversation, a fixed point, resistant to the dialogic flux. Physically, Bates follows a similar course. Although he says, echoing Treece, " 'If you don't touch up against people, you are nothing; you never define yourself, you never exist' " (146), Bates never does just "touch up against people"; he bumps up against them, hard. Emma's description of him as shabby and simian may be ungenerous, but it is not especially inaccurate. Even the detested Bates, however, has his humanities. While he is certainly not one of "the civilized liberal middle class that Treece [as usual, thinking in cliches] saw as the salt of the earth," neither is he (as Emma's Bishops are) "self-engrossed" (211). Instead he seems merely unformed. The danger for Bates is that he can so easily become a younger version of Carey Willoughby, the novel's most overtly parasitic character, an angry young novelist whose social rebellion is little more than a cover for his own self-centeredness.

Not that Bradbury entirely detaches himself from Willoughby, whose criticism of Treece echoes what much of the novel strongly suggests about Treece's liberal failings. Precisely where Bradbury stands in relation to his novel and its characters remains unclear, and it is precisely the absence of such dogmatic clarity that makes Bradbury's first novel especially interesting and rewarding despite its several weaknesses, including the occasionally overplayed satire. In the introduction he wrote for the novel's 1976 reissue, Bradbury, speaking not as author but instead in his role as author-writing-after-the-fact, notes that he had written *Eating People Is Wrong* "from the innocent, fascinated standpoint of the stu-

dent, in fact the first-generation student, for whom universities
were both a novelty and a social opportunity" ("Introduction"
1). For Melvin Friedman this means that as author Bradbury
more closely identifies with his character Bates than with
Treece (109). It is a plausible but not entirely convincing claim.
It is, after all, Treece who interests the reader (and the author/
narrator) most, just as it is Bates who most interests Treece,
Emma who most interests Bates, and the Bishops who (most?)
interest Emma. Moreover, as Bradbury also notes in that same
introduction, Treece "was considerably based upon my twen-
ty-year-old self, or was, rather, a projection of my own commitments about the liberal humanism I . . . [then] both espoused
and questioned" (2).

It is the questioning that seems to dominate in the novel's
final chapters, which are set in the same kind of open hospital
ward of the National Health Service where they were written
in 1958 while Bradbury recovered from surgery. This "fact,"
Bradbury has said, "explains something of the texture and
tone" of these chapters ("Introduction" 3). Perhaps it does,
but there is as well a certain logic at play. On the working
class ward where, much to Treece's liberal dismay, everyone is
treated as an inferior, Treece, recovering from a mysterious
illness, hears a song played, over and over. It is the same aptly
titled song that he and the reader heard earlier in the novel,
"I Was a Big Man Yesterday." One line of that song, "but oh
you ought to see me now," neatly and ironically sums up
Treece's situation. But as a piece of fifties' pop culture, it also
reminds the reader of another song, the one from which
the novel draws its title. "Eating people is," Treece knows,
"wrong," or should be; but in the world in which Treece, like
Bates, finds himself an outsider, all moral absolutes are at best
suspect and at worst anachronistic. Confined to his bed, Treece
is no better able to make liberalism's case than is Bates, whom
Treece discovers is on the same ward following the most recent
of Bates's romantic gestures, attempted suicide. This time,

however, Treece and Emma, being what they are, have no choice but to take some responsibility for Bates's behavior: it was Emma's telling Bates of her affair with Treece that led to his nervous breakdown and eventually to his attempted suicide. (That Bates should fail even at this seems appropriate in a blackly humorous way.) Still unable to act, or even walk, Treece can, however, still think, pondering his own situation in light of Bates's example: "what was proper," he tells himself, "became less and less what was viable. . . . The moral passions can drive one too hard, until, as with Gulliver, home from his travels, ordinary life is hardly to be borne" (241). Treece is right, but his comparing his predicament with Gulliver's reminds the reader of Bates's comparing himself with Hamlet; the reference seems to be made unironically and is, therefore, like Bates's, pretentious, mere posturing. It is a disconcerting lapse in Treece's usual degree of ironic detachment, subtly distinguishable from, for example, his earlier identification of Pilate and himself as "brothers under the skin" (26). And the lapse continues until the every end of the novel where Treece sees Emma, presumably (Treece feels) for the last time. "She went away and he lay there in his bed, and felt as though this would be his condition for evermore, and that from this he would never, never escape" (248). His "never, never" measures the extent of his fall into that usual Batesian mode: selfpity.

Earlier in the novel, Treece's pragmatic Vice Chancellor asks Carey Willoughby why his novels don't have " 'proper endings, why aren't they resolved, why don't people die or live happily ever after?' " (198). He might well have asked the author of *Eating People Is Wrong* the same question, for no one in Bradbury's novel triumphs and no one, not even Bates, dies. Instead they linger on, feeling contingency exert its ever increasing pressure on characters and author alike in novels whose plots (to use Seymour Chatman's useful distinction) are revealed rather than resolved. Not being a reader of contemporary novels (they depress him too much), Treece does seem to deserve his fate, which is to embody the liberal spirit in a post-liberal age. As a character in Bradbury's television play, "The After Dinner Game," points out, "the weakness of liberalism [is], you might say, its chief virtue. . . . To see both sides of a question is to risk being frozen into inaction but it is also the gift of recognizing contradiction, tension, complexity without ceasing to function. The liberal is a man of conscience, but a man whose conscience is a real force in the world. He must be able to act" (31). But to act is precisely what Treece, and Bradbury's later liberal characters, including the speaker of these lines, cannot do.

3

Stepping Westward:
Dangerous Pilgrimages

"THE FLUTE IS not a moral instrument: it is too exciting." Bradbury might just as appropriately have chosen for the epigraph to his second novel, *Stepping Westward*, a line from Bernard Malamud's own novel of academic westward ho, *A New Life*, published four years earlier: "The past hides in the present" (32). In part it is Malamud's Jewish-American story that hides in Bradbury's Anglo-liberal novel. But it is also his own first novel, for like his half-self, Stuart Treece, the author of *Stepping Westward* has not, perhaps cannot, free himself from his alter-ego/echo, Louis Bates, who returns, reshaped and reimagined, as an integral part of *Stepping Westward*'s plodding, largely passive protagonist, James Walker. Compared at one point to "a stout predatory station pigeon," Walker is a "slightly thyroidic, very shambling person in his early thirties, victimized by the need for twelve hours' sleep a day" (47, 31). Tending towards pratfalls as well as somnolence, Walker never quite achieves (as Treece does) the level of Chaplinesque pathos, though he indeed comes close. He is, after all, like his creator, an English liberal and, like the author conjured by reviewers of *Eating People Is Wrong*, a not-so-angry-young-novelist, or, as Bradbury has described his own late fifties' self, the one who travelled to the United States, "a niggling . . . uneasy figure struggling in my Englishness, fighting to get out" (*All Dressed Up* 11). Moreover, while it is true that Walker has withdrawn from his world, his world (in the form of provincial postwar England) has paid him little attention, rejecting the novels that America has accepted so enthusiastically, though not necessarily on the author's preferred terms. Consequently, when the nationally neglected but internationally known Walker receives an invitation to become writer-in-residence for a year at an American university, he interprets—or rather misinterprets—this invitation as a validation of his existence as a writer.[1] As his name suggests, Walker is on the move, but slowly and uncertainly, beset by many of the same liberal doubts and misgivings that at once ennoble and paralyze Treece. To go to the United States, for example, entails leaving his wife (a nurse) and young daughter behind; his liberation from England and all it represents is, therefore, tainted from the very start by guilt and, more especially, by Walker's awareness of his own limitations. He knows, at least dimly, that his is a minimal morality, barely adequate even for his own needs and certainly unable to withstand any real test, least of all the formidable ones to which it is about to be subjected in the United States.

However, there is no "Walker," for Walker is plural, a multi-voiced being that exists in the form(s) of internal dialogues and in the versions—subfictions in effect—conceived by the other characters. There is, for example, James Walker husband and father, and then, quite apart, there is James Walker the novelist known to others chiefly, or even exclusively,

1. As Bradbury has pointed out in an essay entitled "One Man's America," "on the whole being a writer in England, certainly in the 1950s and probably still, seemed a lonely amateur occupation" whereas "the climate in the States was much more explicitly favorable" (99).

through his fiction, his iconoclastically titled novel *The Last of the Old Lords* in particular. But even this James Walker exists in different versions: as the subject of a *Time Magazine* article, of a piece in the university town's local newspaper, and of the verbal remarks made by Bernard Froelich, the man responsible for bringing Walker to the all-too-American town of Party. The different versions of Walker shed important though often contradictory light on his character and never do quite come together in the form of a single, well-focused image. At times they even seem to overwhelm and supplant the "real" self that Walker conceives himself to be. Froelich's wife, Patrice, for example, likes the Walker novels she has read but nonetheless finds them " 'confused, disoriented, and a bit too obviously uncommitted and unfeeling' " (256). Hers is a persuasive enough reading, given what Bradbury's reader already knows about Walker's character. Julie Snowflake, another of Walker's readers, younger but presumably more sophisticated, on the other hand, finds it difficult to reconcile the stiff and unnatural man she meets with the dynamic author whose works she has read and about whom she is writing her senior thesis. The reader would like to trust Julie's reading of Walker's character, but the fact that she accepts as true the *New York Times* article which transforms the "predatory station pigeon" into a political hero makes clear the reader's dilemma, which parallels Walker's. The same holds true when another character, the Nabokov-like Jochim, tells Walker, " 'You are an optimist and live on hope. I am a pessimist and live on experience' " (353). It is (once again) a plausible claim, even though not entirely accurate, for "hope" is too grand a word to apply to Walker, who lives not on hope, not on Dickensian great expectations, but, instead, on limited possibilities, vague abstractions, liberal ideals, and twelve hours of sleep per day. Moreover, as Patrice points out, again plausibly, Walker doesn't actually believe in innocence; what he believes in is complexity, on not permitting anything to be easy. She is, of course, right, even if, like the other characters, only partly.

Like the reader, Walker wants the kind of assurances that the novel withholds. He wants, for example, to be redeemed, though from what and for what he never makes especially clear, either to himself or anyone else. Like the reader who wants to remain loyal to Julie's reading of Walker (or alternately to Patrice's or Jochim's, etc.), Walker wants to be loyal to himself, which is to say to his idea of the liberal self. He wants to be, in Jochim's words, "a loyalist of nowhere," or, as he prefers to call it, "a loyalist of the imagination" (301). Walker's dilemma becomes increasingly more difficult for him (and the reader) because he gradually develops a deeper awareness of just how "thin," "bland," and "uncreative" his British liberalism actually is (40). As he becomes increasingly disoriented, he grows increasingly loyal to the provisional life he now shares with his American students and American friends. This new loyalty, however, does not lead either Walker the man or Walker the author to produce anything more substantive or imaginative than a few hastily written letters and telegrams to his wife, asking for a divorce, and his *Lucky Jim*-like speech in which he drunkenly explains why he cannot, as required, sign a loyalty oath. Stepping to the podium, the plodding hero acts freely, which in his case means impulsively and, as he soon realizes, unwisely. Choosing to forego his prepared text—"It was a decision of panic and fear, and he knew that he would regret it" (309)—Walker lurches on. He came to America to be "uncommitted," he says, adding that it was "disloyal" of him to come, that he had "come to be loyal to being a writer," that being a writer means "not being limited," and, therefore, he concludes, he should not have to sign the loyalty oath (311). There is a certain reasonableness to Walker's claims, even if these claims are couched in the form of a drunken babble in which Walker speaks not only to his audience but, perhaps more importantly, to and with himself. That he ought not to have to sign the oath is clear, but that fact does not mean that he is right to speak as he does. Walker is in fact surprised by his own words, or rather, by the words he has spoken: words which may not be his at all, but merely the words he assumes appropriate to this situation and this audience and in which the reader hears Walker's cadences but Julie's and Froelich's ideas. He is, above all, "surprised that his own mouth should have come round to this position before his heart did" (311). This comment, though it does not actually deny the validity of what Walker has said, does nonetheless put his remarks in some doubt (in quotation marks, as Bakhtin would say). It stretches the head-versus-heart conflict of classic nineteenth century American fiction one stage further along, though whether towards Norman O. Brown's vision of a redemptive "polymorphous perversity" or something akin to Gogol's nose, an emancipated mouth, is left uncertain. In speaking as he has, Walker may have betrayed his heart, either by giving away its deepest secrets or, perhaps, by mistakenly opposing its (and therefore his) "true feelings." According to (university) president Coolidge, it is the university's hospitality Walker has betrayed. Such a betrayal would, of course, make Walker a Benedict Arnold at Benedict Arnold, an institution that is at once the embodiment of "America" and its antithesis: home of the liberated (if not of the free and the brave) and, alternately, a bastion of illiberalism, the dark side of the American dream. Bradbury's (implied) pun has, therefore, its own serious dimension. Walker's refusal to sign the loyalty oath is his most distinctly "American" act: a Thoreauvian resistance to civil government's usurpation of the rights of the individual. His "no," though hardly made in Melvillean thunder, is an affirmation of the freedom and independence that America claims to represent. Yet his act of civil disobedience evokes in the reader little, if any, sense of Walker's moral superiority; it is depicted in such a way as to remind the reader less of

Thoreau, Emerson, the Boston Tea Party, and the signing of the Declaration of Independence than of that most British of fifties' fictions, *Lucky Jim*. It is not merely that the echoes of Jim Dixon overwhelm those of Henry David Thoreau, for Walker is unAmerican, though not, of course, in the Cold War sense of the word. His English past hides below the surface of his American present, and as a result Walker is unable to adapt to life in the United States. He is, as one character points out, too stiff, too much like Treece or Henry James' Europeanized American, Winterbourne. But if Walker is not quite the moral touchstone that he might, in a less ironic and ambiguous age, have been, neither is he entirely a figure of fun for either his author or his reader. Rather, he is, for all his comic bumbling and indecisiveness, one in that long line of expatriates to be found in twentieth century literature who, as Bradbury has elsewhere remarked, demonstrate those "tensions about location and nationality, obligation and independence, which mark modern art" ("Second Countries" 38) and which *Stepping Westward* foregrounds.

The America to which Walker is slowly, and at times reluctantly, drawn is, at first, an idea that gradually becomes substantive, more tangible, less mythic. It is a word made flesh, and made more various as well, though the result of this variety is not necessarily a Whitmanic celebration of the nation's diversity, "its varied carols." One of the most important of these new voices is that of Julie Snowflake, the attractive undergraduate whom Walker meets while in transit to the United States and with whom he later travels around the American West and Mexico. Physically his opposite and temperamentally put off by his self-restraint and evasiveness, she is nonetheless drawn first to his fiction and later to the man, whom she finds "encouraging" in that he hasn't "exhausted normality yet" (132)— any more than the English novelists, including Bradbury and Walker, have exhausted realism. Like Whitman, she seems to contain if not multitudes exactly then at least contradictions.

Virtually a caricature, as Daisy Miller was, of "the American girl," she nonetheless prefers Europe to America, which she claims to detest. Dispensing sex and Kierkegaard in nearly equal measure, she seems to embody what D. H. Lawrence defined as the essential paradox of the American character, which (he noted) is at once idealistic and pragmatic, as concerned about redeeming the world as fixing the plumbing. Whether she indeed loves Walker, as she once claims, or simply, in typically American fashion, wants to redeem him by remaking him in her own image, is impossible to say. What is clear, however, is the degree to which she understands Walker's character and, especially, his limitations. As she explains, or rather accuses, near the end of their trip, " 'You gave in. You lost style. You let it beat you. There were two of us and you acted like there was only one' " (397). She is right, of course, but her emphasis is nonetheless disconcerting, if only as an undertone, for what it suggests is not only her dogmatic assertiveness and preference for style (and stylishness) over that stubborn sense of substance that Walker holds so dear, but her failure (playing as she does her Lolita to his Humbert, her Daisy to his Winterbourne) to attain his level of self-criticism and self-awareness. It is a failure that in turn seems to have been fostered by the family wealth, which insulates her from having to consider the results of her actions and which allows her to move through America as effortlessly as Walker moves through it slowly, ponderously, pondering what he sees. Although she is not, as Fitzgerald's Daisy certainly is, one of "the careless people," neither is she as humanly concerned as she may at first appear. Her economic advantage is not shared by Walker, Jochim, or Julie's opposite, Miss Fern Marrow, the thirty-two-year-old English virgin whom Walker also meets while in transit to America. As ludicrous as her name ("like the vegetable," she says [102]), Miss Marrow nonetheless serves to remind the reader of that moral marrow, that inmost or essential part, that Julie discounts as she travels rapidly through time and space. In its way, Julie's surname is no less connotative than Miss Marrow's, suggesting, for example, a certain childlike quality as well as some of the same iciness that characterizes James's Winterbourne. And her name may be no less ludicrous than Miss Marrow's either, recalling the Indian maiden Princess Summerfallwinterspring who used to appear on the popular 1950s American television show for children, "Howdy Doody."

Bernard Froelich is another manifestation of the "idea" of America, as Martin Green has noted, and his name, too, suggests a similar dualism or ambivalence. The Germanic harshness of its phonemes works against what the name means literally: gay, cheerful, merry. Happy as the ever-grinning Froelich often is, his cheerfulness is itself as ambiguous as his reasons for bringing Walker to Party: to further his book, part of which concerns Walker's fiction; to explode the complacency of his departmental colleagues, especially his chairman, Harrison Bourbon, who would reduce art "to simple order" (12); to acquire for himself a "soul mate," a living reminder of his brief stay in Britain; and, finally, to test the English character, its complacency and relevance. As the narrator—adopting Froelich's point of view and sounding a good deal like the narrator of *The Education of Henry Adams*, another transatlantic narrative—points out: "he [Froelich] wanted to confront an Englishman with confusion, and see what part of the equation would change" (316). The fact that his chief American antagonist is the teetotaling arch-conservative Harrison Bourbon, the author of *The Bucket of Tragedy*, in which he condemns "all art not formally tragic in structure" (24), is certainly in Froelich's favor. But while his praenomen may suggest altruistic service, his actions imply not a certain respect for but (on Bradbury's part) a certain criticism of the concept of the imperial self. In Bernard Froelich we find more than a merely acronymic echo of Benjamin Franklin, patron saint of pragmatism and self-advancement, cut free, however, from Franklin's interest in social meliorism. The goal of Froelich's "militant" liberalism is to spearhead a cause, but the causes he spearheads seem invariably to involve solely his own personal advancement. Thus Froelich illustrates once again Bradbury's sardonic point that eating people is indeed wrong. "This was yet another reason for wanting the man," Froelich reasons; "he could feed his life into Froelich's book, he could be kept perpetually under observation" (26). In such fashion Froelich effects the transformation of American liberalism into the American behaviorism of B. F. Skinner.

It is not the only transformation in *Stepping Westward*. In James's "An International Episode," being American (Bessie Alden claims) means being able to make all the mistakes one wants. For Froelich, it means something a bit different: doing anything one wants. The American Adam becomes the American ego, a Mr. Hyde-like creature lurking in freedom's shadow, resembling less a monster than an exhibitionistic child demanding and usually getting his own way. Such satisfactions as the child, or the child-like Froelich, achieves prove ultimately unsatisfying, however. Froelich's desires outstrip that ironic sense of Lodgean limitations which the novel's very form implies. *Stepping Westward* ends as it began, with a meeting of the creative writing fellowship committee. At the earlier meeting, Froelich got what he wanted: Walker. Now, having subsequently effected Bourbon's fall from power and his own rise to departmental chair, Froelich gains yet another victory. The committee approves his request to use the fellowship money to fund a new journal which Froelich will edit and in which he will publish chapters of his oft-rejected book on "Twentieth Century Plight, with special reference to Post-War plight." Yet even as he gains this victory, "all that Froelich could think was that he, since he *was* human, was missing Walker very, very much" (415). The Walker he misses may be Walker the friend, though one suspects that, even more, it is Walker the audience, the dutiful student willing to learn the lesson of the master, Froelich. In either case, the doubling of adverbs here, as at the very end of *Eating People Is Wrong* ("never, never") serves to ironize Froelich's losses. The reader hears, as it were, an undertone of sadness and longing, but it is an undertone that is undermined by a further irony. The effect of this deeper irony suggests the depthlessness of Froelich's character, his tendency (and Julie's) to skim the surface while the hapless and seemingly anachronistic Walker continues slowly on his pilgrim's progress, comically, yet in a way deeply, pondering the plight of self and other in the postwar world.

Citing Norman O. Brown's *Life Against Death*, Martin Green claims that "what Froelich has, what 'America' has, and what Walker has not, is an egotism of the body," which is to say the spontaneity of instinctual drives rather than, as in Walker's case, the repression of cultural abstractions (58). Walker is drawn to the idea of America made flesh (in the person of Julie Snowflake) and to American egotism (as exemplified by Froelich in particular). Walker the Anglo-liberal wants to "eschew definition"; Walker the would-be American wants, as he says, or rather as he thinks, "to work in with the wheels of history," or what he alternately (and I believe more accurately) comes to judge as the "myths of dispossession" (387). Walker opts for people over myths, commitment over liberation, reality over possibility, England over America. In making this choice, he manifests that "marked disposition" of the English novelist to "distrust all alternate lands of the imagination" (Bradbury, "Dangerous Pilgrimages," Feb. 1977: 58). Consequently, Walker chooses to return to his English home, to his drab but faithful wife, the nurse and mother who will nurse and mother him, and he chooses as well to accept the role of the good "squire" while wistfully recalling his Kerouac-ean "days on the road" (402). Unlike his precursor, Dickens' Martin Chuzzlewit, the wistful Walker cannot proclaim that he "left home on a mad enterprise" and that his only hope "is to quit this settlement for ever and get back to England. Anyhow! by any means!" (233). What Walker feels is not exclamatory and certain, only "sorry, very sorry, for he knew already that it was pleasanter by far to be that man" (402), that man being Walker as the American, or Anglo-American, Adam.

Walker's willingness to settle for so little disappoints his Virgil and Beatrice, Froelich and Julie, and it seems to have disappointed Bradbury as well. But the Bradbury whom Walker disappoints is not so much the author of *Stepping Westward*, who creates in Walker's "sorry, very sorry" another ironic echo of Treece's terminal inconsequentiality and an equally ironic anticipation of Froelich's sad but superficial longing at novel's end. No, the Bradbury whom Walker disappoints is chiefly the writer who has subsequently described Walker as "my undoubtedly negative hero" ("Introduction" xii), one who is unable to "defeat his own innocence, though he knows that he should" ("Dangerous Pilgrimages," Feb. 1977:64). The novel in which Walker appears is not, however, nearly as simple and straightforward as Bradbury's after-the-fact description of its protagonist would make it seem. Rather, it is, as Bradbury has said of Kingsley Amis's *One Fat Englishman*, published two years earlier, "a very ambiguous text, half patronising, half anxious . . . aware of the English limitations" ("Dangerous Pilgrimages," Feb. 1977: 62–63). Although his image of America may be far more appealing than Amis's, Bradbury is nonetheless well aware of the American limitations, or so his novel implies. Walker may be wrong to forego the "existential releases" that Julie offers him, but such resistance is entirely in keeping with Bradbury's own wish to preserve, as well as to test, the essence of British liberalism and the viability of the liberal novel. Walker may understand that it is the existential American Adam that he would like to be, but he is also dimly aware that "the wandering wilful self he had spent these last months upon was already starving to death for lack of sustenance" (402). The language here betrays

Walker's feelings of guilt (perhaps deserved, perhaps not). It also suggests Bradbury's necessary ambivalence towards both America and England—the one a visionary world elsewhere devoid of historical as well as moral substance, the other an all too solid land devoid of imaginative alternatives. It is possible to say of Walker at the end of *Stepping Westward* what Malamud says of S. Levin midway through *A New Life*, that "his escape to the West had thus far come to nothing, space corrupted by time, the past contaminated self" (154). However, the English past that corrupts Walker's American present and therefore prevents his existential release is also what saves him from, for example, Froelich's undeserved egotism and grinning manipulation of others. "In the circumstances in which we see his hero placed," Walker reads in Harrison Bourbon's copy of A. C. Bradley's *Shakespearen Tragedy*, "his tragic trait, which is also his greatness, is fatal to him. To meet these circumstances something is required which a smaller man might have given, but which the hero cannot give" (225). Given where the reader sees Walker "placed"—not in *Hamlet* or *Macbeth* but in a comic novel, and more specifically, sitting on a toilet in a town called Party—there is obviously something ludicrous in applying Bradley's definition of the tragic hero to Bradbury's decidedly unheroic Walker, whose indecisiveness is not Hamlet's, not even Prufrock's. Yet, however grotesquely, Bradley's words do apply. As Edwin Morgan has pointed out, "Walker's various defeats" have to be weighed against "a certain respect he rouses . . . in the reader."

We need to remind ourselves that the author of *Stepping Westward* is also the author of a doctoral dissertation entitled "American Literary Expatriates in Europe: 1815 to 1950," as well as a teacher who "throughout the fifties . . . shuttled the Atlantic," who was offered faculty appointments on both sides, and who, married to an "Ur-English wife," eventually settled down "by the Humber in buttondown shirts reading Bellow and Mailer" ("Introduction" ix), fascinated by an America that seemed (as he points out in his *Introduction to American Studies*) at once a utopia and a dystopia (1). For Bradbury, America and England are not merely different geographical locations; they represent contrasting metaphors and alternative ways of perceiving life that he not only juxtaposes but also allows to challenge one another. Just as nineteenth century American writers such as Hawthorne and James were drawn to Europe by the richness of its history, the British writer has been drawn to America by its unformed vastness and boundless energy. The Walker who arrives in New York sees before him a magnetic New World of possibilities and contingencies which simultaneously attracts and repels. As the dissolution of the European past in the American present suggests, the boundlessness of the new world presents its own difficulties, moral as well as perceptual. " 'Ah, that's the problem,' " Walker begins to understand even before he reaches the American shore, " 'where to start and where to stop' " (61). The America Walker imagines is "a universe of energy in which he might find himself at home" (34), but the America he actually finds is a country that grows before his eyes "vaster and vaster, less and less controllable" (194). It is a land and a landscape that is at once everything and nothing, a realist's version of a Beckett set combined with Henry Adams' idea of multiplicity. It is a realistic landscape that hints at both the slapstick and the surreal, the existential and the photographic: a world of architecturally imitative buildings gathered together as a huge and aesthetically tasteless collage college. It is a world in which each township can vote its own time and where Walker, like everyone else in this reductively pragmatic America, is expected to make choices without having any basis for the choices he makes. For Froelich and Bourbon, the American liberal and the American conservative, respectively, this defines "real democracy." For Walker, it signifies something quite different: confusion and "anarchy." Together these constitute one view of manichaean America, the other being the arch-conservatism of loyalty oaths spawned by Froelich's brand of radical liberalism. The same point is made more directly late in the novel when a cab driver tells the departing—or is it "fleeing"?—Walker about Manhattan traffic: " 'One automobile too many and this island stops. . . . We live on the edge of chaos here' " (408).

" 'At bottom,' " Froelich explains to Walker, " 'America is freefloating and anarchic . . . I sometimes figure that this is why American novels are more experimental than English ones. In your novels the narrative line runs chronologically, and why? Greenwich Mean Time. In American novels, time and law are jumbled; point of view goes all over the place; that is because our visions and our experiences are more fragmentary and separate. We each live in our own time and value zone' " (197–198). In *Stepping Westward*, Bradbury attempts, structurally as well as thematically, to mediate between English and American narrative modes, as well as between English and American cultural sensibilities. In its opening sections, the novel follows a simple, indeed at times a tediously reductive, chronological pattern that causes the reader to experience time, as Walker does, as a confining presence, a spatial restriction. But as the novel progresses, it becomes, in setting and in style and pacing, less constrained, more expansive. This is not to say that *Stepping Westward* ever becomes the kind of American novel that Froelich describes—a *Moby-Dick* or a *Sound and the Fury*. In fact, the frame device that Bradbury adopts provides an interesting and ironic commentary on the paradoxical nature of American political and narrative freedom: what the reader sees at the end of the novel is a group of Americans reenacting the same academic ritual portrayed at the very beginning. His comments about his "undoubtedly negative hero" notwithstanding, I strongly suspect that Bradbury agrees with his bewildered Walker, who is attracted to American freedom but who wants something less extreme, something closer to an elusive middle way between commitment and anarchy, between English torpor and American (com)motion.

The question that David Lodge raises directly in his sixth novel, *How Far Can You Go?*, is implicit in all of Bradbury's fiction and in a good deal of his criticism as well. How far, Bradbury seems to be asking in *Eating People Is Wrong*, can Anglo-liberalism go before it degenerates into either moral paralysis or moral cannibalism? And how far, he seems to be asking in his second novel, can the English liberal and the English liberal novelist go—how far west can they step—before they lose their hold on what is best in the liberal and realistic traditions? How far can American liberalism go before it transmogrifies into either chaos or its opposites, psychological behaviorism and political McCarthyism? And just how far can Walker go in his attempt to break free of his culturally induced repressions and be reborn before he becomes nothing more than a performing self, an object to be observed, or merely a means to other people's ends? More and more this is precisely what Walker does become. Seeking to situate himself in history, wanting to be the man that Froelich (a vicarious novelist as well as critic manqué?) has imagined him to be, Walker finds that he has become, like Party, only "a concatenation of circumstances" (181), a man engulfed by the sands of American contingency. Returning to England surely represents a defeat for Walker, who, thanks to his sojourn in America, has become physically stronger and psychologically more determined. But in returning to hearth and home, Walker does more than simply resist change. He resists as well the drift towards dehumanization that seems to afflict the novel's various American Adams, the party of hope in Party, whose chief articles of faith are: (1) a not especially enlightened self-interest, and (2) a firm belief that the past does not hide in the present, that the individual can indeed change his or her character and so can effect his or her secular salvation. The dialogue of English and American voices in the novel is never resolved, even as they go their transatlantic ways at book's end. Instead of resolution, Bradbury provides a ceaseless juxtaposition of voices in which each voice modifies the others, leaving the reader poised somewhere between belief and clerkly skepticism and in possession of not so much an ending to this particular novel as a sense of an ending. He finds himself dispossessed of both the more or less stable irony to be found at the end of *A New Life* (Gilley's " 'Got your picture' ") and the lyrical intensity at the end of *The Great Gatsby* ("And so we beat on, boats against the current"). Instead of separating the voices, as he does in *Phogey! How to Have Class in a Classless Society* (1960) and *All Dressed Up and Nowhere to Go* (1962)—the one a satire on English traditions, the other a send-up of the British version of American consumer society— Bradbury dialogically mingles them in *Stepping Westward*'s very texture and on every one of its pages.

4

The History Man:
Engulfed by Sand

STEPPING WESTWARD DEALS with the Englishman's as well as with the English novelist's need to cast off his cultural restraints, a need that is, however, complicated by Bradbury's decidedly ambivalent portrait of America. His next novel, *The History Man*, published ten years later, deals with the problem that this ambivalence implies and that the author's subsequent comments concerning his "undoubtedly negative hero" tend to mask, or monologize, namely, what happens when the past that Walker (for example) tries, but fails, to escape is successfully cast off? The novel's answer seems to be that—to borrow a line from Bradbury's poem, "Wanting Names for Things"—"a little past would help" (*Two Poets* 46). Such a modest claim is, however, complicated and dialogized in that (1) it is in danger of being drowned out by the more insistent and clamorous voice of cultural fashion, and (2) it will undoubtedly sound merely reactionary, a literary echo of Margaret Thatcher's (and Ronald Reagan's) political conservatism. In another early poem, Bradbury articulates his dilemma in a self-consciously dated idiom, in effect exaggerating a voice he even then presumed to be marginal:

> And I, who have lived so long in the comfort of
> A relative happiness, and whose general affections
> Are in the family, wife and son, a bourgeois bore,
> Nostalgic for big houses, well-kept lawns,
> Look, I'm afraid, like being out of business.
> (*Two Poets* 29)

The tone here is as wistful as it was genial in the first two novels. But in *The History Man*, the liberalism that Bradbury previously sought both to test and to preserve, that he then placed under various "strains," is now under "threat." In fact the word "threat" begins to appear in his writings from the early 1970s on with considerable frequency and urgency, as in *The Social Context of Modern English Literature* (1971). In that work, Bradbury's aim is "to consider the ecology of modern writing in England, and to explore it . . . as a difficult and a challenging environment, potentially a threatening environment" (258). Like his own character, James Walker, but less sleepily, more acutely, Bradbury the writer feels "out of business." He finds himself displaced, under historical pressure, suddenly made more clearly marginal in an age in which literature no longer enjoys the support of its culture, an age which has turned away from the novel and imagination and towards film, television, and sociology. These changed circumstances necessitate a renegotiation on the writer's part of his place and practice in the culture. The crisis is particularly acute, Bradbury feels, because so many of "the liberal and humane virtues close to much art, if not all, have become not only socially but intellectually at risk."[1] Bradbury accepts the sociological perspective that has largely usurped liberalism's place; what he rejects is the definitiveness of that or any perspective which puts "society first and man in it second."[2] Although Michiko Kakutani has commented as recently as 1983 on the British writer's clear sense of vocation, it is precisely this sense that the sociological perspective has effectively undermined. As Bradbury explained to an American audience in the early 1970s, "The British writer is less confident now about his audience, his own role, his language. New novels seem timidly technical. The latest Amis novel is merely a scared *Lucky Jim*" (Honan, "Symposium" 211). Four years and one novel (*The History Man*) later, Bradbury makes much the same point: "we live in an age in which fiction has conspicuously grown more provisional, more anxious, more self-questioning, than it was a few years ago" (*Novel Today* 8). But Bradbury makes the point in a manner which suggests that he has found a way to transform his anxiety into art, to fashion his own

1. Liberalism, as Bradbury has defined it, is "a set of virtuous principles which are secreted in our culture without necessarily being functional in our culture" (Interview with Bigsby 66). Elsewhere he has noted, "In a sense my liberal humanism might be said to be a capacious envelope which I am prepared to put around many different things, to the point where they become totally inconsistent with each other" (Interview with Haffenden 51).
2. Bradbury's critique of sociology began some years before with his comments in *Phogey!* (1960) and *All Dressed Up* (1962) where he claims that with the rise of sociology "conscience was replaced by pure behaviour, emulation by ego, tradition by trauma, ancestors by angst" and that although novelists and sociologists use the same basic material, sociologists "do a random sample first" (*All Dressed Up* [1986] 125, 92). A writer who shares Bradbury's concern over the misguided importance attached to sociology in the modern world is Walker Percy: ". . . sociology is a simplification, an abstraction from what is the case. A novelist should be concerned with what is the case in the world, the facts, the richness, the intricacy and the variety of the way things are" (19–20).

brand of Lodge's "problematic novel." He seems to have discovered the necessary means by which (as John Barth pointed out in his "Literature of Exhaustion" essay) "an artist may paradoxically turn the felt ultimacies of our time into material and means for his work—*paradoxically* because by doing so he transcends what had appeared to be his refutation . . ." (78).

The same cannot be said of the fictive novelist who appears briefly in *The History Man*. Looking a good deal like Bradbury and possessing a similar academic appointment and list of publications, he is a man who had, ten years before, published two novels of "moral scruple" but who has since been silent, "as if, under the pressure of contemporary change, there was no more moral scruple and concern, no new moral substance to be spun" (204). Asked to divulge the heroine's address to the novel's perhaps dastardly, radical-chic-mau-mau protagonist, Bradbury's out-of-business novelist refuses and, Vonnegut-fashion, feebly asks the protagonist to cease and desist. Richard Todd considers this encounter between protagonist and authorial clone "a very crucial passage." The novelist, he claims, "is unwilling to relinquish Miss Callendar to the forces of radicalism, yet this relinquishment has been implicit in the very act of writing his novel. The moral paradox," Todd adds, "is a very poignant one" (177). Todd's language betrays his rather sentimental reading of Bradbury's rather unsentimental novel. Instead of dwelling on the "poignancy" of the novel's moral paradox, it would be better, I believe, to distinguish more carefully between the novel's elusive author, Bradbury, and the all-too-easily defined writer who appears briefly in it. And it would be much more fruitful to attend closely to their quite different responses to the situation in which both, as Anglo-liberal novelists, find themselves in the age of both Aquarius and Sociology. The fictive writer withdraws into the same silence from which he emerged. The author of *The History*

Man enters into a dialogue with his age, manifesting, largely through subtle parody, a keen awareness of his cultural milieu, responding obliquely and in decidedly contemporary fashion rather than directly and anachronistically, in a novel of great risks and equally great achievement.

Rather than lamenting the loss of characters, and of character, in the modern world and the modern novel (as Bradbury's whilom novelist undoubtedly would do were he one of Forster's rounded creations), Bradbury writes in such a way as to incorporate the loss of character into the very texture of his novel. In doing this, he transforms the fictive novelist's impotence into a remarkably effective and distinctly contemporary moral style. In a novel in which even the modernist-looking universities are managed like factories, the characters appear interchangeable, playing their assigned parts in the novel's various plots, Bradbury's as well as each other's. Thus, we find a woman "whose name is Flora Beniform, a social psychologist," for example, and "some people called the Kirks," Howard and Barbara. "There are many roles for a Howard to perform in a modern society," including lover, though not his wife's lover. That is a role played by "an actor called Leon" who, when Barbara says she doesn't know what she will do while he's away on tour, responds, " 'I'm not the only one like me' " (53, 1, 68, 52, 196). The novel's characters are almost entirely their roles, their professions, their names. In some cases they are rendered as nothing more than human causes of observable effects: "A window smashes . . . the cause is Henry Beamish, who has put his left arm through and down, and slashed it savagely on the glass" (93). Like the fictive novelist who would save Annie Callendar if he could, and save as well the idea of character that she represents, most of the novel's collection of names, roles, and causes feel dissatisfied. Aware, however dimly, of their diminished selves, they wish to be more of the essence, less merely of the existence. As one of them tries to explain to Howard, " '. . . it's hard to know you're little . . . people like to make themselves matter' " (126). They do so, either like Henry, by making "a minimal suicide attempt" (118) as Flora calls it, or like Annie, by rising from the level of sub-plot to main narrative, or like Mrs. Prokosch in Bradbury's short story, "Nobody Here in England," "angling for a little place in history" by peddling her bottle of George Bernard Shaw's sperm to the highest academic bidder (*Who Do You* 88). Such pleas are, however, both more and less than what they may at first seem. " 'I don't think you understand what I'm telling you,' " Barbara tells her husband; " 'I'm telling you that your gay belief in things happening doesn't make me feel better any more' " (17). In such a line the reader detects the sound of authentic anguish and human longing, but, as with so much of what Barbara says in this novel, her authenticity is undermined by her habitual self-pity, her understandable yet nonetheless largely fashionable feminist claims about having been exploited.

The exploiter in this case (and in most others in the *The History Man*) is her husband, Howard Kirk, a latterday Don Giovanni who enjoys what virtually all of the novel's other characters lack. He is the essential character, the center towards which all the others gravitate and around which they revolve, the "presence" against which their relative "absence" may be measured. He is a decidedly ambiguous character in a double sense. On the one hand he is the novel's most fully realized, rounded figure, and on the other hand he is a walking abstraction, a thoroughly dehumanized history man, wholly and solely a man of his particular times. At once loathesome and likable, cankerous and charismatic, Kirk is, as Bradbury later felt compelled to point out, "more serious and competent than to some reviewers he has seemed" ("Dog," Jan. 1979: 42). From his long hair and Zapata moustache to his "Habitat" alarm clock, Kirk, who wants "to turn style into quality" (Interview with Haffenden 26), is nothing if not "relevant." He represents the next stage in the secular pilgrim's progress, first described by Jung, from priest to psychiatrist, and now to sociologist; as his wife points out, he is " 'what we have instead of faith' " (8). Although conscientiously opposed to bourgeois individualism and privacy, Kirk is rather possessive; he keeps his van locked and the manuscript of his new book, *The Defeat of Privacy*, carefully out of sight (or, rather, not so carefully; it is as if Kirk wants to have his manuscripts discovered and read, his privacy violated). Having completed his new book (like *The History Man*, the author's third), Kirk now feels the need "to be back into, to intervene in, the larger, grander, more splendid plots that are plotted by history" (6), or, as a postmodernist would argue, plotted by people like Kirk, novelists and history men. Where Kirk differs from the novelist, whether liberal or postmodernist (or some combination of the two, as Bradbury seems to be here), is that instead of using characters in his historical plots, he uses people. On his magic island, England, Kirk is both Prospero—an "impresario of the event," a "great magician of the feelings"—and Caliban, a cannibal, for whom eating people is anything but wrong. Like Froelich, he espouses liberation, but his politics seem closer in practice to those of B. F. Skinner than to those of Wilhelm Reich: ". . . as Howard always says, if you want to have something that's genuinely unstructured, you have to plan it carefully" (6–7).

Howard possesses a "passion to make things happen" (53), to order the chaos, to make reality (a reality that is full of theories and action but devoid of people and values). However, for all his manipulative and imaginative power, Kirk is in fact considerably less liberated than he believes. He appears locked in a vast Skinner box of his own making, blind to the limitations and factitiousness of his sociological point of view. That his Socsci 4.17 class meets in "an interior room without windows, lit by artificial light" (127) serves metaphorically to underscore the narrowness of his perspective in general and of his particular brand of sociology in particular. (By "sociology" Kirk means "social tensions, twilight areas, race issues, class-struggle, battles between council and community, alienated sectors, the stuff, in short, of true living" [41]). Where Bradbury finds a world that conforms less and less to his Anglo-liberal ideals, Kirk sees a world that confirms his vision all too well—or perhaps just all too easily. Observing the clerk in a wine store, "Howard sees with gratification the indignation of the employed and oppressed, the token resistance" (13). What does not correspond to his vision of the world, to his sociological theories, Howard simply reasons away. Part of his problem is that he can make monological sense of everything, even suicide. His limitations are evident as well in his tending towards monologue. When his wife reads his account of "the exemplary Kirk story" in his first book, she claims that it reveals him as a " 'poseur' " who has " 'substituted trends for morals and commitments' " and who has turned their lives " 'into a grand plot. [It is] a big universal story' " fantasized by " 'a kind of self-made fictionalized character who's got the whole story on his side just because he happens to be writing it' " (31, 32–33). Howard's response—" 'you've not read it properly' "—is especially illuminating when read in the context of a remark Bradbury makes a short time later in an essay on moderism and postmodernism in which he notes that "the danger [for literary critics] is to reach the point of critical closure too soon and too confidently, a danger always present in the critical ambition" ("Modernism/Postmodernism" 327).

The History Man—but not the history man—not only avoids this danger, it takes the tendency towards such closure as its underlying subject, placing all interpretations in figurative quotation marks. The "exemplary Kirk story" mentioned above, for example, is "an attractive and popular story for the times"; the "earlier tellings" of "the exemplary case of the Kirks" (as it is alternately but not quite synonymously called) "had concentrated on the liberation plot. . . . But after a while, there were certain elements of skepticism that needed to be introduced for probability's sake, not utterly disconfirming the tale of a couple moving buoyantly, self-realizingly, through the exploding consciousness of man in history, perhaps even complicating and improving it" (31). Here, and indeed throughout the novel, Bradbury emphasizes a postmodernist blurring of fact and fiction as well as an open-ended multiplicity of arbitrary versions, readings, and misreadings of events and people. Individual readings are never corrected or cancelled ("erased") completely; "traces" invariably remain in a novel that successfully mingles Anglo-liberalism and "endless semiosis." Howard, for example, interprets one ambiguous occurrence—Henry's injury—as "a happening, a chance or a contingent event" upon which no "meaning or purpose" has been imposed. But as Flora Beniform points out to Howard, and therefore to the reader, to call the occurrence an accident imposes its own meaning. "The trouble with our profession," psychologist Beniform tells sociologist Kirk, "is, we still believe in motives and causes. We tell old-fashioned stories" (113). So too does Bradbury, but like Flora he is aware that the story he tells is old-fashioned (in its Anglo-liberal preoccupations), and it is precisely this awareness that marks *The History Man* as a distinctly contemporary novel. That is to say, it is a novel in which, as Frank Kermode has noted, the reader finds "a kind of crisis in the relation between fiction and reality, the tension or dissonance between paradigmatic form and contingent reality" (133).

In *The History Man* this crisis is dramatized in the conflict between Kirk, the high priest of paradigmatic (and entirely abstract) History, and Annie Callendar, who, as her name suggests, represents the escape from the plot of History (as Kirk defines it) to the contingency and freedom of individual days: the openness of her "calendar" versus the closure of his very full appointment book. Not that the opposition is narratively quite so clearly defined. Howard is, after all, as appealing as he is loathesome, and while Annie represents the strengths of the liberal aesthetic, she (like Treece and Walker) also embodies its limitations. She stands for the figurative over the literal, connotative possibilities over denotative meanings, the moral conscience over the merely social (or totalitarian). Her views are noble but, in a world made in Kirk's image, no longer viable. Although she may at times sound up-to-date— " 'It must be nice to think there is a true reality,' " she tells him, adding " 'I've always found reality a matter of great debate' " (143)—her views, derived from Henry James and Lionel Trilling, are in fact as anachronistic (and therefore vulnerable) as Howard's are fashionable (and therefore seemingly impregnable). Just as Howard molds contingency into his sociological image, Annie recoils from it. She seeks refuge in the illusory stability of a Victorian neighborhood (from which cars are banned) and in the formal perfection of lyric poetry. All of this makes her easy prey for Kirk's brand of urban and psychic renewal. The "humanistic balance" between "the reality of persons" and "the reality of society, or history," that is the hallmark of the liberal novel is precisely what Howard and Annie, in their quite different ways, fail to achieve (*Possibilities* 13). *The History Man* is not, therefore, as one reviewer has confidently claimed, "a defence . . . of the traditionally liberal fiction, where life's contingency is welcomed and the otherness of other people is lovingly insisted upon" (Cunningham). Nor is the novel weakened, as Ronald Hayman has charged, by Bradbury's allowing Annie to succumb to Howard's sexual (and ideological) advances—a criticism that tells us less about the novel than about the reviewer's nostalgia for the moral supremacy of the liberal view (43). In her critique of Howard's third book, Barbara complains that Howard is trying to do away with action and people; in response, Howard claims that Barbara is trying to do away with theory. In his third novel, *The History Man*, Bradbury brings the two sides together, as neither Howard nor Annie can, and in doing so he extends the boundaries of liberal fiction. What he achieves is not a "humanistic balance" of self and history, the individual and the abstract, the contingent and the paradigmatic, but something more significant because it is more viable: a dialogue between the individual self and the abstract theory, between liberal novel and postliberal, postmodern fiction. The dramatic conflict between Kirk and Callendar is therefore of no more interest than what it implies concerning the conflict between the liberal tradition and the postmodern example. It is for this reason that the novel is of far greater interest and complexity than the prefatory "Author's Note" suggests.

Insofar as it rejects the novel's mimetic function, the note makes clear its affinity to literary postmodernism. However, to read the note as an explanation of the novel which follows it rather than as an integral part of that novel, one that is subject to the same degree of irony, would be, I believe, a grave mistake. It would be as grave a mistake as choosing to overlook or undervalue the "Author's Note" in order to facilitate one's reading of *The History Man* as conventional, "consumable" fiction. To read the note as explanation would not only univocalize as well as privilege the postmodernist "author's" commentary on his text, it would also render that text superfluous by explaining it away in advance. The novel would be nothing more than the inevitable result of the postmodernist theory which conditions it. However, if we accept Roland Barthes' contention that who speaks is not who writes and who writes is not who is, we will form a clearer idea as to why it is necessary to distinguish between the author of the note and the author of *The History Man*. The author of, or in, the note is not Bradbury; instead, it is one of a number of voices to be heard in a dialogic novel whose own Bradburyan author is himself nothing more and nothing less than the uncertain intersection of authorial-narrative voices. In this capacity, he plays old against new, realistic liberal tradition against both the behaviorism which Kirk practices (even if he does not espouse it) and the postmodern play towards which Bradbury seems increasingly, but also reluctantly, drawn.

The dialogic novel resists both the abstraction of dialectical thinking and the reductiveness of manichaean dichotomies. It is true, however, that *The History Man* does at times tease the reader with the possibility of simple oppositions, such as old versus new, or liberal versus behaviorist (or postmodernist). The history of the University of Watermouth, for example, is, "in encapsulated form, the history of modern times" (64), which is to say that it is an academic remake of Charlie Chaplin's *Modern Times*, made (again) in Kirk's exemplary image. (The two are, in fact, very nearly coextensive.) It is less a university than a factory devoted to high productivity, a non-place where privacy is impossible, where every person and every action is observed and analyzed, where everyone must conform to the rule of non-conformity, and where the rooms are "all like this, stark, simple, repetitious, each one an exemplary instance of all the others" (62). In such an aggressively and architecturally modern environment, conservatives such as Annie Callendar and Henry Beamish, "a social control and delinquency man" (167), appear not merely freakish but psychologically deviant. The curmudgeonly George Carmody, one of Annie's advisees, suffers from a severe "mental condition": he has a "linear mind" (132). Even worse, "Carmody wants to be what he says he is" (131)—a sure mistake at Watermouth where mythotherapy has supplanted the liberal self. Bradbury often depicts these characters in decidedly comic, even slapstick fashion. Beamish, for example, tends towards pratfalls, while Carmody appears as an undergraduate T. S. Eliot. Cloaked in a blue school blazer, he has all of the (liberal) tradition but little if any of the individual talent to shore the fragments against his, or anyone else's, ruin. Bradbury, the liberal novelist, distances himself from his liberal characters. He recognizes both the truth and the inadequacy of their views in a world of Kirks and Watermouths. Interestingly, he depicts Annie's opposite, Flora Beniform, in a far more appealing way, despite the fact that she is in many respects simply the embodiment of the same illiberalism to which Kirk and Water-mouth are committed. She refuses "to be counted on," turns all personal relationships into grist for the mill of her research into the politics of family life, and manages to reinvest for-nication "with new purpose and significance. She has con-ceived of it as a tactical advance on the traditional psychiatrist's couch . . ." (177). Although clearly a member in good standing of the therapeutic society that Bradbury satirizes (and a few years later, that Christopher Lasch, in *The Culture of Narcissism* rebukes), Flora gains a measure of the reader's and the au-thor's approval. She understands Howard at least as well as do any of the other characters; she is also the only character in the novel whom Howard is unable to dominate, or even manipulate, either sociopolitically or sexually. As physically attractive as she is intellectually (and physically) imposing, Flora has had a special appeal for Bradbury who has included her as a character in two variations on his *History Man* theme, the short story "Who Do You Think You Are?" and a television play entitled "The After Dinner Game."

Like Annie, Flora attends closely to language, especially to those interpretive ambiguities that Howard avoids. In parallel fashion, Bradbury attends closely to his novelistic language, certainly more closely than in either *Eating People Is Wrong* or *Stepping Westward*. It is not merely that he has become a more experienced writer but that he has shifted his interest from narrative action to narrative texture. And he has done so, not because this is the fashionably postmodernist thing to do, but because "to write, to paint, to produce a piece of music is to enact and attempt to realize a form of historical consciousness" ("Modernism/Postmodernism" 311). Attempting such an aes-thetic has become an increasingly self-conscious activity in the past few decades. Consequently, in the contemporary age, this historical consciousness must inevitably center on the commu-nication processes that are no longer merely the means to some higher truth (content) but are the end (subject) themselves. Thus, in *The History Man* we have the foregrounding of what, according to Bakhtin, is characteristic of all novelistic discourse. In the novel, Bakhtin has claimed, language "not only represents, but itself serves as the object of representation," self-referentially "criticizing itself." As Bakhtin goes on to point out, "the central problem for a stylistics of the novel"—and of course for the novelist—is "the problem of representing the *image* of a language" (*Dialogic* 49, 336; my italics). It is precisely in meeting this formidable challenge that *The History Man* succeeds so well.

Shortly after *The History Man* was published, Bradbury wrote an introduction for a reissue of his first novel in which he pointed out that *Eating People Is Wrong* "is a more generous comedy than I would write now, in a world that has so changed. . . . Writing more recently, I have found it harder to write in this spirit, because style is indeed a facet of history and changes with it. I have found comedy needs to become a more precise, a more economical, a harder instrument, if the contradiction between our humanist expectations and our sense of ourselves as exposed historical performers is to be expressed" (7–8). The harsher world of the 1970s demands its own "accelerated grimace," a harsher style equal to but also critical of, and so in dialogue with, the age it reflects in what may at first appear to be either a conventionally realistic or merely funhouse mirror. For George Steiner, Bradbury's style suggests considerably more: an "intense [Jamesian] stylization." Steiner's comparison is especially interesting given Bradbury's remark, in "A Dog Engulfed by Sand," that James's later fiction "owes much of its complexity to the problem of finding a grammar accurate to the act of perception" (Nov. 1978: 56). But the problem of finding a grammar, or style, equal to the act of perception is itself compounded by the writer's sense that, in the 1970s, "moral convictions had been displaced by a sense of style" (*After* 16). It was a displacement Bradbury not only perceived but had to avoid as he became increasingly preoccupied with novelistic texture. In *The History Man* Bradbury turns the merely stylish (and therefore morally substanceless) against itself. Instead of surrendering moral depth to surface texture, Bradbury masters it parodically. "Perhaps," Bradbury has written, "what we live in is indeed an age of parody: an age when . . . the feeling of substantial reality is dissipated by plurality and irony. Parody is, I take it, an ironic renegotiation of the relationship between style and substance, so that stylistic presentation passes into the foreground, and content is minimalised in the background; the result is that in some sense both become absurd" ("Age" 44). Compared with the *The History Man*, the nine parodies included in *Who Do You Think You Are* (1976, reprinted with an additional parody, "Mensonge," a send up of deconstruction) are fun but obvious; they please but they do not bring about the kind of renegotiation of style and substance that Bradbury wrote about. And the same can be said of Bradbury's very recent bestseller *Cuts: A Very Short Novel* (1987), which is not a novel at all; it is not, that is, a Bradburyan renegotiation. It is instead and at best a pleasurable but hardly blissful satire on the plight of the academic novelist seduced into writing for British television. Unlike *The History Man*, Bradbury's meditation on the fate of liberal man in the postmodern, postliberal age, and unlike *Rates of Exchange*, an elaborate exploitation of a single metaphor, *Cuts* is merely self-indulgent and redundant: a blot on the literary landscape. It strongly suggests that Bradbury requires the relative expansiveness of the novel form (as he defines it) for his imagination to best realize itself. *The History Man* is much more subtle and much more effective, largely due to the very element that had to be omitted in adapting the novel for British television, this being the novel's distinctive and complex narrative voice.

In his review of *The History Man*, Jay Halio writes that "The key to Bradbury's satire is the primer type of narration he uses to show how the Kirks, so far from being the free people they think they have become, are really automatons wrapped tightly in a rigid set of maoist principles, cliches, fashionable attitudes, and cant." Halio is right about the Kirks but wrong to impose a monologic reading on Bradbury's most dialogic novel, for in *The History Man* there is no single interpretive key which can be used to unlock the novel's meaning. There is no dominant key and no dominant language either, only languages and minimalist variations in this, the most artful and the most artificial of Bradbury's four novels. The "primer type of narration" identified as such a key is indeed pervasive and, more importantly, instructive in its own devious way. It hints at the flattened, reductive nature of contemporary reality and, as in Donald Barthelme's fiction, of contemporary speech: ". . . says Henry, 'it's a good place for a serious talk.' The good place for a serious talk is down in the city," for example, or "the floors are being cleaned by a cleaner with a cleaner" (164, 163). The language clearly mirrors the redundancy and emptiness of Bradbury's all-too-contemporary characters. However, the novel's language proves unstable; it slides and metamorphoses continually, though never so radically as to dispel entirely the illusion of narrative sameness.[3] The apparent seamlessness of the novel's narrative voice masks a multiplicity of vocal shadings, minute variations on the novel's liberal-linguistic theme. The primer style, for example, turns almost imperceptibly into something that reads like—or sounds like—the voice-over for a documentary: an anonymous voice describing what the panning camera-eye "sees." But there are other identifiable (if not narratively identified) voices as well. At times, for example, the narrative echoes the strained objectivity and pseudo-scientific syntax of a sociology textbook

3. In *What is a Novel?* Bradbury distinguishes between Thackeray, who chose to intrude on the action and editorialize about it, and Forster, who preferred "to make a delicate adjustment to the tone of the telling" (35). In *The History Man*, Bradbury clearly follows Forster's example.

("They had married, it is quite evident in informed hindsight, in the adult modern version, in order to reconstruct precisely that sort of family situation in which they had grown up" [23]), and elsewhere it mimics Howard's own prose style (in which "urgent feeling breaks up traditional grammar, methodology and organization" [6]). The childlike and the contemporary exist side by side and at times merge into what may best be described as the style of an adult fairy tale, in which the language mirrors the coyly self-conscious naivete of the Kirks and of the modern age they exemplify:

And that, more or less, give or take an element of self-interest here, a perceptual distortion or two there, a dark ambiguity in this place or that, is the exemplary and liberating story, as Howard explains, of how the little northern Kirks came to be down in Watermouth, with its high sunshine record and its palms and its piershow and its urban demolition, buying wine and cheese and bread, and giving parties; and, of course, growing some more—for the Kirks, whatever else they have done, have always gone right on growing. (35)

It is, above all, a chameleon style that takes on the protective coloration of its immediate environment—a deliberately centerless prose equivalent of its glossy but morally depthless age. In recording a meeting of the sociology faculty, for example, Bradbury adapts his pace and language to mimic the brusqueness of an actual meeting and more especially the biases and idiolect of professional sociologists. But when the narrator describes Flora's "compact, modern service flat," the narrative turns into that of a sales pitch, echoing the subtle suck and sell of these modern hard times: "They lie there in the master bedroom of Flora's compact, modern service flat, with its good-sized living-room, well-fitted galley kitchen, its second bedroom that doubles as study, its bathroom with bath and fitted shower, in the elegant block in the landscaped grounds in the leafy suburb, all described by the letting agents as perfect for modern living, and ideal for the professional single person"

(175). The sense of the times has entered into the very texture of Bradbury's prose in the same way that the verbs "prod" and "penetrate" appear with dismaying frequency in order to suggest the sexual aggression that underlies Howard's conception of society.

"In *The History Man*," Patricia Waugh has written, "the stable ironic voice of the author ensures that the reader can observe and evaluate Howard's version of the past and his imposition of various images and plots upon the present" (51). However, as we have already seen, the narrative (to say nothing of the authorial) voice in this novel is hardly stable. Except for characters such as Annie Callendar and George Carmody, there are no moral or narrative still points from which to evaluate Kirk. (And Callendar and Carmody are not simply stable but static and therefore anachronistic.) The reader can play the part of neutral observer, of passive consumer of Bradbury's product, only at his own peril, and herein lies the novel's moral strength and aesthetic integrity. The novel's matter-of-fact language invites effortless consumption but in fact demands the reader's close attention and even active participation if the linear thrust of the novel—and the culture it mirrors—is to be resisted successfully (which is to say on grounds other than those proposed by Callendar and Carmody). The easy-to-read, often sing-song descriptions mask a cultivated simplicity, a deceptive disingenuousness. Bradbury's prose implicates the reader, who can at times detect the more obvious ironies and so congratulate himself on his own perceptiveness, but who more often than not moves serenely and effortlessly through Bradbury's narrative minefield, lapsing into passivity as he reads a text that both delights and detonates. The novel pretends to objectivity, but this objectivity is deceptive in that it reflects not "the stable ironic voice of the author" but instead the "chosen blindness" of Bradbury's narrator and, more insidiously, Kirk's own point of view (Interview with Bigsby 74). We can see the way in which Bradbury achieves this effect by comparing a sentence from the novel with a very similar one from "Who Do You Think You Are?" In that story, Bradbury foregrounds his satirical intent; in effect he invites the reader to share in the authorial narrator's detachment and sense of moral superiority: "One thing about the house was that it was very conveniently placed for the kinds of social problem that, over the last few years, had become Edgar's stock-in-trade. There were squatters two streets away, and a hippy commune nearer still; there was a handy abortion clinic, and a twilight area with a severe problem of immigrant overcrowding within walking distance, and an active Sinn Fein group accessibly by" (*Who Do You* 39–40). But in the novel, the number of clever ironies ("within walking distance," "accessibly by," etc.) have been reduced and the distance between subject and narrator/reader shortened to the point of being virtually nonexistent: "It is an ideal situation for the Kirks, close to the real social problems, the beach, the radical bookshop, the family planning clinic, the macrobiotic food store, the welfare offices, the high-rise council flats, and the rapid ninety minute electric train service up to London, close, in short, to the stuff of ongoing life" (4). A second, slightly longer example from the novel will better illustrate the way in which Bradbury (like Kirk to a certain disconcerting degree) manipulates the narrative distance and therefore the reader's relationship to and acceptance of the views that are presented. The subject here is an essay Carmody has written for Kirk:

It is dull, dogged stuff, an old scheme of words, a weak little plot, a culling of obvious quotations surrounded by obvious comments, untouched with sympathy or that note of radical fire that, in Howard's eyes, has so much to do with true intellectual awareness. . . . The paper is like an overripe plum, collapsing and softening from its own inner entropy, ready to fall. It is the epitome of false consciousness; its ideas are fictions or pretences, self-serving, without active aware-ness; it moves towards its inevitable fate. (133).

By taking the passage out of the larger narrative context, we will be in a better position to see the way in which the narrative voice only seems to detach itself from Kirk's point of view and frame of reference. Clearly, the phrase "in Howard's eyes" has the effect of misleading the unwary reader. Denotatively it assigns a certain and very limited portion of the passage and of the valuations presented in it to Kirk. Connotatively, it implies that the remainder of the passage presents the narrator's completely independent and entirely trustworthy valuation of Carmody's essay. Like the "present-tense grammar" that Bradbury adopts throughout the novel and that serves to create that aura of immediacy, of things happening, of which Kirk would surely approve, this pretense of narrative objectivity serves to reflect as well as to lament the loss of historical detachment and moral responsibility in the world according to Kirk ("Dog" Jan. 1979:41).[4]

The reader of *The History Man* is—as many of the novel's characters are—awash in the immediacy of the present moment. That Bradbury excessively details this situation is not, as one reviewer claimed, an aesthetic mistake, for *The History Man* is not a realistic novel but a parody of and a challenge to "innocent realism" (Lodge's phrase). It is an attempt to make realism viable in the postmodern age. Bradbury uses details less to create a Jamesian solidity of specification than to produce a numbing effect, a sense of reductive equivalence. This narrative strategy is evident in, for example, the postcoital scene involving Howard and Flora in which what they say and what articles of clothing they don are accorded equal status (181–182) and in the scene in the university cafeteria in which eight speakers carry on a bewildering number of sometimes independent, sometimes overlapping, conversations (146–

4. In his interview with Haffenden, Bradbury explains that he uses the present tense throughout the novel in order to suggest "moral displacement" (45–46).

151). More interesting is the way in which Bradbury handles dialogue. On the one hand he tends to foreground his speakers by obsessively adding the "he/she says" tag to every spoken line. On the other hand, the lines of dialogue are not recorded individually; instead they are grouped together in long paragraphs in which individual speakers are engulfed by the larger context. Moreover, what Bradbury records are never conversations as such, but merely one-sentence exchanges. The characters seem not so much to be talking as playing a form of verbal Ping-Pong. Instead of the fullness we have come to expect of realistic fiction, Bradbury provides a sharply angled prose that serves both to reflect and to criticize the contemporary mass culture. "In the hardened acryllic realism of Hockney," Bradbury has written, "in the cityscapes of Antonini, in the arbitrary, contingent psychology of Handke, we can see a tone that is ours" ("Putting" 208). And precisely the same holds true for *The History Man* as well as for the novel it most resembles in style and substance, Walter Abish's *How German Is It*, published five years later.[5] In these major works of literary superrealism, reality and conventional realism are engulfed and supplanted by the style of contemporary reality. *The History Man* is Bradbury's most up-to-date, most parodic, and most richly ambiguous novel. In it he mocks and replenishes at the same time; he takes delight in his verbal inventiveness but also suggests his own degree of sadness and dismay over

5. Bradbury's description of Abish's novel is appropriate here: "Another formally very exacting return to the subject of Germany, in its flat modern materialism a world of signs without meanings under which dark meanings hide, where crisis relations between history and form persist, where the writer's task is to unlock the hidden code and penetrate the chaos inside. His work, bleak, detached, and bearing strong stylistic resemblances to that of Italo Calvino or Peter Handke, reminds us that 'postmodernism' is a more than American phenomenon, a ranging quest of the troubled contemporary imagination to find a style that faces our kind of world" (*The Modern American Novel* 184–185).

the contemporary human comedy, especially as it is perceived by the novelist aware of his limited options in the wake of the collapse of the liberal novel. As Bernard Bergonzi has pointed out in *The Situation of the Novel*, the contemporary writer seems to have but two choices, neither of which appears particularly inviting. One is to continue to produce works of liberal realism, works that will perforce have no importance. And the other is to abandon liberalism and embrace art so as to produce "an energetic, but an implicitly totalitarian or illiberal, fiction, in which the individual agent is dwarfed, diminished, often verbally violated" (Bradbury's summary; *Possibilities* 205). A novelist at the crossroads, Bradbury resists the extremes. He chooses neither nostalgic liberal realism nor totalitarian postmodernism. Neither a novel of wistful regret nor an example of dehumanized art, *The History Man* is a novel about dehumanization, aesthetic and moral.

According to the publisher's blurb on the front cover of the Penguin paperback edition, *The History Man* is "the classic sixties campus novel which gleefully skewers radical chic." Of course, the novel is considerably less gleeful than it may at first glance appear, and given the time between original hardback (1975) and Penguin paperback (1985) publications, the novel is a "classic" only if one accepts the very obsession with the present that the novel criticizes. Unlike the Penguin blurb, the Goya painting that Bradbury chose to appear on the dust jacket of the 1975 Secker & Warburg edition provides a less unintentionally ironic gloss on the novel's style and substance. "A Dog Engulfed by Sand," as the painting eventually came to be called, is one of those "grotesque surrealistic . . . studies in pain" that are collectively known as Goya's "Black Paintings"— black because of their grim subject matter as well as their narrow range of dark colors. What has particularly attracted Bradbury to this one particular work in the series is its ambiguity, the fact that it is impossible for the viewer to know whether there is indeed a figure being posed at all, and if there is whether it is a head, and if it is a head whether the head is to be seen as emerging from the sand or being engulfed by it. And what Bradbury finds especially fascinating is the way in which the painting "both qualifies and insists on the figure." The painting captures so perfectly the tension between realism and abstraction that lies, as Bradbury rightly insists, at the heart of modern existence and all modern art ("Putting" 205). Henry James's *The Golden Bowl*, Bradbury has noted, is "a novel of hardened form, of aestheticism grown ironic. The characters may *live* as consciousnesses, but they are positioned as objects, indeed *objets d'art*, vessels of being with cash value" (*Modern American Novel* 33). In the *History Man*, the situation has become still more extreme and the aestheticism more pronounced. The characters no longer exist as objects, but only as vague abstractions within the larger abstraction of History. Bradbury depicts this world with chilling though often comic accuracy, but at the same time he resists it. He insists (as Goya did) on the living figure, perceiving and presenting in narrative form not just the contemporary malaise but "the pain in the strangled victim" ("Putting" 208).

There is a special irony at work here, for, as I noted earlier, the novel's most fully "rounded" character is the very Kirk, Captain of the Starship (Sociological) Enterprise, who remains blind to the tension that animates both Goya's painting and Bradbury's novel. Not only is he the novel's only "rounded" character. He is also a novelist of sorts, either (as was briefly noted before) a spinner of old-fashioned tales involving causally related plots (as Flora claims) or (Bergonzi's alternative) the postmodernist maker of aesthetically totalitarian fictions. Just as Bradbury has dubbed John Fowles "the novelist as impresario," he has his narrator describe Kirk as an "impresario" of the various "happenings" he stages and directs. There are, however, significant differences between the two. One is that whereas Fowles (like Bradbury) manipulates his fictive characters as if they were real people, Kirk as impresario manipulates mimetically real people as if they were fictions. They provide grist for the mill of what Kirk contends is History but that the reader suspects is nothing more than Kirk's own excuse for imposing his egocentric fictions on others. The second and perhaps more important difference is that whereas the novelist as impresario self-reflexively calls attention to his fictions as fictions, Kirk does not. He remains unaware of, or at least unconcerned about, the ways in which fact and fiction affect one another and, more especially, the ways he furthers the process by which the individual figure is lost to abstraction. Kirk's plot to have Carmody expelled from the university illustrates this point rather well. Getting rid of Carmody enables Kirk to become the focus of student attention and to rise to new heights of radical fame, but the means by which he achieves these and other ends is less historically inevitable than narratively contrived. Terming Carmody "a juvenile fascist" (142), Kirk transforms himself into a "martyr of Carmodian persecution" (128) by a sleight of wits that elevates Kirk and trivializes that real-life example of the process of abstraction carried out on a mass scale, the Nazi extermination of Jews and other "enemies of the Reich." By invoking "the plot of history," which he calls "inevitable" (230), Kirk effectively excuses himself from complicity in and responsibility for the plots he himself has set in motion, even though the purpose of these plots is to serve Kirk's own egotistical ends. Foremost among these plots (or so Kirk would have her believe[6]) is the

6. It is impossible for the reader to determine whether Kirk is indeed as much in control as he would like Annie Callendar to believe or whether he is turning contingent events into Kirkian necessity in much the same way he usurps (of course without attribution) the language of others as his own. His explanation as to why he had sexual relations with his student, Felicity Phee, for example, echoes (with appropriate change of pronoun) Flora's earlier explanation as to why Beamish slashed his arm: "She was crying out for attention" (208).

wooing and bedding of Annie Callendar. Seducing Annie
entails eliminating Carmody, the whilom humanist who, in the
course of the novel, has transmogrified into a Kirk-like social
scientist observing and making public Kirk's sexual activities.
When Kirk tells Annie not to worry because Carmody is no
longer around to spy on them, she replies, " 'I rather wish he
was. . . . The critical eye' " (229). Lacking the necessary sense of
critical (and moral) detachment that she ascribes to Carmody,
Annie and Kirk come to exist entirely within Kirk's fiction. As
a result, neither hears the noise of a window breaking: "The
cause is Barbara who, bright in her silvery dress, has put her
arm through and down, savagely slicing it on the glass. In fact
no one hears; as always at the Kirks' parties, which are famous
for their happenings, for being like a happening, there is a
lot that is, indeed, happening, and all the people are fully
occupied" (230). Barbara's accident is not so much a variation
on the earlier one involving Henry Beamish as it is a repetition;
and as such, it serves as the most dramatic, and blackly humorous, illustration of the closure that—Howard's rhetoric notwithstanding—betrays the baselessness of his version of liberation sociology.

The ending of *The History Man* does not form, as Todd has
claimed, "a kind of existential question mark" (42); rather, it
is a subtly ironic commentary on Kirk's illiberalism in a novel
in which the characters are not condemned to one hundred
years of solitude but are "sentenced to history." "Who's
Hegel?" asks the novel's epigraph, borrowed from Gunther
Grass:

"Someone who sentenced mankind to history."

"Did he know a lot? Did he know everything?"

On the evidence of *The History Man* (but, again, not the history
man), the answer is clearly no, as it is as well in Derrida's

Glas, published one year earlier. In *Glas* Derrida juxtaposes (typographically as well as philosophically) Hegel and Jean Genet, using the latter to deconstruct the former. *Glas* begins with a question—"*quoi du reste aujourd'hui, pour nous, ici, maintenant, d'un Hegel?*"—and ends with this problematically open-ended answer or fragment—"*Aujourd'hui, ici, maintenant, le debris de.*" In its own quieter, less aggressive, and less opaque manner, *The History Man* forms a similar circle and reaches a similar goal, neatly undermining the authority of abstract Hegelian history, which Kirk espouses, without quite denying its validity. *The History Man* is, then, as Michael Church has noted, "a technical tour de force as well as a quietly devastating piece of social commentary." It is a work in which the liberal and the postmodern are juxtaposed in an effort to answer the question upon which Bradbury has based all of his work: "whether there is an individualism that can be reconstituted" (Interview with Bigsby 75). *The History Man* does not provide a definitive answer. What it does provide is a dialogical "loop-hole." As Bradbury has said, "what I hope that people will do when they put down a book of mine is actually to seek the cause of the dehumanization I'm representing, and that there-fore the elements of humanism—which are very much in the books as presences but not as solutions—will matter" (Inter-view with Haffenden 43–44).

5

Rates of Exchange:
The Liberal Novelist's Quarrel
with the French Algebraists

" 'YOU CANNOT BUILD a city with words only,' " says a character in Bradbury's fourth novel, *Rates of Exchange* (174). He alludes, presumably as unwittingly as the book's author does quite self-consciously, to Tony Tanner's highly influential study of the postwar American novel, *City of Words*. In *Rates of Exchange* Bradbury accomplishes precisely such a construction: a purely verbal architecture, a lexical landscape that, like the American works discussed by Tanner and by Richard Poirier in *A World Elsewhere*, has its basis in something deeper than its own linguistic surface. It is, like *The History Man*, a deceptive novel, as well as being a novel of deception, as we shall shortly see. Not the least of its deceptions is the way in which the novel not only builds a city of words but often borrows its materials from other, usually far less self-consciously composed, cities of lex. *Rates of Exchange* is very obviously indebted to recent American fictions by John Updike and Saul Bellow that have also dealt with western observers in eastern Europe: *Bech: A Book* (1970) and *The Dean's December* (1982). This indebtedness, which includes borrowed characters, plots, and themes, borders at times on plagiarism, but it is a plagiarism so obvious as to more nearly constitute what Raymond Federman (borrowing from Jacques Ehrmann) calls playgiarism. In effect, the extent of Bradbury's borrowings from Updike and Bellow serves to foreground them in a novel that is both linguistically and literarily rich. Like John Gardner's *The King's Indian* (with which it was on at least one occasion reviewed), *Rates of Exchange* is filled with literary echoes, from Baudelaire and Melville to Heller and Federman. There is even a last minute, self-consciously obligatory bow to Kingsley Amis, or rather a nod in the direction of those reviewers who have, often disparagingly, commented on Bradbury's indebtedness to the author of *Lucky Jim*. The novel's "implied author" makes a guest appearance of his own, pipe in mouth and tongue in cheek, sounding a good deal more self-confident than the reclusive novelist who appears so briefly and so ineffectually in *The History Man*. In fact, Bradbury's third novel appears in his fourth as well; the absence of any copies of *The History Man* from the bookstalls at Heathrow airport ensures its presence in *Rates of Exchange*. One of Howard Kirk's colleagues from the earlier book makes his way into the later novel in similar fashion. He is the Dr. Petworth with whom the Dr. Petworth of *Rates of Exchange* is twice confused. The latter Petworth comes to take the former's place along the novel's diachronic plane of action as the result of a metaphoric substitution (an "exchange") from among the choices available along the novel's synchronic axis. Thus does Bradbury's parodically structuralist novel proceed. *Rates of Exchange* is in fact filled with such echoes and allusions: linguistic and literary theories (including structuralism of course); fairy tales; the voice of one of eastern Europe's best known exports to western pop culture, Zsa Zsa Gabor; the spy novels of Deighton, LeCarre, and others; as well as the postmodern parodies of this subgenre written by Thomas Pynchon, a writer Bradbury especially admires.

Of the various ways in which Pynchon's fiction influenced the writing of *Rates of Exchange*, one of the most important is the manner in which Pynchon develops his narrative by exploiting some one dominant metaphor. In *Gravity's Rainbow*, as Lodge has pointed out, Pynchon "takes the commonplace analogy between rocket and phallus and pursues its ramifications relentlessly and grotesquely through the novel's enormous length, while the V. motif in the same author's first novel . . . mocks interpretation by the plurality of its manifestations" (*Modes* 235-236). *Rates of Exchange* is a quieter and less aggressive, though no less relentless, exploration—or exploitation— of the dominant metaphor that gives the book its title. Comparing the novel to the works by Bellow and Updike mentioned earlier, Martin Amis found *Rates of Exchange* wanting and "uneconomical—prohibitively so." Amis's judgment neatly misses the novel's point, for *Rates* is only as uneconomical as the long chapter on "Economy" with which Thoreau begins his exploration of the rate of exchange between the material and the transcendental in mid-nineteenth century America in *Walden*. Adopting Pynchon's mode and adapting it to his Anglo-liberal purposes, Bradbury considers narratively what the rate of exchange metaphor both denotes and connotes. There is the literal exchange of currencies as well as the figurative exchanges of various kinds—economic, cultural, diplomatic, linguistic, sexual, and—in the forward thrust of the novel's storyline versus the disarming simplicity of the novel's densely woven verbal texture—narrative. Moreover, as in *The History Man*, Bradbury evidences his interest in the rate of exchange between theory and fiction, abstract history and the literary imagination. *Rates of Exchange* is, in effect, Bradbury's second narrative attempt to give fiction its due in a world made hostage to dehumanizing abstractions of various kinds. The world he depicts is one in which—as the structuralists and poststructuralists like to say (and as the novel echoes)—"everything is a language" and, therefore, only a language, including the language of novelistic discourse which has lost (or perhaps mistakenly relinquished) its once-privileged place.

In the opening sentence of the novel's prefatory "Author's Note," one hears an echo of the realist writer's formulaic disclaimer of any correspondence between fact and fiction—a tactic designed, once upon a time, to forestall possible libel actions. But in the phrasing of this sentence—"this is a book, and what it says is not true"—rather than in its ostensible content, the reader also hears a note of self-deprecating postmodern irony, as well he might; for as the "Author's Note" goes on to explain, "like money, this book is a paper fiction, offered for exchange." Bradbury, or rather the novel's "implied author," seems to agree with Roland Barthes who, to quote Bradbury quoting Barthes in one of the novel's four epigraphs, has defined narrative as "legal tender." The second of the epigraphs, from Poe's "The Purloined Letter," concerning Dupin's "quarrel . . . with some of the algebraists of Paris," complicates matters even further (even before the first words of the "novel proper" have been read) insofar as Barthes is read as a contemporary "French algebraist," along, of course, with Derrida. Indeed, the "novel proper" will rather strongly suggest that the author of *Rates of Exchange* has his own quarrel with the French algebraists, a quarrel of a special kind. The best of the parodies included in *Who Do You Think You Are?*, "Mensonge," is a flawless sendup of deconstructionist practice, but as with similar works in the collection it evidences what Bradbury has called his "love-hate" relation with the subjects he parodies.[1] Skeptical as he is of deconstruction, Bradbury appears to be equally skeptical of a naive affirmation of the liberal assumptions upon which he once based his narrative art.

As *The History Man* and *Rates of Exchange* clearly attest, Bradbury has become increasingly interested in language and preoccupied with the linguistic surface of his novels. At the same

1. "Mensonge" appears in the paperback edition of *Who Do You Think You Are?* published by Arena in 1984 but not in the original Secker & Warburg edition (1976) or the new Arena edition (1987).

time, he objects to the tendency on the part of many contemporary critics, including Barthes in *Writing Degree Zero* and "The Death of the Author," "to deny to writers an appropriate freedom of will and invention, and to explain writing according to large-scale systems of causality." He objects as well to "the tendency in a good deal of recent criticism to stress not the separate internal energy of literary language but its relation to all language, to explore not the conscious control of the artist but the substrata of literary language. . . . For [as Bradbury goes on to explain] it is precisely with the conscious, created, persuasive features of making and shaping that give it its essential existence and essential independence, that the test of an adequately literary criticism lies" ("State" 36, 37). However, although he claims that "there is no gainsaying the personal source of a book," he nonetheless does acknowledge that the individual author's "signature can be a very curious and angled thing" (Interview with Haffenden 43). In attending so closely to his novelistic language, deliberately and painstakingly foregrounding it in *The History Man* and *Rates of Exchange*, Bradbury manages a double feat. On the one hand, he takes account in typically postmodernist fashion of the reality of language, of its existence as a determinant of reality rather than a transparent means to a higher end. On the other hand, he continues to explore the possibilities of the liberal novel in and for a postliberal age by insisting on the individual novelist's mastery of, rather than surrender to, his medium. He insists as well that while "estrangement . . . is a very important part of contemporary writing," the "moral function of literature" involves a two-part process: "to estrange, but then to reacquaint" (Interview with Bigsby 32). Early in the novel the protagonist, a linguist, is asked if he still follows Chomsky's transformational grammer or if he has converted to structuralism. "In his own mind, he knows whether the mind is, or is not, a *tabula rasa* before language enters it, though he will not be divulging his answer [to this "crucial question"] directly in this book" (33).

It is not just the character who does not divulge his answer, but the author as well. Bradbury seems to have been as fascinated by language (and theories of language) in the writing of this novel as he was with Goya's painting in the composition of *The History Man*. He appears to have discovered in language theory yet another illustration of the modern drift towards dehumanization and, at the same time, the means by which what remains of the liberal self may continue to resist being swamped by the historical tide.

As in *The History Man*, Bradbury successfully resists the drift towards abstraction and dehumanization by paradoxically appearing to give in to it, substituting for "plot" the idea of plot and for "style" the idea of style. Each novel masters, as well as mirrors, what Bradbury has elsewhere termed the "extraordinary profusion" of the present "polyglot" age ("Foreword" xii) in which moral depth has been supplanted by—or exchanged for—stylistic surface. Style—the word as well as the literary quality it denotes—appears everywhere in *Rates of Exchange*, even when it is absent, as in the case of the novel's "styleless" protagonist. Katya Princip, Bradbury's version of Updike's (and Bech's) Bulgarian Poetess, is, on the other hand, a very stylish dresser and, moreover, possesses a very distinctive literary style, that of magic realism. London appears to Petworth as "a fancy fiction, a disorderly parade of styles" (*Rates of Exchange* 21), whereas Slaka, the eastern European city he visits, is just the opposite: social realism on an urban scale, a visual monologue. "Yet," as Bradbury's narrator notes at one point, adopting a structuralist axiom, "inside likeness there is difference" (26). And inside each of the novel's many simple oppositions—East and West, capitalist and communist, male and female, and so forth—there exists a dialogic complexity that manages to ambiguously suggest both the essential ineffableness of the liberal self upon which Bradbury insists and that spectre of multiplicity gone amok that Henry Adams believed had already overwhelmed (and eventually would extinguish) not only the individual but all mankind. (Significantly enough, it is with a lengthy discussion of *The Education of Henry Adams* that Bradbury begins his study of *The Modern American Novel*, written concurrently with *Rates of Exchange* and published one year before.)

As with *The History Man*, there exists a significant discrepancy between what many reviewers believed was the uniformity of the novel's style and the fact that this uniformity is, like virtually everything else in this seemingly simple novel, a deception. As in *The History Man*, the seeming uniformity masks parodic multiplicity. Accounting for the *apparent* uniformity is fairly easy to do. A good deal of the novel, especially in the opening pages, comically parodies the English as a Second Language (ESL) prose found in all of those eastern European guidebooks, customs forms, airline regulations, etc., written for the English-speaking tourist, which is precisely what the novel's "implied reader" often becomes, guidebook and map in hand. To this form of ESL-speak, Bradbury adds a lilting rhythm that serves to further distance the prose from Standard English, and that is especially obvious in the novel's opening sentence: "If you should ever happen to make the trip to Slaka, that fine flower of middle European cities, capital of commerce and art, wide streets and gipsy music, then, whatever else you plan to do there, do not, as the travel texts say, neglect to visit the Cathedral of Saint Valdopin: a little outside the town, at the end of the tramway route, near to the power station, down by the slow, marshy, mosquito-breeding waters of the great River Niyt."[2] Going well beyond the conventions of "indirect discourse," the seemingly seamless, ceaselessly parodic narrative voice incorporates into itself

2. Bradbury uses a similar but certainly less pervasive lilting style in a number of earlier works, particularly "A Goodbye for Evadne Winterbottom" (collected in *Who Do You Think You Are?*) and in *The History Man*.

pieces drawn from various linguistic environments. The ESL solecisms that are predictable enough in the dialogue of Slakan speakers also frequently enter the authorial narrator's supposedly neutral narration in a comically disconcerting way, as in his description of Slaka as "a place of dangers and treacheries, courages and cowardices" and in his offhand reference to "our patriotic workers" (18). In similar fashion, the narrative voice often echoes Petworth's professional vocabulary and his linguist's frame of reference. It adopts (as well as adapts) everything from "grammar," "noun," and "sentence" to Derrida's terms "presence" and "absence." The novel is filled not only with ESL-speak and guidebook prose but small talk, "lecture talk," body language, and, in orthography as well as typography, a form of computer speech (thus the chapter titles: "1/ARR.," "2/RECEP.," "3/ACCOM.," etc.).

In addition to emphasizing the multiplicity of languages, *Rates of Exchange* emphasizes the ambiguity of language, as comically rendered in a host of Slakan mispronunciations and Petworthian misunderstandings: e.g., "no smirking" for "no smoking" and "are you thirsty?" for "are you turstii [i.e., a tourist]?" (30, 60). In a similarly broad comic vein are the stutterings of the British Embassy representative, Steadiman, whose unsteady speech results in one-liners such as, " 'if you need a bit of ass, a bit of assistance call me, any time' " (182). Such lines tease the reader; they invite him or her to jump to understandable but nonetheless incorrect interpretive conclusions (including a reading of the entire novel as being similarly obvious and superficial: a mere joke). Bradbury exploits the potential ambiguity of language for comic effects but at the same time he provides an object lesson on the ways in which we seek to make sense of what we hear and read. In the case of Steadiman's stuttering, comic surprise is always followed by a clarification of the intended meaning: "a bit of ass" becomes "a bit of assistance." Elsewhere, however, the novel insists upon the ambiguity of its own language and of language in general.

In his attempt to provide a brief but authoritative history of Slaka, for example, Bradbury's suddenly Borgesian narrator makes the following prefatory comment: "A certain reputable encyclopedia, consulted in an old edition, authoritatively observes (if I have read it accurately, and if my hastily scribbled notes, gathered amid the distractions of the great round Reading Room of the British Museum, where white-eyed Italian girls shout hotly for company around tea-time, tempting serious scholars, of whom I am not one anyway, into folly, are correctly transcribed) . . ." (2). The parenthetical aside qualifies and deflects from the point the narrator ostensibly wishes to make; in this way it undermines the very authority of the imaginary source it sets out so confidently to establish. Not only does the aside allude to several of Borges's best known stories; it also defines and enacts the narrative garden-of-forking-paths quality that characterizes Borges' *ficciones* and Bradbury's novel. "In Slaka history is a mystery, and it is not surprising that the nation's past has been very variously recorded and the facts much disputed, for everyone has a story to tell. Perplexities abound, accounts contradict, and accurate details are wanting" (2). The same may be said of *Rates of Exchange*. Like the interpolated story of Saint Valdopin, the imaginary patron saint of the imaginary and anonymous country of which Slaka is the capital, the novel "can be read in many fashions" (7). In fact, one needs to go further. The novel demands to be read in light of this awareness of critical pluralism that undermines the authority of any one interpretive mode that would impose closure on so "elusive" a text. ("Elusive" is a word that appears frequently throughout *Rates of Exchange*.) Although the narrative "I" claims that he is "a writer, not a critic," he demonstrates an obvious awareness of and interest in critical theory. And although he claims to prefer that his "fictions . . . remain fiction" (9), the very statement of this preference disturbs the creation of that "vivid and continuous dream" (to borrow John Gardner's phrase) to which Bradbury's narrator claims to aspire.

Such linguistic and narrative[3] disturbances plunge the reader into the poststructuralist pit. However, like Petworth, who orders a different breakfast each morning only to be served the same one, Bradbury seems to posit the existence of a resistant reality that lies beyond the novel's various and arbitrary sign systems, including language, upon which his characters must necessarily rely. When Katya Princip tells Petworth she wants to take him somewhere and asks, " 'Do you want it?' " (195) the reader, schooled by Steadiman's stutterings, detects the sexual double entendre. But the humor here is not only not as heavyhanded as in Steadiman's case; it also hints at some deeper, more human, level than that of mere verbal play. Even as it points to a plurality of possible meanings, Katya's question affirms the reality of those human emotions and relationships that lie beneath the novel's dense and delightful linguistic surface. And so in this indirect, even duplicitous, way, *Rates of Exchange* circles back to the Bellow

---

3. Although the overall structure of *Rates of Exchange* is one of linear progression, beginning with Petworth's arrival in Slaka and ending with his return to London, Bradbury frequently and quite self-consciously disturbs this simple narrative movement. In just four pages (16–19), for example, the narrative switches first to a view of Slaka from the air, even though (1) Petworth's plane has already landed and (2) Petworth's actual flight will not be described for nine more pages, then to descriptions of Slaka culled from guidebooks, then to a paragraph in which the plane comes to a halt and Petworth rises from his seat (prematurely, as the reader learns when this part of the narrative is resumed some fourteen pages later); only then does the reader learn why Petworth has come to be where he is—a flashback that itself begins with a flashforward (in Genette's terms, an analepsis which begins with a prolepsis): "Indeed, as brilliant, batik-clad, magical realist novelist Katya Princip will remark, somewhat later in this narrative. . . ."

and Updike books, mentioned earlier, that it parodies and plunders; though quite different in texture, *Rates of Exchange* is ultimately quite close in spirit to *The Dean's December* and *Bech: A Book*. As such, it serves as oblique but nonetheless convincing proof of the viability of Bradbury's renegotiated liberal-realist aesthetic in the postliberal, postrealist age. Accepting "the fundamenal recognition of modern criticism, that all things in fiction are mediated through words," the author of *Rates of Exchange* makes a convincing case "that certain things can be held logically and temporarily antecedent to those words, as a matter which the words mediate" (*Possibilities* 283).

For Bradbury, the fate of language and the fate of character are inextricably linked in a dehumanized age. It should, therefore, hardly come as a surprise that in *Rates of Exchange* he should place such stress on language and linguistic surface and at the same time further explore the attenuation of character in the modern world where style, including verbal style, has supplanted human substance. Like Treece and Walker, the protagonist of Bradbury's fourth novel has, at best, a tenuous hold on his own identity. More than five thousand words go by before the reader is introduced to "Dr. Petworth," who is "white and male, forty and married, bourgeois and British," a TEFL specialist and frequent "cultural traveller" for the British Council (14). And another fifty thousand words go by before the reader learns Petworth's first name, which is Angus, " 'like the steak' " (160). During the course of the novel the name Petworth, like that of Joyce's Bloom and Earwicker or Pynchon's V. goes through a host of transformations in the mouths of eastern European guides, hotel clerks, officials, et al.: Petwurt, Pervert, Petwit, Pumwum, Perworthi, and Patwat. Having so little identity himself, this thin, "styleless" man is often confused with that other Petworth, the University of Watermouth sociologist mentioned in *The History Man*. Insignificant himself, the Petworth of *Rates of Exchange* must rely on outward manifestations to establish his own minimal self. There is the puce and magenta British Council tag, for example, which, since there is no British Council in Slaka, becomes a "sterile sign, a meaningless meaning" (54). Under the influence of "the strange dulling grammar of airports," Petworth becomes less a subject, more an object, less the doer than the one to whom things are done (302). His situation is, of course, comic, particularly the three hours he spends waiting in the Slakan airport while his guide looks in vain for the other Dr. Petworth whose photograph she has been given. (Exploiting the language difficulty, Bradbury crosses from one literary medium to another and renders the entire scene as a kind of silent film comedy.) A traveller who hates to travel, who dislikes planned itineraries but passively accepts them, who visits foreign lands only to sit in his hotel room and revise his lectures, Petworth seems to well deserve his fate, his inconsequentiality and insignificance. It certainly does not help that, like Treece and Walker, he speaks so blandly and in such an old-fashioned manner. At a dinner given in his honor, for example, he makes a toast " 'to language. . . . The words that bring us all here, and bring us closer together' " (125). Geographically and physically language has indeed brought all the people at the table closer together; it is the "pretext" of their meeting and of Bradbury's novel. But in a novel and in a world in which words both "explain and estrange," Petworth's toast must strike the reader as hopelessly naive and as beside the point as Petworth's lectures on "the Uvular R" and on the difference between "I don't have" and "I haven't got."

Bradbury's attitude towards Petworth is nonetheless complex. Even as he savages his protagonist, Bradbury seems intent on salvaging him as well.

The business of a lecturer is, of course, to lecture; this is why lecturers exist. Petworth has not come this far, crossed two time-zones, found other skies and other birds, simply in order to answer toasts, to visit tombs, to worry about domestic disorders, to catch himself in the thorny thickets of sexual confusion, split loyalties, divided attachments, to know desire or despair, to fall in love with lady writers; he has come to perform utterance. This is why planes have flown to bring him here, hotel rooms been booked, food set before him on plates; this is why he has left his house, home and country, brought his briefcase, made his way to this point. His head may ache with peach brandy, his wrist may hurt, his split lip blur his talk a little; his heart may be troubled, his spirit be energyless, poor, lacking the will to be, let alone the will to become. He may be a speech without a subject, a verb without a noun, certainly not a character in the world historical sense; but he has a story to tell, and now he is telling it. And telling it, he becomes himself an order, a sentence that grows into a paragraph and then a page, a page and then a plot, a direction incorporating due beginning, middle, and end. His text before him, he becomes that text; and, though he may be before an audience that has come to hear another lecture, from another lecturer, it does not matter. Petworth, for this moment, exists, in his hour of words. A bell rings in the corridor, and he knows his words and his existence are up. But, sitting down, in the great auditorium, while Mrs Goko utters a few last sentences of translation, Petworth knows that he has been. (193–194)

At the end of one of Twain's "Mysterious Stranger" manuscripts, Little Satan explains to Theodore that what men claim to be reality is in fact a dream; then he advises his young friend to dream other dreams, and better. The author's advice to Petworth seems to form a postmodern equivalent: to tell other stories, and better. Petworth has a story to tell, the lecture that momentarily defines him and gives him his being, but the reader also has Bradbury's story of him, the novel *Rates of Exchange*. According to the narrator, Petworth's is "a version of the old and familiar story, the lecturer's tale, with stock theme and minor variations" (53). This description of Petworth's "simple story" of "everyday life" (56, 57) is, however, clearly disingenuous. It is not a description at all; instead, it is a device used to defamiliarize Petworth's "familiar story" in order to revitalize both the liberal novel and the idea of character at a time when both are (at best) suspect. Petworth steps eastward rather than (like James Walker) westward, but he does step nonetheless. He wants something more than the safe domesticated life that has left him, as well as his "dark wife Lottie," outwardly secure and inwardly dissatisfied. His "I want" may not be as clamorous as Eugene Henderson's, but it is no less real. It is as real as Bradbury's desire to pass through self-apparent language, which can no longer be assumed to be a transparent medium that brings us all closer together, to some realm that language, once upon a time, was assumed to mediate.

In *The Dean's December*, Bellow establishes a number of thematically, as well as structurally, significant oppositions: Chicago and Bucharest, West and East, capitalist and communist, terra firma and space, journalism and science, and so forth. For his own twice-told tale of two cities, Bradbury creates a number of similar oppositions but adds to them a Pynchonesque twist. In effect, he transforms his tale of two cities into a postmodernist text of two-plus plots, each having its own literary as well as sociopsychological significance. Stepping eastward, Petworth moves from the domestic to the fantastic, from realism to fable. As his official guide, Marisja Lubijova, explains to him, " 'You have some wishes you cannot make real at home, so you go somewhere and hope they will happen' " (82). They will not happen with Marisja, however, who for most of the novel embodies in her actions and her language the aesthetic of social realism. It is Marisja who hands Petworth his itinerary, the plot of his days, and who tries her best to have him follow it. "The brilliant, batik-clad magical realist novelist Katya Princip," who meets Petworth at the Restaurant Propp and later takes him to the Cafe Grimm, represents just the reverse, politically, physically, and aesthetically. Each serves as Petworth's guide, and each wants him to learn the lesson she tries to teach. Each, in her own way, acts as a Bellowian reality instructor even though the realities in which they try to instruct Petworth are in fact quite different. For Marisja, to exist means to possess a passport; but for Katya, to exist is not enough. " 'The problem,' " she claims, " 'is not to exist at all, it is to make importance of it' " (219). Her phrasing suggests the limits of her English language skills, but it implies as well Bradbury's preoccupation with how "the human" is to be defined in a dehumanized age in which abstract history matters but the individual person does not, and in which language determines the speaker, not the other way around.

Katya rejects both the State and "reality" (as well as realism) as "bad" fictions which imprison the self. Against them she posits her own postmodern fables which liberate her from the narrowness of the totalitarian state and (to borrow Mas'ud Zavarzadeh's term) of the totalizing novels which attempt to explain the world in univocal terms to the passive reader. As Katya Princip explains, " 'reality is what happens if you listen to other people's stories and not to your own. The stories become a country, the country becomes a prison, and the prison comes in your mind. And everywhere more of the same story. . . . Soon it is the only story, and that is how comes reality' " (204). Katya understands that all people feel about their existences as Petworth does about his. Their lives too are "empty" and "meaningless," and so to overcome their guilt and to fill the void they accept the readymade fictions of the State and of History. Marisja wants Petworth to be cautious and to accept; Katya on the other hand wants him to take risks and to possess " 'a will' " and " 'a desire' " (213, 219). Of his two guides, Katya is obviously the more aesthetically, politically, and sexually appealing. Whether Petworth and the Petworthian reader can or should trust the batik-clad magic realist novelist is, however, another matter. The narrator's words, "but it is as Katya Princip, that deceptive novelist, has said to him," at once invite the reader to believe Katya and yet be skeptical about her (271). By quoting her, the narrator establishes her authority and encourages the reader's trust in her judgment. By calling her "deceptive," he produces a more ambiguous result. Her deceptiveness may be a necessary strategy given the general intolerance on the part of Communist governments to un-censored literary works, or it may suggest an evasiveness that has less to do with free expression than with personal gain. The narrator's words thus constitute a distillation of the reader's necessarily ambivalent response to her. Other factors contribute to the reader's uncertainty. According to Marisja, Katya may speak of taking risks, but nonetheless, she is always sure to cover her bets. (And perhaps her tracks as well: Petworth's unofficial guide "looks like a very elegant shepherd" [121] but may be a predatory wolf in a sheepskin coat; whatever she is, Petworth remains the perfect sheep.) If Katya takes an interest in Petworth, then she must have some ulterior purpose, some self-serving plot in mind, or so goes Marisja's reading of her. The reader can neither accept Marisja's reading nor reject it. He cannot say for sure that the reason Katya finds Petworth attractive is that he is " 'not a character in the world historical sense' " and there-fore outside the political-sexual intrigues that characterize and corrupt the lives of her countrymen, for whom, as Katya admits, " 'all life is an exchange' " (212). Nor can he say for sure that Katya uses Petworth to advance her position by seducing him into playing an important but nonetheless expendable role in her affairs. If the latter is true, then Katya is simply a version of those Bradburyan characters, Froelich and Kirk, who manufacture plots and manipulate others in order to achieve their own self-serving ends.

With Katya, Petworth's all too quotidian life becomes an adult fairy tale in which he is raised (much as Annie Callendar is by Kirk) to the level of main plot. However, despite her words concerning the need to create one's own reality, Katya, "that deceptive novelist," proves remarkably attentive to the historical/political facts of life: the ringing of the telephone brings their brief and utterly fantastic interlude to an abrupt end. Like the stroke of midnight in "Cinderella," the ringing of the phone summons the characters back to the real world. It effectively transforms the ethereal Katya Princip into a version of the clearly earth-bound Marisja Lubijova, whose heavy-sounding name not only contrasts with the crisp, lighter-than-air quality of "Katya Princip" but serves to link her as well to the Petworth who stands in his "flat earth shoes," firmly rooted to reality. Interestingly, however, Marisja undergoes a similar transformation, one that takes her in precisely the opposite direction. After travelling through a dark forest, arriving in a strange city, and nearly becoming Petworth's lover, she confides to him those misgivings that clearly echo Katya's remarks earlier:

Because if you are interpreter, it is easy to grow a little afraid. You speak all the time, but always the words of others. Then you wonder: is there inside me a person, someone who is not the words of those others? You think: can I have still a desire, a wish, a feeling? But of course if you think like this, it is bad for your job, you must forget it. You are not here for that, you are here to make those exchanges, to let the others talk, so the world can go on. But, excuse me, please, sometimes I do have a little feeling. And now, I am sorry, it is jealous. (273)

In echoing Katya's remarks to Petworth some sixty pages earlier, Marisja's words reveal not a structuralist "difference," where sameness was once perceived, but instead a shared humanity. This common core of values and desires lies beyond all rates of exchange but one, the exception being the novel *Rates of Exchange* itself. Petworth proves his humanity when, after first Katya and then Marisja have revealed themselves— that is, their true (?) selves—to him (another of the novel's fairy tale motifs), Petworth manages to do what he had previously neglected to: he calls each by name. Much to their delight, he acknowledges their individual existences, affirms their common humanity, and in this way saves them from being engulfed by the sands of historical (including postmodern/post-structuralist) abstraction. To name and thus to acknowledge the existence of Katya and Marisja may be the least startling and yet the most important result of Petworth's trip to Slaka.

Such a seemingly insignificant affirmation may go entirely unremarked. It may itself be overwhelmed—or engulfed—by the novel's verbal play and deliberately overrich plotting. However, the reader's desire to unlock the novel's mystery by singling out some climactic scene or event can misfire, as it seems to have done in the case of the reviewer who claimed to have discovered, in Petworth's smuggling Katya's manuscript out of Slaka, the "hidden purpose of his visit" (Morrison). To read *Rates of Exchange* as if it were a mystery novel (as this reviewer evidently did) or to attempt to read it along conventional lines is to indulge in an understandable but nonetheless misguided desire to impose a plot on a novel that artfully and ambiguously balances narrative form and contingent event in an effort to reinvent, or at least renegotiate, the liberal aesthetic and the liberal self. Within the simple narrative thread that follows Petworth's itinerary, Bradbury pursues a bewildering number of plots, none of them "sub-," all of them pluralistically interwoven to one degree or another. Or, more accurately, what he pursues is less a multiplicity of plots than the idea of multiple plots. He creates a structural or narrative parallel to the more obvious exploitation of semantic multiplicity to be found throughout the text. Each plot—or rather, the possibility of each plot—like the possibility of multiple meanings for individual words, utterances, and characters— serves to interrogate ironically all the others, to place them (as Bakhtin would say) in quotation marks, putting them in doubt by undermining their authority. As the novel progresses, the plots proliferate, and the explanations of and the connections between them become more and more tenuous. Contrary to the reviewer's conclusion quoted above, the reader can never be entirely sure why Petworth has come to Slaka. His lecture tour cannot be separated from or entirely linked to his wanting to escape momentarily from the numbingly realistic novel that his domestic life has become. But neither can it be separated from Katya's new manuscript or from Professor Plitplov, who may be exploiting both Petworth and Princip, or from the British government's wanting to test the political waters, or from a host of other possibilities. Similarly, Petworth's relationships with Marisja Lubijova and Katya Princip cannot be separated from either his erotic fantasies or the advice of the British Council worker who warns Petworth of the secret police's (HOGPo's) favorite tactics for entrapping unwary foreigners. A young female interpreter, he is told, should be considered " 'forbidden fruit. . . . And don't bring papers or documents out of the country, however compassionate the story; that's another favourite' " (51–52). Thus, in *Rates of Exchange*, Henry James meets Thomas Pynchon insofar as the multiple plots cannot be separated from Petworth's sexual desires and psychological apprehensions. Some must be evidence of Petworth's paranoia, but which ones isn't clear. Similarly, certain coincidences suggest intrigue, others mere contingency, but most suggest both.

Marisja Lubijova and Katya Princip, for example, are clearly opposites, physically as well as politically. Yet it is Marisja who presents Petworth with a copy of Katya's newly published novel, *Nodu Hug*, which translates "do not be afraid" though for an English speaker it immediately suggests a warning or command to avoid intimacy, do not hug. Marisja contends that despite the language barrier Petworth will come to understand the novel before he leaves Slaka, and she claims that " 'there is another reason why you must have it. I cannot tell it to you yet, but you will see' " (112). What Petworth and the reader eventually see is never made clear, though her comment does evoke a multitude of possible meanings, including having Petworth help Katya smuggle her manuscript out of the country. In other words, the social realist plot of their approved itinerary, as well as Marisja's caricature of the eastern European guide, may be a cover for the "real" story going on at some deeper, covert level. But if this is true, then who is scripting the deeper story? Is it Plitplov, the cartoonish figure who conspicuously shadows Petworth's every move, who claims to have been responsible for Petworth's visit, and who " 'likes to make plans' " for his " 'friend' " (278)? And do his plans include using Petworth as a courier? Or is it Katya herself who is in control, turning life into art as well as art into life? The plots of her novel and of her story about a character named Stupid either parallel or orchestrate Petworth's Slakan adventures. In a phone conversation, Katya—or someone Petworth and the reader assume is Katya—says that she will tell Petworth the end of Stupid's story when they meet at the cathedral. Throughout the novel, the narrator insists (four times in the first ten pages alone) that the reader should visit the cathedral even though it is not included on any of the official tours. His insistence makes both the cathedral and the narrator conspicuous by virtue of their absence. More importantly, it seems to implicate the (perhaps Plitplovian) narrator in some or all of the novel's many conspiratorial plots. At the cathedral, Petworth is met by his comic double, Plitplov, who tells him about the plan to smuggle the manuscript of a collection of stories that Katya has dedicated to him and in which he appears as a character. "That night, in the hotel, Petworth eats a solitary meal in the great dining-room, where the sad singer sings again, songs of love, songs of betrayal; he sits and thinks of obscure processes, strange machinations, stories perhaps of love, perhaps of betrayal, in which he has some unexpected part. He does not know whether these stories started before he arrived, or because he arrived" (298).

And neither does the reader, who remains aware that every possible explanation is not without its Bakhtinian "sideward glance" at another equally probable explanation. "Not, finally and conclusively, to know—this is his achievement," Jay Martin has said of Henry James (312). Bradbury makes this "not knowing" his narrative subject as well as his narrative technique. In his short story, "Composition," which ends Fowles-fashion, with alternative conclusions, an American graduate student tells his British colleague that although they have read all the critics and know even the most sophisticated critical approaches, they still cannot be sure whether a letter written by an attractive freshman means love or blackmail or both. *Rates of Exchange* implies a similar but far more exhaustive indeterminacy, motivated as much by Bradbury's wish to preserve the liberal self and the liberal novel as it is by his attraction to postmodern fiction and the postmodern aesthetic.

According to the Russian formalist Propp, it is not character that is important but the character's narrative function, the part the character plays in the plot. *Rates of Exchange* follows Propp's formalist theory but in a self-conscious, parodically critical way. Bradbury's target is not formalist criticism per se; instead, it is those theoretical systems—whether literary, linguistic, economic, or political—that transform characters into caricatures, into mere functions. The language reform that is briefly effected in Slaka involves changing all "i" endings to "u." The "i" and the "u" as well the I and the You become pawns in a political language game. In this context it is significant that Petworth, in his tentative efforts to speak the native language, intrudes a redundant "i." He is himself a redundant "I' in this wholly ironical and all too real "people's republic" with its even more ironically named capital, Slaka. Described by its author as "a comedy of gloom and bleakness" ("Introduction," *Stepping* vii), *Rates of Exchange* succeeds in large part because Bradbury artfully plays the comic and pessimistic elements against one another, using each to comment on and modify the other. It is possible to detect in his comic despair and postmodern play some of the same movement towards romantic affirmation that Bradbury has detected in the fiction of that bleakest of contemporary Austrian writers, Peter Handke (rev. of *Slow Homecoming*). What Bradbury stubbornly affirms—or wants to affirm—is the continuing presence of the individual self in a world that is largely committed to denying its existence. And he affirms as well the need for fiction in such a world. Without a guide, without a "voice to tell its story, Slaka does not seem very different from any city anywhere else" (288). And without a voice, without a story of his own, Petworth too is in danger of disappearing entirely. "Of course, everywhere, even in Slaka, there are the politicians and the priests, the ayatollahs and the economists [and the linguists who 'explain that every transaction in our culture . . . is a language'], who will try to explain that reality is what they say it is. Never trust them; trust only the novelists, those deeper bankers who spend their time trying to turn pieces of printed paper into value, but never pretend that the result is anything more than a useful fiction" (8). At the end of the year in which *Rates of Exchange* was published, Bradbury was asked to comment on what he wished the future to be like. "May we have imagination instead of politics," he said, "aspiration instead of history. A pretty vain hope, I think" (quoted in Interview with Haffenden 27). Much of this same pessimism infects the ending of his fourth novel in which on the one hand the reader sees "the men of history" go, like the posters that bear their images, up and down according to which way the political winds are blowing (300),[4] and on the other Petworth returning to England, to "his dark wife" Lottie, and to that state of "self-

4. Whether source or analogue, it is interesting to note the line, "all the portraits of Krushchev had vanished," from *The Stories of John Cheever*, which Bradbury reviewed in the 29 June 1979 issue of *New Statesman*.

nullifying passivity" from which only fiction has momentarily rescued him (Interview with Haffenden 48). "I have a moral agony going on in my guts about what it is we actually are as human beings," Bradbury told Ronald Hayman in April 1983—an agony that *Rates of Exchange* did less to relieve than to bring into even sharper focus.[5]

5. Recall that Robert S. Burton posits a considerably more optimistic Bradbury: ". . . like Angus Wilson, he is able to read the signs clearly and ultimately find his way back to a home rooted in a stable domestic and literary tradition from which standpoint he writes conventionally moralistic fiction, mixed with stylistic ingenuity." To quote Jake Barnes's words to Brett at the end of *The Sun Also Rises*: "Yes, isn't it pretty to think so." Widdowson also takes special notice of the *Nostos* motif in Bradbury (and Lodge); like Burton, he finds no possible irony in Bradbury's (or Lodge's) use of such returns. For Widdowson they represent Bradbury's acceptance of bourgeois values; for Burton, the bliss that comes to hero, author, and critic upon discovering that all loose ends are tied up, all questions answered, all problems resolved: they all live happily ever after.

6

The Picturegoers, Ginger, You're Barmy, and the Art of Narrative Doubling

TAKEN TOGETHER, David Lodge's first two published novels provide a useful introduction to his increasingly dialogic—and increasingly self-conscious—practice. Many of the same dialogic concerns and techniques that inform his later works appear here in embryo, as it were, in stumbling, exaggerated form, writ large not so much for the near-blind reader (or critic) as for the tentative would-be novelist. Clearly, *The Picturegoers* is a far less successful and subtle work than the similarly titled *The Moviegoer*, another first novel by another Catholic writer, published one year later. Walker Percy's novel is an existential fiction of a special, even unusual, kind. This comic successor to Dostoevsky's fiction distills the Russian's dialogic breadth in the person, or rather the voice, of Percy's narrator-protagonist, the genial underground man, Binx Bolling. Within the moviegoer's seemingly flat discourse one hears echoes of Kierkegaard on the one hand and American popular culture on the other. *The Picturegoers*, as the plural of its title suggests, takes a sociological rather than an existential approach. For Percy's version of Gabriel Marcel's homo viator (sovereign wayfarer), Lodge substitutes a "mass" of Joycean narrative focalizations. He permits each of his picturegoers to speak in his or her own turn and in his or her own voice within the novel's fictive space and limited carnival freedom (Interview with Haffenden 146–147). In his subsequent reading of Bakhtin and Gerard Genette, Lodge found the theoretical rationale behind his inchoate use of essentially dialogic narrative techniques. As he discovered, "the more the characters are allowed to speak for themselves in the narrative text, and the less they are explained by an authoritative narrator, the stronger will be our sense of their individual freedom of choice—and our own interpretive freedom." In overall structure, if not in complexity and execution, *The Picturegoers* anticipates *Changing Places* and especially *Small World* (despite differences in tone), *How Far Can You Go?* (with which it shares a similar religious doubt or reservation), and *The British Museum Is Falling Down* (in which the concatenation of parodies is but a variation on Lodge's dialogic aesthetic, the carnival freedom of styles in this later work parallelling the convergence of characters at the cinema in *The Picturegoers*).

The Palladium Moviehouse, formerly the grander Palladium Theatre, serves the same purpose on the thematic level that the novel itself does in the larger structural sense. It acts as a meeting place, not only for people but for styles, forms, and languages as well. Just as the characters go to the Palladium for a variety of reasons—to be entertained, to be titillated, to fantasize, to rest, to kill time, to earn a living—the reader experiences a similar diversity in the novel as a whole—a variety of characters and overlapping, or intersecting, but nonetheless largely discrete plots. There is Mark Underwood, a lapsed Catholic and aspiring writer, who seems much like Blatcham, the hometown he has left; located midway between city and country, it has elements of both but "belong[s] to neither" (39). Then there is the Mallory family in whose traditionally Catholic home Mark becomes "a willing prisoner," as attracted by the "warmth and humanity" that his own family lacks and to the older daughter Clare, as he is repelled by their simple religious faith. There is the parish priest, Father Kipling, who launches an unsuccessful counteroffensive against the Palladium and its manager, Mr. Berkeley, whose loveless marriage leads him to have an affair with Doreen, one of his young employees. Then there are Bridget and Len whose love leads to marriage but whose marriage seems likely to be dogged both by poverty and their film-induced romantic illusions. And there is the young thug, Harry, who goes to the movies to fuel his sadistic sexual fantasies and in this way to find some release from his desperate loneliness. And finally there are two characters that we do not actually see at the Palladium: Clare's former student, Hilda, who has turned from religion to a nearly lesbian love for Clare and now finally to movie idols in order to satisfy her own need for love, and Damien, a priggish Catholic whose desire for Clare is as abhorrent as it is chaste.

The separate narratives not only focus on different characters, they are narrated in variously stylized ways in the manner of Joyce's "scrupulous meanness" or what Park Honan has called Lodge's "cinematic style." "Lodge's manner with narrative viewpoints is innovative," Honan contends. "In *The Picturegoers*, the novelist's own camera—in that familiar maneuver of impressionism—is set behind the characters' eyes. 'Reality' is perceived and felt by representative South Londoners. But the viewpoints are not developed in the showily imitative fashion of dialogue. Instead, there is a subtle shift between kinds of vocabularies as viewpoints change" (171). Honan's description is accurate, especially insofar as it correctly links Lodge's novel with his theory of the language of fiction. It is nonetheless open to two objections, one because Honan goes too far and the other because he does not go far enough, which is to say not nearly as far as Lodge the novelist does, even in this, his flawed first novel. To begin with, Honan claims that Lodge achieves "the linguistic variety he wants within the limits of cinematic unobtrusiveness" (169). That is, he does not call attention to the stylistic variations themselves, for his goal here is to achieve a heightened realism, not a postmodern self-consciousness. Whatever he may have intended, what Lodge achieves is anything but unobtrusive in a novel marked, or marred, at every turn by the same melodramatic excess that also characterizes (though less noticeably) *Ginger, You're Barmy* and *Out of the Shelter*. Lodge learned to overcome this tendency towards melodrama by gradually adopting, or adapting, a number of distancing poses borrowed from the English comic novel and from postmodern fiction. In *The Picturegoers*, the language is indeed stylized, but the stylizations too often only reflect what the characters all too allegorically "mean": Mark the skeptic and writer-to-be, Clare the whilom nun moving towards sexual love, etc. To a large extent, the novel Lodge wrote reflects all too well the limitations that Mark discerns in himself: "Were other people like this, he wondered—always observing themselves in a spontaneous emotion? It was the penalty of being (or trying to be) a writer. To create characters you took a rib from your own personality, and shaped a character around it with the dust of experience. But it was a painful debilitating process. Usually the characters were still born, and the old Adam got weaker and weaker, less and less sure of his identity" (93). After reading such lines, Lodge's reader may very well agree with the author's own assessment of *The Picturegoers* as "an immature work . . . which I cannot now read without embarrassment" (*Write On* 61).

Although Lodge's execution is considerably less success-ful—his prose less cinematically unobtrusive—than Honan claims, his reach is far greater than Honan allows. This narrative cinematism is, I believe, one aspect not only of the modern novel in general as an essentially dialogical genre but of Lodge's novels in particular. They have become so increasingly self-conscious in their dialogism that Lodge the dialogical novelist has in fact come to merge with Lodge the critic who has gone from propounding the language of fiction to working with structuralism and, more recently, to finding in Bakhtin's theoretical writings the articulation of his own aesthetic practice. Thus, *The Picturegoers* includes not only various stylized languages but numerous interpolated and carnivalized forms as well; the sheer number and extent of these carnivalizations suggest that Lodge's first novel may have as much in common with *Ulysses* as it does with either *Dubliners* or *Portrait of the Artist as a Young Man*. The reader finds not only summaries of films, as one would naturally expect in such a novel, but Mark's notebooks, Doreen's fantasies, Damien's imagined conversations with Clare, one of Father Kipling's sermons, hymns, psalms, parts of the Catholic mass, excerpts from Christopher Marlowe's writings, and even a scene from a cheap novel which Harry has apparently memorized: "A blade glinted, and as if by magic a crescent appeared on the man's cheek, with little beads of blood seeping out like juice from an orange" (140). It is not only the content and style of, for example, films and cheap novels that manifest themselves in a given character's language—both his external speech and, more especially in this novel of and about private longings, internal discourse. It is the form as well, as in the case of Mark's thinking, which begins to resemble the trailers he and the other picturegoers watch before the feature film commences. Thus, even as the novel itself is made up of alternating stylizations, these stylizations often recapitulate the novel's larger structure insofar as they are themselves not uniform and whole but dialogized still further. The passage in which Harry "quotes" from a cheap novel illustrates in the simplest possible way the kind of further internal dialogization which pervades the entire novel and which manifests itself in still

more striking fashion in a number of passages that deal
with Mark and Clare. Thinking back to the sexual passion
he has released in Clare, for example, Mark writes in his
notebook:

But not tenderness she wanted now. Passion now.
    If dishonoured her, must then make an honest woman of her?
Marriage with Clare. Nothing said, but it was expected. Suppose
could do worse. Logical really, after what he had said to Pat. Merge
with the Mallorys; marry a Mallory. Name the day, bride in white,
radiant, nuptial Mass. Our Lady of Perpetual Sucker, till death do
us, special graces, Mendelssohn, the happy couple, pause for photo,
confetti, into the car, what to say, what the hell does one say—roll on
bed? The reception, a buffet, so glad you could come, yes didn't she,
yes I am, O ha ha Uncle Tom's sozzled ha ha good Old Uncle Tom,
unaccustomed as I am to public speaking, a glass of champagne cider
each. I give you the Bride's parents! My own parents looking a bit
sick of all the tipsy Irish. Thank God we're going, kippers in the car,
confetti, small hotel, double bed, a baby started, could do worse. (172)

Or Clare, later in the novel, feeling oppressed by the heat and
"incapable of sustaining any longer the intolerable labour of
love." "How long was this fencing going to continue. She was
impatient for the heavy swing of blunt, simple statements: 'I'm
sorry'—'I was a bitch'—'It was my fault'—'I love you' " (198).
And again, towards the end of this same scene, Clare wonders,
"Was that all then? Well good-bye, it's been nice knowing you,
I've enjoyed running my hands up and down your spine, it
was so nice of you to give me my faith back, we must keep in
touch, I do hope you have a nice life, cheerio" (202). Her
language captures all too well both her own dismay and Mark's
posturing, the hollowness of his spiritual rebirth. In the words
that Mark "cries out"—" 'I can't be true to the old evil in me,
and be false to—whatever may be potentially good in me
now!' " (200)—the reader hears echoes not only of Clare's
former innocence but of Damien's self-righteousness as well.
We witness in their language the fact that Mark and Clare have

in effect traded characters. She has become more skeptical and self-consciously dialogical, and he more strident and mono-logically certain. In the thoughts and words of each we hear the echoes of what the other formerly was, though in a form modified by some essential feature of their characters: in Clare's case, her authenticity, in Mark's his posturing.

Earlier in the novel, Mark says of the abrupt, unexpected ending of *Bicycle Thieves*, the picture he and Clare have just seen, " 'that's just the brilliance of it. No American or English director would have dared to end it there. . . . The point of the film is the plural of its title' " (141–142). The same cannot be said of *The Picturegoers*. Although its plural title suggests its dialogical point and method, as well as its sociological perspective, Lodge chooses not to end his novel abruptly or brilliantly but, instead, "cautiously." He resembles, in this regard, his own character, Mr. Berkeley, whose showing of a rock and roll film in order to save his ailing theater brings about an unexpected result. "It awaken[s] many dead souls to life." However, when the dead not only awaken but begin dancing in the aisles, Mr. Berkeley decides that things have gone too far. Lodge would undoubtedly understand and sympathize. In *The Picturegoers*, and indeed throughout his career as novelist and as critic, he has always tempered his willingness to explore new narrative and theoretical modes with a healthy sense of caution, or skepticism. The dialogic play of these two tendencies, or voices, is particularly evident in Lodge's second novel, *Ginger, You're Barmy*.

In comments on his second novel, David Lodge has identified three major literary influences ("Introduction" 4). One, the most localized, was Norman Mailer's war novel, *The Naked and the Dead*, which provided Lodge with a simple means for dealing with a then troubling aspect of the book's realism, the obscenities in his characters' speech. Another and far more important influence was John Osborne's play, *Look Back in Anger*, a performance of which Lodge attended while on leave from the same National Service that forms the ostensible subject matter of his own contribution to the literature of Britain's angry young men. As for the third influence, it was only long after the novel had been written that Lodge became aware of how completely he had cast it in the structural mold of Graham Greene's *The Quiet American*, from which he borrowed, "subliminally," that novel's "systematic flashback technique" as well as the final "e" of his protagonist's surname. Looking back on *Ginger, You're Barmy* and on the roles Mailer, Osborne, and Greene played in its conception and composition, Lodge seems to have been afflicted with a belated case of the anxiety of influence, pointing to what he feels are weaknesses in the novel that are clearly the result of a young author's failure to go it on his own. He has come to judge his second novel as a work of "missed possibilities" and has located the chief source of these missed possibilities in the genesis and composition of the novel as "an act of revenge," an angry look backwards at his two-year stint in the National Service ("David Lodge Interviewed" 112). Despite its shortcomings, *Ginger, You're Barmy* is, if not a major novel, then certainly an interesting, even impressive, one. Its strength derives much less from its overt subject matter and Lodge's "angry" response to it than it does from the ways in which he solved "the technical problem" that the writing of the novel posed and from the relation between Lodge's solution to this problem and the ideas about narrative theory and practice that he was then formulating—ideas that he would later bring together under the title *Language of Fiction* ("David Lodge Interviewed" 113).

In an interview with Bernard Bergonzi, published shortly after a second, revised (deMailerized) edition was published in paperback in 1970, Lodge explained the nature of this technical problem. The task he set himself was to create for the reader a sense of the tedium of peacetime military life without actually making the novel itself tedious to read. Lodge hoped to overcome the problem in two ways: one was to concentrate on the first weeks (of basic training) and on the last few days before the protagonist-narrator, Jonathan Browne, is mustered out, and the second was to add to this story a prologue-and-epilogue frame that would allow him to justify the narrative method he had adopted and "to convey some kind of moral comment on my ["somewhat unsympathetic"] narrator. . . . So the prologue-and-epilogue was partly an answer to a formal problem, partly an answer to a moral problem" (113). It was also an answer that seemed to insist upon the protagonist-narrator's development, morally and, as we shall see, aesthetically as well. Later, however, in the introduction he wrote in 1981 for a third (reMailerized) edition (in which "fugg" and "c——t" are restored and the novel transformed into a period piece), Lodge questioned whether his handling of this "technical problem" did not in fact constitute "a failure of nerve" on his part (3). Insofar as the frame insists upon a development of the protagonist's character that the rest of the novel does not adequately prepare for, then, the intentional fallacy notwithstanding, Lodge is undoubtedly correct in his assessment. This "failure of nerve" can, perhaps even should, be understood in a quite different way, however. Rather than constituting either a *deus ex machina* imposed by the author or an unconscious borrowing by a young Catholic novelist from another and more experienced one, Lodge's frame-and-tale structure forms part of a much larger pattern of doublings that in effect makes up the novel's underlying structure, that provides a structural metaphor for the novel's moral substance, and that anticipates as well his later interest in Gerard Genette's structuralist theory of narrative grammars.

To begin simply, the addition of the prologue-and-epilogue frame entails a chronological doubling: "now," in the narrative present, Jonathan looks back on events that occurred "then," during his two years of National Service, and becomes in the process "a *voyeur* spying on my own experience" (12). And there is as well a similar doubling within the framed tale, a constant shuttling back and forth of the narrative between the last days of Jonathan's tour of duty at Badmore and his first weeks at Catterick (the flashback technique mentioned earlier). The military experience is thus itself doubled—beginning and end, Catterick and Badmore—and within this doubling contrasted with civilian life: "For us soldier-commuters 'home' and 'camp' were two disparate, self-contained worlds, with their own laws and customs; every week we passed from one to the other and back again, changing like chameleons to melt into the new environment" (127). The changes are never quite so complete, however, either for the narrator-protagonist or for the reader. The soldier-commuter is never either wholly soldier or wholly civilian. Each carries the residue, or trace, of the other into their respective environments. The reader, whose reading of the framed tale doubles Jonathan's reading of his manuscript, faces a similar dilemma, for the story he reads not only concerns different temporal and geographical settings but has been composed by Jonathan at different, but not always distinguishable, times. That is to say, we do not read the "confessional outpouring" Jonathan wrote (although we may forget and think we do). What we read is that text as it was subsequently revised—lengthened and "polished." The result may be a Wordsworthian emotion recollected in tranquility or something quite different and far more self-serving. The reader cannot be sure because, while the idea of revision is a textual fact to which Jonathan admits in his prologue and epilogue, the textual evidence of these revisions is missing. To complicate matters a bit more, our reading of the framed story's two textual levels cannot be separated from the fictive author's (Jonathan's) commentary on them in the appended frame and, for readers of the third edition, from Lodge's commentary on them in his introduction. This is not to say that Lodge consciously and meticulously labored to create chronologically discrete compositional stages of Jonathan's narration. He may have, of course, but he did not need to. He needed only to create a Borgesian sense of their presence to lead the reader to intuit that "Jonathan" is not single, or even, as he himself claims, double, but more accurately, multiple, a series of images in a funhouse mirror. In this respect, the character development of which Lodge writes in his introduction to the third edition may be said to constitute a failure of nerve insofar as it attempts to reduce the dialogic complexity of Jonathan's character to the level of simple monologue. As narrator, Jonathan comments on the self he was then, but this is another, different Jonathan who is (was?) already at least double (geographically and narratively split, Catterick and Badmore). And as narrator Jonathan is further multiplied. He is the writer, the reviser, and finally the commentator who addresses the reader directly in the prologue and epilogue. Instead of remaining entirely discrete, these separate selves, each having its own distinct though not always or even often distinguishable voice, merge dialogically to create a surprisingly rich and troublingly complex characterization in a novel that, in the surface texture of its seemingly artless, conventionally realistic prose, suggests a similarly deceptive easy-to-understand narrative depthlessness. As in the case of those realistic novels which Lodge discusses in *Language of Fiction*, *Ginger, You're Barmy* demands the kind of close critical reading it seems least to invite.[1]

At times, the narrative voice speaks not only as "author" (which Jonathan of course is, fictively) but for its author, Lodge, who in writing *Ginger, You're Barmy* appears, narratively speaking, to have split himself in two. "My response to the Army," Lodge has written, "shifted from an indignant

---

1. "But in so far as the study of the novelist's language is limited to those who most obviously invite it, because their use of language answers immediately to our view of how literary language works, we risk implying that the language of other, earlier novelists [i.e., the realists/premodernists] is less integrally integrated to their achievements . . ." (Lodge, *Language of Fiction* 30).

moral resistance to its values . . . to a pragmatic determination to make myself as comfortable as possible and to use my time as profitably as possible" (2–3). That Lodge managed to use his time wisely is evidenced by the fact that he wrote much of his first novel, *The Picturegoers*, while in the National Service. More interesting is the way in which Lodge assigns the halves of his own divided response to army life to two different characters, Jonathan Browne and Mike Brady. Although (to put the matter in a crudely biographical way) Browne and Brady do, almost allegorically, represent sides of Lodge's own mind during his tour of duty, the significant fact is that whereas in his monological introduction the two are conveniently and easily separated, in the novel they exist and intersect dialogically. On the surface of Lodge's narrative, they are in simple opposition to one another. Mike is impulsive, gregarious, idealistic, and naively credulous. Jonathan is calculating, self-centered, pragmatic, and agnostic. The one is virtually a caricature of Irish Catholicism and "grotesque individuality" (50), the other a study in secularism and self-promoting anonymity. Mike suffers from claustrophobia and requires considerable physical as well as psychological space (paradoxically so, given the narrowness of his religious beliefs). Jonathan, on the other hand, though ostensibly a free thinker, actually seems to prefer various forms of confinement, metaphorical "boxes" in which he can prosper in his own preferred narrow fashion. As he explains at one point, "success consisted in determining which box would be most pleasant for you, and getting into it. If you were forced to inhabit an unpleasant box for a time, then you could make it as comfortable as possible until you could get out. . . . [I]t was better to be in the most uncomfortable box than outside, in the confusion of the elements" (196–197). Better to be inside reading William Empson's *Seven Types of Ambiguity* (as Jonathan does) than to be outside and therefore paradoxically *in* the uncertain ambiguous world.

Keeping the spatial metaphor in mind, we can say that Jonathan is correct in his summary analysis of his and Mike Brady's differences: "My temperament was prudence and my destiny success, as surely as Mike's were foolhardiness and failure" (217). However, Jonathan's syntactically balanced assessment is not without its own ironic double: " 'I may not have the virtue of Christian prudence,' " Mike tells him, " 'but God help me from the unchristian sort' " (160). The point is not that either Jonathan or Mike is right, but that they somehow share the truth between them. Each qualifies the other, though never to the point that Lodge is able—or at least willing—to posit a monologic synthesis that will resolve the characters' and the reader's moral dilemma. It is, however, difficult to like Jonathan and so to accept that his views have any moral validity whatsoever. If Mike's conscience works overtime, then Jon's appears to work not at all, replaced by selfishness, self-consciousness, and voyeuristic detachment. "I have always tried to avoid occasion for regret, the most lingering of all the unpleasant emotions, by prudent foresight" (46), Jon explains as he ponders whether or not to deflower his girlfriend, Pauline. It is hard to like such a "reasonable" character, especially one as prone as Jonathan is to self-pity, to making himself (Henry Fleming fashion) the object of the world's injustice. On the other hand, it is impossible not to agree that his judgments about himself and others are often correct and that his self-pity is at times warranted. The comment recorded in his army file, for example, "educated up to the university level: thinks too much of himself" (52), is at once accurate and yet (given the context of the army's distrust of and distaste for "education") patently unfair. The syntactical parallelism in this comment reflects the balance of objectivity and subjectivity, of fairness and injustice, as well as the larger dialogical character of the entire novel. Similarly, Jon's voyeurism and reasonableness, although objectionable, cannot be entirely separated from that awareness—especially self-awareness—which so clearly contrasts with Mike's narrowness and which identifies him as a distinctly "modern" character, one who is willing to expose himself, "warts and all," to the reader's own voyeuristic gaze.

The prospect of parting with Mike . . . aroused ambiguous feelings in me. I could not deceive myself that our friendship had been deep and instinctive: it had been almost artificially forced by our mutual distaste for the Army. On the other hand I viewed with little enthusiasm life in the Army without Mike's moral support. I mean "moral" literally. Mike's hostility to the Army seemed to have an essentially moral basis, which somehow sanctioned my more self-centred grievances. But it was becoming increasingly clear to me that Mike's "morality" was an unreliable guide to conduct, and I did not wish to become involved in some wild, quixotic crusade against the Army. (152)

Mike's rigid moral code is as archaic as the army's feudal infrastructure and the "who goes there, friend or foe?" (159) challenge that Jonathan cannot bring himself to take seriously. For Mike, the army is " 'evil' "; it deprives him of his " 'free will' " and thus makes it impossible for him to fulfill his purpose on earth, which is, he says in a "pedantic," catechetical way, " 'to exercise my free will, and to save my soul' " (158). For Jonathan, the army means something quite different: the interruption of his academic studies, the limiting of his personal freedom, and the loss of certain creaturely comforts. It is difficult not to credit to some degree his realistic if self-centered point of view, even as the reader questions the value of a life in which amorality and selfishness are so rigorously pursued.

Instead of promoting a moral position, the novel creates a morally and textually ambiguous world. This ambiguity is most pronounced in Lodge's handling of one of the novel's central narrative events, the death of Percy Higgins. Whether Percy's death is accidental or a suicide is a crucial question that Lodge deliberately leaves unanswered. The novel focuses on the survivors', especially Jonathan's and Mike's, efforts to deal with this ambiguity. (Lodge blurs further all simple distinctions by developing parallels between Percy and Mike on the one hand and Percy and Jonathan on the other. Percy is, for example, like Mike a Catholic fundamentalist and like Jonathan a sheltered loner in need of Mike's help.) The novel in fact opens with an invitation, or rather a challenge, to the reader to read Jonathan's story according to a literary equivalent of the physicist's laws of uncertainty and complementarity. "It is strange to read what I wrote three years ago," the novel begins. "It is like reading another man's writing. Things have certainly not worked out as I expected. Or did I deliberately prevent them from so working out?" (11). If Lodge is concerned with the question of ambiguous meaning, then we would have to say that his narrator is obsessed by it. The book Jonathan reads just before he gains his release from the service, Empson's *Seven Types of Ambiguity*, not only symbolizes this obsession but seems to have influenced his writing as well.

It is true that much of the narrative parallelism in the novel serves a *too clearly* ironic, and therefore nearly monologic, purpose. The soldier who scoffs at Mike's grief over Percy's death, claiming that what actually troubles Mike is the loss not of Percy but of part of his leave, ironically echoes Jonathan's own selfishness and insensitivity a page or two earlier. But in a later scene, one which in turn echoes the first, we find ambiguity rather than irony. Mike has just been taken into custody after clubbing Sgt. Baker, whom he holds responsible for Percy's death. As he waits to discover Mike's fate, Jonathan lashes out at a small group of soldiers who have (in this case unjustly) claimed he was " 'not being very worried about his mate.' " Jonathan calls them " 'stupid, selfish bastards' " and especially (and rightly) condemns their "Fugg you Jack, I'm all right" attitude (174–175). Immediately after making this Brady-like outburst, Jonathan discovers that he has been assigned to guard duty. His response—" 'Fugg the Army' "

(176)—puts him in the same moral as well as linguistic realm as those whom he has just criticized. However, the irony here, while it clearly underscores what appears to be Jonathan's dominant and certainly least appealing trait, does not cancel out what the novel's parallel structure implies: that Jonathan is poised somewhere between self-pity and moral concern. Both the critical irony and the moral ambiguity deepen in a later, and again parallel, scene in which Jonathan visits Mike at the military stockade where, following his escape from his first imprisonment (for striking Sgt. Baker), he has been confined for taking part in an IRA raid on the Badmore camp. Lodge handles the raid much as he handled Percy's death earlier in the novel. He compounds the irony to the point that individual ironies dissolve (though not without leaving a trace) in the larger ambiguous whole that results. For example, Mike is one of the attackers, but his part in the raid is the condition upon which his release from the IRA (whose violence he abhors) is predicated. That Mike should find it necessary to gain his release from the very group, the IRA, that helped free him from his first captivity contributes to the novel's pervasive irony and general blurring of clear-cut distinctions. Similarly, in foiling the IRA attack, Jonathan becomes—at least in the minds of his military supervisors—what for two years he has managed to avoid being: a good soldier. Doing his duty, he saves the camp's officers, whom he loathes, from the same kind of embarrassment he himself suffered moments before when one of those same officers launched his own surprise attack in order to test camp security—and to win a bet. As the ironies multiply, the stable point of view upon which the successful use of moral irony is said to depend dissolves. As a result, the reader finds himself adrift in a morally ambiguous textual world that offers him certain simple facts and connections (Jonathan, for example, foils the IRA raid and so is indirectly responsible for his friend's capture), but that teases the reader with moral conundrums (Jonathan was unaware that Mike was among the attackers, but what would he have done had he known?). As their visit draws to an end, Mike says, " 'It's all right, Jon. You were only doing your duty' " (215). His words echo Jonathan's own remark, "It's all right, Jack," just a few pages before. Whatever Mike intends his words to mean, for his auditor and for Lodge's reader they serve both to console and to condemn, as does the sign Mike makes as Jonathan departs, lifting his hand "in a gesture of . . ./. . . of what? Reassurance? Dismissal? Benediction? Would I ever know?" (216). Admittedly, the ironies and uncertainties here and elsewhere in the novel are laid on in a heavy-handed, even melodramatic, fashion, but it is a heavy hand that tells the reader more about the workings of Jonathan's mind, I believe, than about the shortcomings of Lodge's writing.

Just as the structure of the novel betrays doubling and parallelism at all narrative levels, from the meanings of individual words to the construction of syntactically balanced sentences, compounded ironies, parallel scenes, and complementary subchapters, so in similar fashion does Jonathan's style evidence a dual tendency towards the melodramatic on the one hand and the religious on the other. While the former suggests the stilted "literariness" and self-pitying sentimentality of Jonathan's character and point of view, the latter points to one of the ways in which Mike has impressed himself on Jonathan's imagination and on his writing. Together they create an interesting tension between Jonathan's largely selfish views on the one hand and his tentative moral gropings on the other. Certain words evidence this moral, or more accurately, this religious subtext directly: "confession," "contrition," "indoctrinate," "covet," "expiation," "benediction," "mission," "conscience," "transubstantiation," "eremitical"(!), among others. Other instances are less direct—Jonathan's Peter-like denials, first of Percy and later of Mike as "friends," for example, and, more effectively, the echoes of Catholic doctrine in certain of Jonathan's phrasings, "occasion of sin" in his "occasion for regret" and "firm purpose of amendment" from the Catholic sacrament of penance in his "possibilities of amendment."

In the novel's religious subtext the reader detects the residue of Jonathan's studied and all too serious literariness (the parallels he draws between military life and Dante's *Inferno*, another of the books he reads during his National Service) as well as Mike's continuing presence in Jonathan's life and writing. The precise extent of Mike's influence and the uses to which Jonathan puts it are less certain. In his epilogue, Jonathan claims that "my relationship with Mike had been a fuse laid in the bed-rock of my self-complacency" (221), but though he offers this view Jonathan also tends to reject or at least modify it, noting elsewhere (in the prologue), for example, that Mike's influence has been far less explosive. "I don't think I am a better person, or even a happier one; but perhaps there has been a small advance" (11). Outwardly the change appears considerable. During the three years since he completed his National Service as well as the writing and revision of his manuscript, Jonathan has, like his Biblical namesake, devoted himself to his friend. He has abandoned his academic studies and taken a teaching position in a small rural school in order to be close to the prison where he can visit Mike as often as possible and minister to his needs. Equally startling, now that his friend is to be released and his own "mission" over, Jonathan hopes to "build a life of modest usefulness" (223) as a teacher, husband, and father. "I hope Mike will agree to stay with us for a while," Jonathan writes. "He has been the focal point of my life for so long that I am curiously jealous of the rest of the world with whom he will shortly resume contact. Also, I feel a certain panic when I reflect that he will no longer need my support. It is not a question of what he will do without me, but of what I will do without him" (222). All that Jonathan writes here is understandable, even—in its high degree of honest self-criticism—commendable. But then, in a verbal gesture that is entirely characteristic of the Jonathan of the framed tale, Jonathan as narrator immediately adds, "now he is free, and I am shackled,—by a wife and family I do not greatly love, and by a career that I find no more than tolerable" (222). Jonathan's honesty disarms and appalls the reader, but does it do so because Jonathan's selfishness makes him such a morally appalling figure in the reader's eyes or because the narrative mode in which his tale is told (or, alternately, in which he has chosen to tell his tale)—the religious confession—requires this kind of self-portraiture?

Beginning his work as a "confessional outpouring" (11), the writer monastically ("eremitically") sets himself apart from the hedonish world, specifically Majorca where Jonathan and Pauline's dream vacation turns nightmare. Their island paradise transmogrifies into an inferno of sickness (Pauline's food poisoning), and frustrated longings (psychological, sexual, and linguistic: Jonathan's ignorance of Spanish makes it difficult for him to communicate with anyone on the island). As a result, Jonathan turns to writing, or more particularly to confession, but even the penitent can be seduced. "The demon Form" leads him to turn his "confessional outpouring" into something more aesthetically crafted, but whether this transformation signals transfiguration or falsification—or both—is not made clear; perhaps it cannot be made clear. For all its seeming transparency, *Ginger, You're Barmy* is very much about the ambiguous relationship between art and life. At one point, Jonathan readily admits that his "mission" has been both an unselfish act and an excuse to be nothing more than a nominal husband and father. Much the same can be said of Jonathan's mission as a writer. The self-flagellation of his self-begetting novel at once chronicles life and competes with it, as Pauline quickly comes to realize when she finds she has to compete with the manuscript for Jonathan's attention. Significantly, what first attracted Jonathan to her was her "femininity" (141), by which word Jonathan seems to mean her feminine receptiveness, less as a sexual partner than as an audience for his repressed monologues. Soon after they meet, she asks him to tell her about army life, a topic on which the usually garrulous Mike Brady has been noticeably reticent. "The invitation could not have been more welcome. This was the audience I had been seeking all the week-end" (137). Jonathan is thus not only a character in search of an author (himself), but an author in search of an audience (in this case Pauline). Later, when he goes to Pauline to tell her what Mike has done (struck Sgt. Baker), Jonathan "considered very carefully what version I should give her of what I knew about the incident, and had decided to tell her what I should say when Mike was charged. My motives were, firstly, to rehearse the story properly, and secondly, to position myself as favourably as possible in relation to Pauline. This latter problem was by no means simple" (162). Read in the light of this passage, the ending of the novel puts Jonathan in a particularly ambiguous position. The reader cannot be sure whether Jonathan has indeed grown morally or whether any claim, or even any narrative hint, of such growth on his part may be nothing more than a calculated attempt to once again position himself "as favourably as possible" in relation to his audience. What complicates the reader's dilemma still further is the fact that Jonathan's willingness to put himself before the reader, warts and all, is disarming.

The form of his narration and of Lodge's novel is therefore especially noteworthy in that the story Jonathan tells appears to be an act of self-incrimination, and by exposing himself in this way the teller earns not only the reader's censure but his sympathy as well. Unfortunately, Jonathan's narrative strategy may not be quite as disingenuous as the credulous reader would like to believe. Given that Jonathan's position as narrator parallels Lodge's as author, the former's remarks quoted above curiously anticipate the latter's, quoted earlier in this chapter, on the "technical problem" that the writing of the novel posed. Such a reading would certainly be in keeping with the pragmatic side of Jonathan's personality, evident throughout both his tale and the frame he appends to it: "even now, it seems, I am not immune from the insinuations of Form. It occurs to me that these notes, which I am jotting down on this momentous morning, might usefully form a prologue and epilogue to the main story . . ." (12). On the other hand, the fact that Jonathan has unearthed—or resurrected—his manuscript and revised it for a second time (by adding the frame) suggests the ongoingness of his search to discover the meaning of his military experience and more particularly, through Mike, of himself. In doing so, Jonathan embodies one of the key points upon which Lodge's *Language of Fiction* theory rests: "in literary discourse, the writer discovers what he has to say in the process of saying it, and the reader discovers what is said in responding to the way it is said" (64–65). What Jonathan could not bring himself to tell Pauline, he confides in his manuscript, and it is the writing process itself that enables Jonathan to begin to understand himself. What the reader experiences is not the act of self-discovery, some Joycean epiphany, but the process through which that discovery may occur. The uncertainty is crucial, for synthetic, univocal readings (including the author's in his introduction) are precisely what the novel manages to avoid. Its author David Lodge and its narrator-protagonist Jonathan Browne are poised, as I believe its reader must be, between belief and clerkly skepticism. What the novel ultimately points to is not any "failure of nerve" on Lodge's part but, instead, the open-endedness and necessary incompleteness of the dialogical process—a process for which the unfinished state of Jonathan's manuscript stands as a metaphor.

Ginger, You're Barmy succeeds to the degree that it embodies and not merely espouses such an interplay of conflicting voices, one in which the relation between the formal and moral aspects of art are given a new post-liberal twist. In the *Language of Fiction*, Lodge quotes "a very characteristic statement of Dr. Leavis's": "when we examine the formal perfection of *Emma*, we find that it can be appreciated only in terms of the moral preoccupations that characterize the novelist's peculiar interest in life." Lodge then "emends" the quotation in the following manner: "when we examine the moral preoccupations that characterize Jane Austen's peculiar interest in life as manifested in *Emma*, we find that they can be appreciated only in terms of the formal perfection of the novel" (68). Whether it is or is not useful to speak of the "formal perfection" of *Ginger, You're Barmy* is a moot point. What we can speak of with assurance, however, is its formal consistency as well as the ways in which the novel anticipates, and in some cases recapitulates, many of the same concerns that Lodge has voiced in his critical writings. Bradbury and others have complained that as a critic Lodge favors linguistic analysis over humanistic values, "the demon Form" over "the confessional outpouring." The charge is at once merited and yet—in light of the numerous disclaimers of any such preference that punctuate the *Language of Fiction*—mistaken:

a true "science" of stylistics is a chimera. . . . [Linguistics can never replace literary criticism because linguistics claims to be science and literature] concerns values. And values are not amenable to scientific method. . . . [W]hile a literary structure has an objective existence which can be objectively (or "scientifically") described, such a description has little value in literary criticism until it is related to a process of human communication which is not amenable to objective description. (55, 57, 65)

In such disclaimers, as in his contention that the rigorous brand of verbal analysis he advocates and practices must be "applied intuitively," we detect much the same play of contending voices as in *Ginger, You're Barmy*. Certainly, the writing of his story of National Service is Jonathan's most ambiguous and most transformative act. In it biography metamorphoses into fictive autobiography, contingent life into formal art, the narrator's examination of conscience into his examination of narrative. Lodge's second novel evidences a profound concern for "formal perfection" that, on the one hand, necessitates a retreat from the values associated with much humanistic (especially realistic, premodernist) art but that may, at the same time, suggest the most viable means for achieving moral clarification, if not moral certainty, in the modern age.

7

The British Museum Is Falling Down: or, Up from Realism

The British Museum Is Falling Down is another of Lodge's double novels—double not in its structure (as in the case of *Ginger, You're Barmy*) but in its very texture. On the one hand the novel tells the comic story of a day in the life of twenty-five-year-old Adam Appleby, a post-graduate student who knows he will not finish his thesis—on the long sentence in three modern English novels—before his scholarship runs out. Worse, and funnier, as his academic prospects dwindle, his alphabetical family (Adam, Barbara, Clare, Dominic, and Edward) continues to increase, the children being the fruits, or rather by-products, of the rhythm method that he and Barbara, as believing Catholics, continue to practice. On the other hand, *The British Museum* is a post-*Sot-Weed Factor* but pre-*Lost in the Funhouse* instance of the literature of exhaustion, English style: a parodic collage in the guise of a seamless comic realistic novel. While early reviewers tended to overlook the novel's parodic side, later readers run the risk of making the opposite mistake and of thus failing to realize that in Lodge's third novel, realism and parody, life and literature, feed on and reflect each other, creating a comical but nonetheless disturbing confusion of realms. Adam Appleby is certainly confused even though he is able to theorize about the very condition that besets him throughout the novel: " 'Novelists,' " he says, " 'are *using up* experience at a dangerous rate.' " In prenovelistic times, literature was chiefly allegorical and fantastical; thus there was little danger of confusing literature with life. But novels deal with ordinary people in ordinary ways and have, Adam contends, " 'just about exhausted the possibilities of life. So all of us, you see, are really enacting events that have already been written about in some novel or other. Of course, most people don't realise this—they fondly imagine that their little lives are unique. . . . Just as well, too, because once you *do* tumble to it, the effect is very disturbing' " (129–130). Although Barbara calls his idea "cracked," the novel explores—and exploits—the narrative possibilities of this and other "jokey relations" ("David Lodge Interviewed" 110), including the one between the novel's two epigraphs, Oscar Wilde's deadpan claim that "life imitates art" and Samuel Johnson's contention that although he has "fear enough" to be a Catholic, "an obstinate rationality prevents me."

One way to approach the relationship between the epigraphs (and what they suggest about the rest of the novel) is to consider briefly the general context in which the work was conceived and composed. Part of this context is religious: the convening of Vatican II and, a few years later, a Pontifical Commission whose task it was to investigate the Church's teaching on birth control. Taken together, they held out to many Catholics—Lodge among them—the promise that a liberalizing of the Church's ban on all forms of artificial birth control was imminent. Of equal importance is the novel's literary context. Begun in England, the novel was chiefly written in the United States during the 1964–65 academic year that Lodge spent there with his family, studying, touring, and in general enjoying the "stimulating and liberating effect of the American experience" ("Introduction" 1). His liberation as a

writer had in a sense already begun some three years earlier
when Malcom Bradbury joined the University of Birmingham
English Department and began to convince Lodge of the liberating possibilities of literary comedy. Together with Jim Duck-
ett, they wrote a satirical revue, *Between the Four Walls*, and
Lodge began *The British Museum*, which he would later dedicate
to Bradbury, "whose fault it mostly is that I have tried to write
a comic novel." *The British Museum* is, however, not simply a
comic novel but a comically parodic novel which evidences
Lodge the novelist's indebtedness to Lodge the critic. Just
prior to beginning his third novel, Lodge had completed his
first critical study, *Language of Fiction*; the close analysis of
language in the one facilitated the writing of the parodic passages in the other, as Lodge has himself explained ("David
Lodge Interviewed" 110). There is, however, another "jokey
relation" worth mentioning: the one that pits the high seriousness of the critical enterprise against the decrowning vitality
of Lodge's comic fiction.

"Comedy is based on contrast, on incongruity" (Lodge, *Language* 250), and *The British Museum Is Falling Down* involves
exposing and exploiting this incongruity, both overtly and
covertly. Looking back at the earliest period of the Applebys'
marriage, the narrator claims: "For three anxious months they
had survived. Unfortunately, Barbara's ovulation seemed to
occur late in her monthly cycle, and their sexual relations were
forced into a curious pattern: three weeks of patient graph-
plotting, followed by a few nights of frantic love-making,
which rapidly petered out in exhaustion and renewed suspense. This behaviour was known as Rhythm and was in accor-
dance with the Natural Law" (14). By exploiting the discrepancy between the mechanical methods and the Church's
designation of it as the Natural Law, Lodge explodes the
baselessness of that "rage for consistency" ("Introduction" 2)
that he feels then characterized British (and American) Catholicism, producing in the process his own artfully inconsistent,

early postmodernist text. Adam Appleby "revolts" against "still repose," "physical restraint," and "the sedation of routine," including that of the rhythm method (40, 55). Lodge achieves a similar if more effective and more self-conscious narrative revolution by carnivalizing his text in an effort to undermine the monological seriousness of various forms of authority. "On all sides a babble of academic conversation dinned in his [Adam's] ears," Lodge writes in a chapter that is itself a parody of the "sherry party" scene found in many campus novels, including *Eating People Is Wrong* (136). Rather than merely noting the "babble," Lodge records it—records that is, the brief and entirely unrelated snippets from the conversations of various unidentified speakers. This "babble" reflects on the micro-level the general structure of the entire novel: a concatenation of voices transformed into a seemingly sequential and apparently seamless narrative. Lodge is able to carnivalize so adroitly because he cannibalizes so well. The novel comprises a multitude of literary allusions and lengthy parodies of individual authors—Conrad, Greene, Hemingway, James, Joyce, Kafka, Lawrence, Woolf, C. P. Snow, and Baron Corvo—as well as of literary schools. The novel devours and adapts not only literary authors, styles, and works at a bewildering rate, but literary and subliterary forms as well, including newspaper reports, advertising jingles, encyclopedia entries, unpublished manuscripts, plot summaries, letters to the editor, and slapstick comedy. To compound matters, Lodge's novel has as its main character not only a postgraduate English student who feels—or finds—that most of his life has been "annexed" by literature (82), but one who is himself given to parody.

As even this brief summary makes clear, the resemblances between Lodge's slim, seemingly conventional realistic novel and Joyce's mammoth literary museum of densely textured modernist prose, *Ulysses*, are considerable even if on a first reading they are not entirely obvious. As Dennis Jackson has usefully explained, "like Leopold Bloom, Adam . . . becomes increasingly disoriented as his day progresses, and his perceptions of life around him become increasingly phantasmagoric. Like Bloom also, Lodge's hero keeps his mind constantly fixed . . . on his home and his wife; he suffers because of his religion; and he has fantasies of grandeur (which, like Bloom's, are always followed by some sort of comic diminution" (473–474). Jackson's summary of the "explicit parallels" between these two works—including the parodies and the concluding soliloquies of Molly Bloom and Barbara Appleby—attest to the extent of Joyce's influence on Lodge. I suspect, however, that behind these "explicit parallels" lies a deeper and perhaps darker reason for Lodge's intense interest in Joyce's iconoclastic art. The novel's incessant and shifting parodic play delights Lodge's knowing reader who (unlike Joyce's) has little difficulty in subordinating the parodically disruptive surface to the forward movement of conventional narrative. Yet the parodic, disruptive play does disturb insofar as it intrudes, however subtly and smilingly, a note of uncertainty into a text that is otherwise easily read and readily consumed. If the Catholic novelist whose spirit broods over *Ginger, You're Barmy* is Graham Greene, then in *The British Museum* it is Joyce, and therein lies the important difference between these two works. The novel's parodic, Joycean style (and structure) serves multiple purposes. Since "Adam works not only literally but figuratively in Bloomsbury's shadow," Lodge's parodies are, as Robert Burden has pointed out, entirely "consistent with the novel's fundamental realism" (141). The novel's parodic style may thus be read as "a mimetically justified device" which, Bradbury has claimed, Lodge uses "to expose and explore the literariness of the main character and his problems of self-definition" (179). (Whether the novel is as fundamentally realistic as Burden and Bradbury claim is, however, open to question.) The parodies also enabled Lodge to transform critical theory into narrative art. He could draw on his study of the language of fiction and yet at the same time distance himself from a character made in the author's own image, or, rather, in caricature of that image. (Adam's thesis on "The Long Sentence in Three Modern English Novels," for example, may be read as a reductio ad absurdum of *Language of Fiction*.) As Lodge explains in *Language of Fiction*, "it is characteristic of such novels [as *Tristram Shandy* and *Pale Fire*] that the central figure is himself a writer [Adam, too, plans to write a novel], often with autobiographical reference, that there is a lot of parody, many literary jokes, and much discussion of literary questions, and that in this way the author is able to gain a surprising distance on his own literary identity" (261). Further, like Adam Appleby, Lodge felt the weight of the literary past and as a result chose to turn the novel into "a kind of joke on myself" ("David Lodge Interviewed" 110), an act of comic revenge. It was "a way of coping with what . . . Harold Bloom has called 'Anxiety of Influence'—in the sense that every young writer must have of the daunting weight of the literary tradition he has inherited, the necessity and yet seeming impossibility of doing something in writing that has not been done before" ("Introduction" 4–5). Just as Adam feels at the end of his road, his options all used up, so Lodge apparently felt. *The British Museum* is, therefore, his literature of exhaustion, his way of moving ahead by moving back, of demystifying the literary past by parodying it.

The British Museum Is Falling Down undermines authority at virtually every level. This is especially obvious in Lodge's wickedly funny parodies of Lawrence (pp. 50–51), Hemingway (pp. 108–112), and James (pp. 115–118), in which he effectively underscores the least attractive features of their writing. Even the epigraphs which precede each of the novel's ten chapters contribute to the general sense of comic leveling and carnivalistic play. Lodge places various figures and even objects of authority—Carlyle and Ruskin, for example, as well as government statutes and the British Museum Catalogue—

in a decidedly humorous light by excerpting their words in such a way as to deprive them of their serious context (and content). Carlyle, for example, is made to do a comic turn: "I believe there are several persons in a state of imbecility who come to read in the British Museum. I have been informed that there are several in that state who are sent there by their friends to pass away their time" (61). And Yeats metamorphoses into a clownish wimp, a literary Mr. Peepers: "I spent my days at the British Museum, and must, I think, have been very delicate, for I remember often putting off hour after hour consulting some necessary book because I shrank from lifting the heavy volumes of the catalogue" (78). Arundell Esdaile, identified as a "former secretary to the British Museum," contributes an item which, given Adam's preoccupation with sex and birth control, takes on intertextual meanings that the former secretary must never have intended: "Free or open access can hardly be practised in so large a library as this" (96). The general breakdown of authority extends further, for Lodge depicts all of the novel's fathers, husbands, priests, department heads, literary executors, landladies, firemen, even telephone operators—anyone, in short, in any position of authority whatsoever—as incompetent bumblers.

The anxiety of influence that Lodge felt so acutely and managed to turn to comic advantage is, however, itself double: literary *and* religious. The two merge to a considerable extent in the tradition of the Catholic novel in which Lodge necessarily works and to which he has devoted a good deal of his time as a critic: a doctoral dissertation on the subject as well as pamphlet-length studies of Greene and Evelyn Waugh. Since the Catholic novel, as Lodge defines it, is "concerned with the operation of God's grace in the world, with a conflict between secular and divine values in which the latter are usually allowed an ironic and unexpected triumph" (*Evelyn Waugh* 30), it is clear that *The British Museum* represents how far Lodge has departed from the very tradition which Waugh, Greene, and others found congenial but which Lodge considers outmoded. Lodge undermines the authority of his sources, including the Catholic novelist (here represented by the prissy hypocrite, Egbert Merrymarsh, a Chesterbelloc clone), by carnivalizing them; in this way he establishes his own authority by evidencing his technical mastery of their styles, forms, subjects, and voices. *The British Museum* can be described, therefore, as a Barth-like virtuoso peformance that serves to establish Lodge's credibility as a writer and, equally important, at a time when the debate "about authority and conscience" provoked by the birth control issue was just getting under way, his credibility as an individual Catholic able to make his own moral (as well as aesthetic) decisions.

In "The Novel Interrogates Itself: Parody as Self-Consciousness in Contemporary English Fiction," Robert Burden points out that while Lodge and Angus Wilson use parody and pastiche "for comic purposes . . . their burlesque and mimicry include serious concerns about the form of the novel" (154)— and, I would add, about contemporary moral matters as well. Writing specifically of Wilson's novel, *No Laughing Matter*, however, Bradbury makes a point that also seems to apply equally well to *The British Museum*: "These modes of ambiguity and distortion, parody and pastiche, make it hard [for the reader] to discover the authentic register of the novel; there is a decided stabilization of the text in the latter half, but it is an evolution itself somewhat disturbing, since it involves a reduction of rhetorical energy" (*Possibilities* 228). Despite the verbal energy of the Molly Bloom-like soliloquy with which Lodge's novel concludes, something similar can be said about *The British Museum*, not because the novel is flawed in its form (the charge Bradbury levels against *No Laughing Matter*) but because Lodge's aesthetic (as well as the aesthetic integrity of his novel) requires such restraint. This restraint is, in fact, built into his aesthetic and extends to his parodic technique, which not only undermines the authority of his sources but paradoxically validates and even pays homage to them as well. Lodge's dialogically divided attitude towards parody accounts for why on the one hand he worried that the parodies in *The British Museum* would alienate some readers and on the other he wanted a blurb to appear on the dust jacket alerting readers to their presence. (It was a suggestion his publisher rejected, leaving readers and, especially, reviewers free to overlook the parodies, as they indeed did, much to Lodge's dismay.) Lodge understood what his parodic method implied and so attempted to steer a middle course, both aesthetically and religiously. He wanted to write a parodic novel, but not one that would go quite so far as those written by the more gleefully apocalyptic—especially American—writers of the sixties and early seventies with which Lodge was then becoming acquainted. Similarly, he wanted to write a comic novel about the Catholic Church's teaching on birth control that would not go so far as to actually challenge the Church's authority. At that time it would have been impossible to challenge the Church in one area without challenging the Church's authority altogether. Yet, Lodge's later disclaimers notwithstanding, such a challenge to the Church's monologic authority is precisely what his parodic technique implies.

For all its parodic humor and energy, *The British Museum* is a serious fiction about a latter-day poor forked creature, a young Old Adam who finds that his life has been usurped, or "annexed," by fiction, including the fiction of the Natural Method, which as both Adam and Barbara realize, is quite unnatural. The Church reduces sex to simple monologue, but as Barbara points out in her soliloquy, sex is in fact a complicated matter. What the Church preaches abstractly is not what individual Catholics are able to actually practice. Finding a workable sexual policy may be considerably more difficult than trying to find a workable definition of the "the long sentence." As Barbara says at one point in *her* long sentence, the one with which the novel concludes, "there's always a snag perhaps that's the root of the matter there's something about sex perhaps it's original sin I don't know but we'll never get it neatly tied up you think you've got it under control in one place it pops up in another either it's comic or tragic nobody's immune" (174). Appearing twenty times in the final two pages, Barbara's cautionary "perhaps" echoes her husband's similar uncertainty. Asked by some liberal Catholics what it is he wants, Adam says that he doesn't know, though he does "suppose" that no one "really *wants* to use contraceptives. . . . They're not things you can work up much affection for" (70). And one hundred pages later Barbara makes precisely the same point: "there's something a bit offputting about contraceptives" (174). Each understands that while contraception may be necessary, it cannot solve a problem that is essentially religious rather than biological. There can be no adequate monological solutions to concrete dialogical problems. Similarly, *The British Museum* has no uniform monological style, but is instead a dialogue of styles, a mulligan stew. Taken together or individually, they stand in opposition to what Adam at one point disparagingly refers to as the "style of high-minded generality" (68). Thus it is fitting that this novel which seems to be "about" Adam Appleby should end with his wife's soliloquy. It ends, that is, with a voice which echoes Molly Bloom's (as well at times as Adam's) but that is nonetheless her own, syntactically and sexually different from all the voices that have preceded it, closing and so completing *The British Museum*, yet at the same time disrupting it, opening it up and, "perhaps," out.

8

Out of the Shelter and the Problem of Literary Recidivism

THE DOUBLENESS OF Lodge's fourth novel, *Out of the Shelter*, first published in 1970 and recently reissued in 1985 in a substantively revised—or actually restored—edition,[1] is evident even in the history of its composition and publication. Although largely based on a trip that the author made to Germany when, like his protagonist, he was sixteen years old, the novel bears as well the clear impress of Lodge's first trip to the United States, thirteen years later, and it anticipates his second, to assume a visiting professorship at the University of California at Berkeley, which he undertook shortly after

1. In revising the badly mangled text printed by Macmillan in 1970 for the new edition to be published by Secker & Warburg (1985), Lodge restored a number of passages, deleted several others, and "made many small stylistic alterations" but otherwise left the text pretty much as it was in an effort "to discover the effective version of the novel I wrote in 1967–8" (Lodge, "Introduction," *Out of the Shelter* xvi). Around the time he was making those changes, he explained to John Haffenden that "if I were writing it now I would not use that restrained monotone, the conventionally realistic mode; I think I would have more stylistic variety, more differences of perspective" (Interview 151).

completing the manuscript in 1968. The novel is, therefore, as Lodge has pointed out, "autobiographical in origins, but not confessional in intent" (ix). It is confessional in form, however, even if that form is not quite so apparent as it is in *Ginger, You're Barmy*. That *Out of the Shelter* should have more in common with Lodge's second novel (and with his first, *The Picturegoers*) than with his third, the archly parodic *British Museum*, should not be surprising. It was, after all, conceived before *The British Museum* was written (xii). Moreover, Lodge's career as a novelist has had a curious dialogical rhythm of its own involving the alternating publication of serious and comic works. That Lodge should, with Bradbury's help, have discovered the possibilities of comic narration in the writing of his third novel, and then have composed a work that is "in tone and technique" (xii) closer to *The Picturegoers* and *Ginger, You're Barmy* than to *The British Museum*, does not, therefore, necessarily signal an aesthetic retreat on Lodge's part. However, *Out of the Shelter* does look back to and "double" the past—itself double, biographical and literary—in an aesthetically unsatisfying way, and it does so despite the author's large claims for the book's formidable lineage and at times equally large claims for its aesthetic merits. Ironically, it may be because the book is, as Lodge has said, "the most inclusive and most fully achieved" of his first three "serious" novels that it satisfies so little (quoted in Vinson 401).

As Lodge has noted, *Out of the Shelter* merges two literary forms, the *Bildungsroman* and the Jamesian international novel "of conflicting ethical and cultural values,"[2] and has as "its most obvious literary models" Joyce's *A Portrait of the Artist as a Young Man* and James's *The Ambassadors* (with touches of *The Dubliners* and *What Maisie Knew* thrown in for good measure

---

2. "I tried to write a really ambitious socio-cultural novel, in the form of a *Bildungsroman*: it didn't quite come off . . ." (Interview with Haffenden 151).

and added effect) ("Introduction" ix). Of the two, it is clearly Joyce's influence that is by far the more pervasive and that accounts for the novel's being so "fully achieved." What one finds is not the parodic play of *Ulysses* that Lodge adapted so effectively in *The British Museum*; instead, it is the "realistic truthtelling and poetic intensity" of Joyce's earlier style, the aims of which (Lodge then claimed) were "still worth pursuing" insofar as "the heightened realism" of Joyce and the other "classic modernists" had not yet been "exhausted" (quoted in Vinson 401; "David Lodge Interviewed" 116). Lodge may have been correct, but *Out of the Shelter* does not support his claim of continued viablity. Moreover, there is even a certain irony in the fact that Lodge should have written this novel of "personal liberation" in so shackled and disabling a style. The fact that "everything is presented from [the protagonist] Timothy's point of view, but narrated by a 'covert' authorial voice that articulates his adolescent sensibility with a slightly more eloquent and mature style than Timothy would have commanded" ("Introduction" xvi), describes rather well *how* the story is narrated, but sidesteps completely the issue of whether the narrative language is aesthetically effective or not. Much of the prose Lodge wrote ostensibly in imitation and extension of Joyce's early style only seems either to fall flat—"arc lights fixed in the palm trees illuminated the pool, but did not penetrate its depths" (269)—or, despite the book's serious subject matter, to parody it in unintentionally comic fashion:

A squadron of jets suddenly screamed overhead, making the windows rattle. Feeling a commotion beside him, he opened his eyes and he saw Gloria arch her back, kick, and the blue jeans flew off her brown legs. He shut his eyes again. His hand now moved freely under the light tension of her flimsy briefs. He ran his hand over the fine, springy nest of hair, and reached a moist crevice. There was a distant rumble, as of bombs or guns. The sound barrier. He heard her breathing quickly beside him. He scarcely dared to breathe himself. She spread her legs and his index finger slipped in like a seal into a

rock pool, slithering against the slippery walls, and touching something that quivered and contracted, fluttering like a shrimp under
bare toes at low tide, and he thought he must be losing his senses, for
there was a strange smell of shrimps in the room. (240)

Whether this is "heightened realism" or merely heightened
rhetoric hardly seems in doubt, least of all when, his climax
over, the sixteen-year-old hero of Lodge's portrait of the specialist in "planning blight" as a young man has his obligatory
epiphany and, deciding not to rush immediately from adolescent sex to Catholic confession, chooses to lay "his unshriven
soul as a gift at Gloria's feet" (248). If in *The British Museum*
Lodge's parodic technique tends both to undermine the authority of his sources and yet paradoxically to validate them
as well, then the language of Lodge's fourth novel works in a
similar fashion, though in the reverse direction. It undermines
even as the author seeks to validate and extend, so that in
large measure the novel becomes not the work of "heightened
realism" that Lodge intended but (to borrow a line from
Barth's "Lost in the Funhouse") yet another, and not especially effective, story about a sensitive adolescent.

If the novel succeeds at all, then, it does so not in its imitation
of Joyce's verbal mannerisms but in the way it reflects quite
another feature of Joyce's (and Lodge's) writing. This is his
preoccupation with verges and transitions of all kinds, with a
character's (or, in the later works, even a word's) being poised
between two worlds, two sets of values, two meanings. "Ever
since he [Timothy] had come out from England it seemed to
him that he had been looking down from heights, being shown
the kingdoms of the world, like Jesus in the Bible" (150). What
saves such a passage—and such a book—is that Timothy (as
well as the reader) is given more than one world from which
to choose, and the choices are dialogically presented rather
than monologically distinct. This is not to say that the novel
does not seem to posit certain simple oppositions. It is, after

all, a work which is set in a period of (as Lodge saw it) "crucial transition" from "austerity" to "affluence," and which grew out of the author's conviction that there indeed was, as the Sixties' Youth Culture insisted, a generation gap, but one that separated those who had experienced the war from those who had not ("Introduction" x). Leaving the shelter of his family and country for the first time, Timothy is struck by what he assumes is the completeness of the separation. Shaking his father's hand becomes not a sign of emotional attachment but instead is "like casting off a rope that had held him for a long time in safe anchorage" (67). And his final glimpse of his mother, from the departing train, provides a perfect if pathetic image of just what he is leaving behind. "That was the last view he had of his mother: standing on the platform, gasping for breath, disappointment lining her face, still holding outstretched, like a rejected gift, the Lyons' Individual Fruit Pie" (72). Coming out of his various literal and figurative shelters, Timothy enters a world that is not only new and different, but geographically, socially, culturally, religiously, and sexually ambiguous. The novel necessarily involves, then, an epistemological doubling: Timothy comes out of the shelter, presumably into the clarifying light, but his vision is invariably obscured in various ways. The bomb smoke that prevents his seeing the deaths of his playmate Jill and her mother near the beginning of the novel is the first of several physical, psychological, and cultural barriers to Timothy's actually achieving that clarity of vision that the novel's title seems to imply. The ambiguity is further complicated by the fact that Timothy is himself double: on the one hand he wants to experience the world and on the other he is another of Lodge's voyeurs who prefer to live their lives vicariously. As Timothy himself realizes (in sentences that reflect in their very syntax the workings of his dialogical mind and Lodge's equally dialogical novel), "there was something deeply ambiguous about his situation—he could see it alternately, and almost simultaneously, as absurd and exciting—enviable and ridiculous. . . . He could convert it into something positively exciting only by grasping its opportunities, and he was not equal to that. . . . He had added to his experiences lately, but the additions were abysses concealing more than they revealed."[3]

Out of the Shelter is a novel of seeming contrasts—childhood and adolescence, adolescence and adulthood, war and peace, secular and spiritual, male and female, the poetic and the prosaic, etc. The starkest of these are geographical and cultural. England means shortages, drabness, privation, confinement, work, sameness, and the narrowness of lower-middle-class Anglo-Catholicism, whereas Heidelberg, as the center of the American occupation forces, represents abundance, variety, color, freedom, play, and a certain secular expansiveness. That England should continue to suffer economically even though it won the war, while German Heidelberg prospers, is one of the signs in this novel that things are not necessarily as one might expect them to be "out of the shelter." But as Don Kowalski, one of Timothy's unofficial mentors, explains, Heidelberg too is a kind of shelter, "full of people who don't want to go home" (87). Timothy's sister, Kate, makes a similar point, though from a quite different point of view. (She is one of those who won't, or, as she would prefer, can't go home again.) What she and the other non-Germans in Heidelberg have in common, she says, is that "we want to forget. . . . We want to live in the present. We want fun and companionship without emotional involvement, without the risk of getting hurt again. And we do have a lot of fun. . . . But it can't go on for ever" (167). Kate and Don provide Timothy not only with alternative explanations as to why peo-

3. Lodge, *Out of the Shelter* (London: Macmillan, 1970) 145. The revised version reads: "He had added to his experience lately, but as regards sex the additions were abysses concealing more than they revealed" (139).

ple like Kate stay in Heidelberg but with alternative courses to follow in his own life. However, just as the voices of Don, Kate, Timothy's parents, and Kate's friends intersect yet remain distinct in the reader's mind, so in a similar fashion does Lodge suggest that there is no one voice and no one course of action for Timothy (or the reader or the writer for that matter) to follow—not Don's, or Kate's, or Joyce's.

Individual characters are presented in a similarly ambiguous manner. To her family, for example, Kate—or Kath, as they refer to her—is at once a fairy godmother and a fallen woman. The ambiguity of her character and the ambivalence of her family's response to her evidences itself throughout the novel and is distilled in lines such as, "it was as if Kate were accumulating invisible credits, like indulgences, on which the rest of the family could draw,"[4] a description which neatly combines the financial and religious preoccupations of Timothy's lower-middle-class Catholic family. In addition, the Kate that Timothy visits in Heidelberg is quite unlike the Kath he knew in England, for this "Kate" is poised, self-confident, even attractive. But when they go swimming, Timothy makes a second discovery; he sees in her heavy thighs evidence of "the old fat Kath that she [Kate] normally concealed under her skirts" (129). This is the residue of the past that neither Kate nor any of the other characters can ever escape entirely. For better or worse, their pasts continue to haunt them: individual family backgrounds, the world war, original sin, the modernist literary tradition—Barthelme's Dead Father—in whose shadow the contemporary writer self-consciously seeks to find his own distinctive voice. Lodge thus insists upon the presence of the past, on the ways in which it both hinders and helps his characters. And he insists too on their doubleness and upon the similarity or interpenetration of seeming opposites. Creating contrasts and parallels at every turn of the narrative, he causes

4. *Out of the Shelter* (1970) 41.

the novel's characters and their beliefs to alternately merge and separate, to come in and out of focus.

I noted earlier that the novel is, in a sense, confessional in form. It is also a variation on the theme and structure of that traditional religious subgenre, the dialogue between the flesh and the spirit, but one in which the voices merge and the spirit is hardly allowed an unequivocal triumph. The mingling of the sacred and the profane is evident in the phrase, "credits, like indulgences," quoted above and more especially in the fact that Timothy is simultaneously attracted to and appalled by Kate's friends' "insatiable appetite for diversion," an appetite which "affronted his deepest [Anglo-Catholic] instincts and principles" (151). Don articulates in characteristically dogmatic fashion what Timothy, also characteristically, can only contemplate and even then only in the most general terms, being, as he is, entirely devoid of a necessary grounding in historical fact. As Don sees it, Kate's friends are nothing more than well-heeled "camp-followers": "Just when the Germans—and not just the Germans—began to crawl out of their cellars, clear away the rubble, rebuild their cities, open up the hotels and restaurants and the sights and the casinos—they happened to be the only people around with enough money to take advantage of it. The only people with no currency problems, no passport problems, no visa problems. . . . when you think of what happened in Europe only a few years ago, sackcloth and ashes seem more appropriate than Waikiki shirts" (152–153). Don's critical and irreverent attitude towards the war in general and the Allied victory in particular is merited and, for Timothy, a useful corrective to his uninformed chauvinism. Nonetheless, Don's language here and elsewhere in the novel is excessive; he is no less improvident with his moral pronouncements than Kate's friends are with their money. Moreover, although it is true that Don greatly extends Timothy's critical awareness of society and history, he also draws Timothy back in time and place. His preference for "sackcloth and ashes" and the old-fashioned amateur approach still followed at the London School of Economics, where he hopes to do graduate work, echoes Timothy's own English provincialism and Anglo-Catholic morality. It is, therefore, difficult for the reader to know exactly how to respond to Don, who seems to invite both approval and dismissal. As Timothy comes to realize, "that was the trouble with Don's company—it was something of a strain, like taking an examination all the time" (155). Timothy is right, but since Timothy also confuses Auschwitz with Austerlitz, an examination may be exactly what he needs. Moreover, even though he can spot this flaw in Don's character, he cannot make himself immune to it. After going to bed with Gloria Rose, for example, who is "sort of Jewish," Timothy, sounding like Don's echo, asks her what it is like to be a Jew living in postwar, post-Auschwitz Europe. (Gloria is, however, interested in sex, not questions of religious identity and national guilt.) Like so much in this novel, Don's moral concern is at once persuasive and excessive.

His "sackcloth and ashes" frame of mind leads him, as a descendent of Polish Jews, to want to visit Auschwitz, and something similar causes this typically rootless American to want to study at the London School of Economics. Kate on the other hand, intuiting what she feels is the used-upness of both the past (England) and the present (Heidelberg), chooses to step westward into the future (the United States). Their restlessness contributes to Timothy's uncertainty (he is "sort of half-way") and to the reader's as well in a novel which not only blurs distinctions but follows a course that both invites (insofar as it moves through time in a straightforward manner) and disrupts the reader's passive consumption. Structurally the novel is divided into three numbered and titled parts, plus a nine-page epilogue. The three parts progessively increase in length, from fifty-one to sixty-one and finally to 139 pages. Each of these parts is further divided into three numbered (but untitled) sections that are, with one exception, again further divided into anywhere from four to twenty-one unnumbered and untitled subsections of varying lengths (from one page to twenty-eight). Within each of the three major parts, the narration tends to be more or less uniform in style (less so in the first), but between them it is subtly different, the Joycean differences reflecting changes in Timothy's (like Stephen Dedalus's) maturing mode of perceiving his changing world. Part One, "The Shelter," deals with the period from 1940 (the year of the London Blitz, when Timothy is five) to 1949. Though chronologically arranged, the narrative is not actually continuous. It leaps from event to event, following (especially in its first half) what a child might remember of the war and written in a style that reflects a child's (and later an adolescent's) efforts to make sense of what he doesn't understand based upon what little knowledge he has acquired up to that point. It begins, "almost the first thing he could remember was his mother standing on a stool in the kitchen, piling tins of food into the top cupboard," followed by the child's query, "what are all those tins for?" (3). And it ends, appropriately enough, with what might most profitably be thought of as a narrative palimpsest. Sitting on the beach, Timothy recalls Arnold's poem, "Dover Beach," and more especially the essay he wrote about it for his mock O-level exams. As Timothy begins mentally to revise his essay, the reader becomes aware in this single narrative moment of the existence of two Timothy's, one past and the other present, psychologically distinct yet narratively coeval. Though longer by some ten pages, the novel's Part Two, "Coming Out," deals with a much shorter chronological period, covering just the time it takes Timothy to travel by train from London to Heidelberg and his first day and night in this Americanized German city. (There is also, near the beginning, a flashback to the events leading to Kate's invitation and Timothy's acceptance.)

At the beginning of the novel, Lodge moves abruptly from scene to scene but nonetheless manages to achieve a certain degree of narrative continuity based upon the recounting of significant events in a child's life: his perception of these events and his efforts to understand them in the light of his very limited knowledge. The temporal and spatial restrictions of Part Two, on the other hand, are reflected in this section's high degree of narrative continuity. The average length of the ten subsections is 6.1 pages, twice that of either Part One (2.68 pages) or Part Three (3.3 pages). The narrative situation and strategy changes radically in Part Three, " Out of the Shelter," which is set in Heidelberg but which involves numerous geographical, political, theological, psychological, and narrative side trips—as well as side narratives—taken during Timothy's four-week stay. More importantly, the narrative here includes numerous abrupt crosscuts that do more than merely disrupt the narrative flow, for they involve parallel scenes, each serving as an alternative to the other, dialogically qualifying but never monologically cancelling out the other. The result is another kind of narrative palimpsest in which different views and judgments come into conflict in Timothy's and the reader's minds without ever being resolved. Although the subject matter of some of these scenes is undoubtedly overdrawn, the "heightened realism" taking a bathetic pratfall, the technique itself is less obtrusive and far more effective. It enables Lodge not simply to recount but actually to recreate for the reader Timothy's own sense of epistemological uncertainty. Such uncertainty is decidedly at odds with what the novel's title and epilogue seem to imply: development ending in closure.

Like the conclusions of so many nineteenth century novels, Lodge's epilogue serves to round off the story for the reader (and perhaps the author as well) who craves the traditional narrative comfort of knowing how it all turned out. Timothy, now thirty years old, has received a fellowship to study in the United States where he, along with his wife Sheila and their children, pays a brief visit to Kate, now a resident of California. Timothy has done rather well—not as well as he would like, but better certainly than Don (divorced) or Kate's Heidelberg friends Vince and Greg (disgraced) or his parents ("growing dully old") or Jill (dead) or Kate who, though she has returned to the Church, remains vaguely dissatisfied. The novel does not end, however, with the hero's relative triumph, freedom, and happiness. Instead, as Timothy joins his wife in the motel pool, "it came on him again—the familiar fear that he could never entirely eradicate, that this happiness was only a ripening target for fate; that somewhere, around the corner, some disaster awaited him, as he blithely approached" (270). It is of more than passing interest that Lodge makes precisely the same point in *The British Museum*, where, of course, it is rendered in the style of deadpan humor: "Catholics are brought up to expect sudden extinction round every corner and to keep their souls highly polished at all times" (65). Whether the reader of Lodge's novels is to understand the feeling shared by Adam Appleby and Timothy Young as the comic residue of their Catholic upbringing or as a tragic fact of human existence is necessarily and dialogically left uncertain. What is certain is that unlike Stephen Dedalus, Timothy cannot proudly and defiantly—and pompously—proclaim, "I go to encounter for the millionth time the reality of experience and to forge in the smithy of my soul the uncreated conscience of my race" (253). He can only, and desperately, cry out his wife's name, seeking in her what he had earlier hoped to escape, the need for shelter. His need takes on added urgency given the fact that Kate's dissatisfaction is due, at least in part, to her not having married (the sexual and emotional counterpart of her self-imposed geographical exile from Britain and her parents).

Timothy's "Sheila!" concludes the novel but does not quite complete it. His crying out in the California desert exists not as a merely climactic narrative act but in contrast with the point Timothy makes just a few pages/moments before to Kate: "you can be so grateful for being where you are that you don't want to move on, in case things get worse. I recognize that tendency in myself" (265). The contrast here in the epilogue between Timothy's desire for motion and change and his need for stasis and stability reenacts—or re-voices—the similarly dialogical endings of the novel's first two parts. In the first-and the more effective of the two, discussed briefly above—Timothy recalls Arnold's "Dover Beach" and, almost immediately, his own essay about it, and this in turn leads him to reconsider the poem and to revise his essay mentally. Even as he moves ahead, refining his reading with his more mature insights, he moves back as well, not only to his original understanding—or misunderstanding—of Arnold's lines but even further back to the war, until finally, "alone in the shelter, under cover of night, safe from observation, Timothy lapsed into a heroic dream of his childhood" (52). The play of contending forces—past and present, childhood and adolescence—is rendered so that each has its own distinctive voice. (And the same is true in the epilogue where Timothy speaks reasonably of his need to forge ahead and later cries out emotionally when beset by "the familiar fear he could never entirely eradicate.") Though twenty-five years older than at the beginning of the novel, Timothy still faces essentially the same dilemma. He remains discontented not because he has failed to mature but because the process of "coming out of the shelter" and coming "out of [one's] shell" (265) is, as Lodge defines it, continual. His desire for shelter and his counter desire for freedom cannot be reconciled, only dialogized.[5] Timothy's situation is thus analogous to that of the novelist, again as Lodge has defined it. The writer's freedom to invent is limited by the closed universe of

5.   According to Lodge, the epilogue was not intended to show any disillusionment, only that Timothy has been lucky and that he possesses "a temperamental cautiousness which holds him back" (Interview with Haffenden 151).

the narrative continuum having realism and metonymy at one end and fabulism and metaphor at the other. The essentially spatial form of Lodge's seemingly, or deceptively, linear novel implies a similar limitation, leading the reader back and forth rather than (simply) ahead. And Lodge has managed to "cautiously" advance his career as a novelist in a similar manner, for the writing of *Out of the Shelter* resulted in a moving forward that was itself the result of a looking back to James/Joyce and the high seriousness of his first two novels.

9

Changing Places:
Narrative Doublings Redux

AS WE HAVE seen, structural, thematic, and even syntactical doublings have played a prominent part in Lodge's early writings. In his fifth novel, *Changing Places*, Lodge goes much further. He raises doubling more directly to the novel's textual surface in order to ironize it and thereby to gain the necessary level of dialogic detachment that was so largely absent from *Out of the Shelter*, where Lodge's efforts to validate and extend Joyce's style of "heightened realism" chiefly served only to undermine Lodge's own achievement. This is not to say that *Out of the Shelter* was by any means a wasted literary effort; the novel is significant if not entirely successful for both the reasons discussed in the previous chapter and for the fact that writing so limited and limiting a novel seems to have freed Lodge to write *Changing Places*.[1]

At the end of *Out of the Shelter*, Timothy Young, now thirty, arrives in the United States and immediately begins to experience its liberating effect. At the beginning of *Changing Places*,

1. "I don't think I made it as a writer until *Changing Places*" (Interview with Haffenden 150).

it is forty-year-old Philip Swallow who plays the part of the English sojourner. But his story is duplicated by that of Morris Zapp, also forty, the other half of Lodge's narrative exchange program. Zapp is Jewish, apocalyptic, arrogant, and academically distinguished—a full professor at the State University of Euphoria in Plotinus (Lodge's funhouse reflection of Berkeley) and the author of five books, four of them on Jane Austen. Having achieved everything he wanted professionally, Zapp has become more cautious, ironically so given the rationale behind his now abandoned Austen project: to exhaust the interpretive possibilities. Zapp hates (and so likes to "zap") all other critics, especially those who tolerate "opinions contrary to their own" and who begin their essays with a humble "I want to raise some questions about so-and-so" (45), as the tolerant David Lodge often has begun his essays.[2] This is also how Philip Swallow would begin his critical essays, if he wrote any, which he doesn't. Utterly unknown and undistinguished, Swallow is "a mimetic man" (10): unsure, eager to please, infinitely suggestible. As birdlike and as seemingly shallow as his name suggests, he lacks completely what the comic book super-critic Zapp possesses so excessively: will and ambition. It is not will and ambition that drive Zapp to spend a semester at the academic wasteland of the University of Rummidge, however, but the seemingly Swallowian, utterly unZappian desire to save his marriage. He wants to give his stridently feminist wife, Desiree, time to reconsider the divorce that she craves and he fears. Even caricatures, it seems, can have their humanities. Swallow, on the other hand, whose marriage is as moribund sexually as he is professionally, sees in the State University of Euphoria (Euphoric State) and the neighboring

2. See, for example, *The Novelist at the Crossroads* (1971). Lodge's next critical book, The *Modes of Modern Writing* (1977), is more Zappian in both its reach (towards "a comprehensive typology of literary discourse") and to some extent its language as well.

Borgesian city of Esseph across the bay a chance to regain the paradise he and his wife Hilary briefly had on their honeymoon in that same area. However, he will also come to experience the paradise lost of guilt since, like James Walker in *Stepping Westward*, his going to the United States entails leaving his wife and daughter behind. Eventually Swallow does come to feel freer and more confident, and while it would be of some interest to trace the sequence—or mare's nest—of comic improbabilities that lead to this emancipation, Lodge's deliberately coincidental plot is, I believe, of considerably less importance than the way in which Lodge renders Swallow's liberation linguistically. In effect, he finds the way to turn the lessons learned in the writing of his two most Joycean novels, *The British Museum Is Falling Down* and *Out of the Shelter*, to his own novelistic advantage.

Changing Places is a novel that begins as a more or less conventional realistic comedy—a campus novel—but that quickly develops into something quite different and quite effective.[3] At the beginning, the various voices—the narrator's as well as each of the characters—are rendered stably and realistically. Swallow, for example, sounds British, and Zapp sounds like a loud, arrogant American. But slowly the voices (including the narrator's) begin to change—to change places. Admittedly, these changes serve a decidedly realistic purpose—to record or mirror changes in the character's character. But they also serve a distinctly postmodern purpose insofar as each voice not only changes but becomes, as the novel itself does, a pastiche of various parodically rendered voices. The novel's linguistic distinctions are most obvious when the voices speak directly and in a syntactically and/or thematically parallel way: the Euphoric students, for example, demand

3. "Essentially the campus novel is a modern, displaced form of pastoral. . . . That is why it belongs to the literature of escape" (Lodge, *Write On* 171).

that their audience "*Defend the Garden!*" (based on Berkeley's People's Park) whereas the radicalized but nonetheless still sedate Rummidge students politely ask that their audience "Support the Occupation" (158). But, as in Bradbury's *The History Man*, even seemingly neutral descriptive prose can subtly slip its linguistic moorings and take on (in ironic fashion) the colors of its linguistic environment: "The Black Pantheress was explaining to a caller [on a late-night radio talk show] the application of Marxist-Leninist revolutionary theory to the situation of oppressed racial minorities in a late stage of industrial capitalism" (103). Similarly and more subtly, the prose used to record Swallow's and Zapp's thoughts mimics their respective styles of thinking and in this way reflects Lodge's view that thinking is essentially a verbal activity:

Such ideas, that is, never occurred to his [Swallow's] conscious, English self. His unconscious may have been otherwise occupied; and perhaps, deep, deep down, there is, at the root of his present jubilation, the anticipation of sexual adventure. If this is the case, however, no rumour of it has reached Philip's ego. (28)

Why should he [Zapp] suffer with all these careless callous women? He has knocked up a girl only once in his life, and he made an honest woman of her (she divorced him three years later, but that's another story, one indictment at a time, please). (32)

More interesting are the twenty pages devoted to Swallow's wholly mental efforts to draft a letter to Hilary explaining his affair with Zapp's wife, now that the academic exchange has become a sexual exchange as well. The italicized mental-letter passages comprise just two of the twenty pages but serve a number of narrative purposes: to allow the husband to explain himself—or rather his adulterous self—to his wife; to permit Lodge to flash back to events related to Swallow's adultery that have not yet been narrated; to enable Lodge to parody the flashback technique and the epistolary novels in which it is

160
Dialogic Novels

used; and finally but perhaps most interestingly to allow Lodge
to double Swallow's mental voice (itself the double of his speaking voice). There is the voice that is a verbal caricature of
British reserve, one in which even informality sounds oddly
formal and, as Daisy Miller would say, "stiff": "*It all started, you
see, on the night of the landslide. Mrs. Zapp and I had been invited
to the same party again, and she offered me a lift home, because there
was a kind of tropical storm*" (178). His subsequent thoughts
eventually lead him out of his usual maze of uncertainty and
indecisiveness to the climactic scene in which Swallow, while
sitting in a cafe, gazes out at passing humanity (in its California
version) and becomes Whitman's "fluid and swallowing soul,"
absorbing the world and letting it back out again in a three-
hundred-word sentence-long paragraph, a Whitmanic catalogue of "young bearded Jesuses and their barefoot Magda-
lenes," blacks and whites, hippies and junkies, kaftans and
saris, buttocks and breasts, all ending with a lyrical paean to a
girl "dressed in a crotch-high mini with long bare white legs
and high up one thigh a perfect, mouth-shaped bruise" (193–
194). Swallow interrupts his song of himself and the open road
only long enough to invoke Henry James and decide (adding
epiphany to epiphany, James to Whitman) that he is both
Lambert Strether and Little Bilham, both the old man who
learns too late "to live, live all you can" and the young man
able to take advantage of that knowledge. "Do I contradict
myself?" Whitman asked. "Very well then, I contradict myself.
I contain multitudes." At this point, Swallow is swept back into
the Whitmanic flow once more and the meaning of American
literature is suddenly revealed to him. His revelation takes
the form of yet another of Whitman's syntactically parallel
catalogues: "He thought of [Henry] James. . . . He thought of
Henry Miller. . . . He understood American Literature for the
first time . . . understood its prodigality and indecorum . . .
understood Walt Whitman . . . and Herman Melville . . . understood Mark Twain . . . and why Stephen Crane . . . and

what Gertrude Stein . . ." (195, ellipses mine). It would be wrong, however, to think that Swallow simply and merely moves ahead, either psychologically or linguistically. His Whitmanic cadences (and revelations) do not in fact replace his earlier British rhythms (and ideas) but instead alternate with them. Although Whitman frees Swallow to at least complete his letter to Hilary in a page-long burst of automatic mental writing, the prose he uses recalls that other, earlier Swallow, the old Adam from which he will never be entirely free anymore than he will actually post or even write his letter. The linguistic alternations reflect Swallow's comic situation, but they also serve to remind the reader of Lodge's parallel belief in literature as an essentially closed system in which Bradburyan "possibilities" are rendered as narrative permutations to be exploited comically in works such as *Changing Places* and, as we shall see, given a dark twist in *How Far Can You Go?* These are the necessary boundaries within which both characters and author must operate, or oscillate, achieving at best a relative and decidedly problematic freedom.

Swallow's alternations represent in miniature the structure, rhythm, and method of the entire novel. They can be found as well in even more condensed form in the Rummidge folk group, Morte D'Arthur, which appears briefly, singing "pastiches of recordings" by Joan Baez, Judy Collins, and other "folk singers," including the group they most clearly imitate, Peter, Paul and Mary. But the parallel here may be a bit misleading, for *Changing Places* is not merely an imitation, as Morte D'Arthur surely is. Rather, it incorporates into itself the various voices and forms it imitates, not merely to echo and repeat but to renew—not these specific voices and forms, of course, but the voice and form of fiction in an age of fabulism, exhaustion, and film. Milton, Shakespeare, Austen, Whitman, James, Joyce, and a host of other literary masters all have their Whitmanic parts to play, whether great or small. The literary echoings in *Changing Places* extend much further, however, to include late-night radio talk shows and the "split screen" technique of film and television. There is even a two-page/ two-paragraph sequence reminiscent of silent film comedies in which, in one of the novel's many cases of misunderstanding and mistaken identity, Zapp (the academic turned Marx Brother) and Gordon Masters (a department head turned madman) go up and down on a paternoster, that curious British piece of hermaphroditic technology, part elevator, part escalator. And, if I'm not mistaken, Lodge even includes a cartoon strip, in its sixties R. Crumb, Jules Feiffer adult version: Swallow, while taking part in a departmental vigil to protest the presence of armed police on campus, continues to compose his mental letter to Hilary; he has, along with the unwary reader, a narrative flashback that ends with his recalling the circumstances that led up to his making love to Desiree for the first time. " 'Excuse me, Phil,' " Sy Gootblatt whispers. " 'But I think you're having an erection and it doesn't look nice at a vigil' " (192). Even the characters become aware of the literary correspondences, of this being a scene from a film and that "from a Victorian novel, the snow, the fallen woman, etc., but in reverse, because she was coming in instead of going out" (139). (Indeed, it may be said that Lodge's entire method in *Changing Places* is, as its title suggests, one of reversals of various kinds.) Lodge's narrative method is certainly in keeping with Bakhtin's definition of the novel as a metagenre: "The novel permits the incorporation of various genres, both artistic (inserted short stories, lyrical songs, poems, dramatic scenes, etc.) and extra-artistic (everyday, rhetorical, scholarly, religious genres and others). . . . All these forms permit languages to be used in ways that are indirect, conditional, distanced . . . [in order to achieve] a relativizing of linguistic consciousness" (*Dialogic* 320, 323).

In *Changing Places*, narrative language is similarly relativized on all levels, including the structural, which is to say, on the level of narrative grammar. On the one hand, for example, the novel may be said to follow the linear plot of conventional fiction, from beginning to middle to end. On the other hand, the novel's six chapters—"Flying," "Settling," "Corresponding," "Reading," "Changing," "Ending"—not only serve to develop the novel's linear progression, they disrupt and impede it as well. All six chapters are told from what is identified early in the novel as "our privileged narrative altitude" (8)— a phrase which immediately puts the novel into postmodern dialogue with the literary tradition. As with a plane in flight, this narrative altitude will vary during the course of the novel. The first two chapters, "Flying" and "Settling," for example, are more or less conventional in form and stable in narrative structure. Chapter 3, however, "Corresponding," is quite unlike the previous two; epistolary in form, it is made up entirely of letters written by the four principal characters. Chapter 4 is a *Ulysses*-like collection of newspaper items, news releases, student manifestos, flysheets, and printed handouts. Chapter 5 returns the novel to the narrative mode, or altitude, of the first two chapters, to which Lodge adds the three drafts of Swallow's mental letter to his wife. But Chapter 6 disrupts the text yet again, for Lodge's ending takes the form of a filmscript. If, as Swallow realizes in his moment of Whitmanic revelation, Melville's great achievement was his "split[ting] the atom of the traditional novel in an effort to make whaling a universal metaphor" (195), then Lodge's achievement is similar even if it lacks Melville's Ahabian—or Zappian—will to power and inclusiveness.

Within the confines of his more limited though still transatlantic world, Lodge follows Melville's example, splitting and then splicing as he goes. Not content to narrate Zapp's and Swallow's stories in merely parallel fashion, Lodge runs them together as best he can in the absence of the film director's split screen and short of resorting to Derrida's doubling of columns in *Glas* or Nabokov's coupling of text and commentary in *Pale Fire*. Thus, for the first two chapters—112 pages, roughly half the novel's entire length—the story alternates between Zapp and Swallow, consistently and fairly evenly. (Here and throughout the novel as a whole, however, it is Swallow who receives more of the narrator's and therefore the reader's time. This strategy, whether intentional or not, allows the text to compensate for Zapp's being otherwise so dominant a character, both physically and intellectually.) In the next two chapters this pattern, to which the reader has just accustomed himself, breaks down. The twenty-one letters and one tele-gram in the thirty-eight pages of Chapter 3 and the twenty-nine assorted items in the fourteen pages of Chapter 4 follow what the reader assumes to be a chronological order that is disrupted typographically by the blank spaces and narratively by the absence of transitions between the items, which often appear several to a page. The pattern changes once again in Chapter 5, "Changing," where the first three untitled and unnumbered sections are devoted to Swallow (thirty-three and one-half pages) and the next five sections (thirty-six pages) to Zapp, thus creating the highest degree of narrative continu-ity—that is to say, the most continuous single story—in this otherwise highly discontinuous yet nonetheless highly read-able novel. And the sense of narrative continuity is heightened, or at least prolonged, in the concluding chapter, which brings together for the first time all four of the principal characters in narrative time and space, though this continuity is again disrupted by the mode of narration: filmscript.

"And in an age of more leisurely transportation," Lodge writes early in the novel, while the planes in which his twin protagonists crisscross high above the North Pole, Zapp and Swallow might have gestured to one another as they crossed paths by ship or train (7). In an age of leisurely transportation and equally leisurely narration, Lodge might not have felt compelled to disrupt his transatlantic jet-age narrative or to undermine the realistic illusion that plays so vital a part in more conventional fiction by dropping into his narrative and onto the roof of Zapp's boardinghouse a gratuitous block of frozen urine from a passing airliner. As Zapp's pious (as well as hypocritical) landlord claims, "some people might say it was an act of God" (166)—or, the reader suspects, of an altitudinous author. No longer content to stand apart from his creation, paring his fingernails, Lodge inserts himself into his story just as he repeatedly inserts a variety of carnivalized voices, languages, and literary forms. Among them the reader finds excerpts from Beamish's *Let's Write a Novel*, published in 1927, advising the would-be novelist to avoid flashbacks, end happily, etc. And he even finds a character's comments on Beamish's recommendations. "What a funny little book it is," Hilary writes in Chapter 3, "Corresponding." "There's a whole chapter on how to write an epistolary novel, but surely nobody's done that since the eighteenth century?" (130). At every level and seemingly at every narrative turn, *Changing Places* reflects a modern skepticism and instability, from the "time slips" that Zapp experiences (127) to the uncertainty Swallow suddenly feels as student strikes disrupt his teaching and the very words he uses begin to take on strange new meanings ("Black," for example). The novel's thematic, linguistic, and structural levels all either concern or involve disruptions of one kind or another. Yet because the various disruptions reflect and reinforce each other, the novel's wholeness—its aesthetic integrity—grows out of the artful fragmentation of its parts. The entire novel may be said to function as a large-scale narrative paradox, holding together by breaking apart, a literary e pluribus unum. That Zapp has "periods of confidence and pleasure punctuated by spasms of panic and emptiness" is mirrored in another character's having "a pathological urge to succeed and a pathological fear of being thought uncultured, and this game [Swallow's 'Humiliation'] set his two obsessions at war with each other, because he could succeed in the game only by exposing a gap in his culture" (135), and they reflect the larger rhythmical opposition from which the novel's unity may be said to derive. It is entirely appropriate, therefore, that in such a novel simple repetitions should serve both to unify and to disrupt insofar as they remind the reader of the novel's arbitrary ontological status as well as its problematic but still existent relationship with reality. The repetition of lines such as "at exactly the same moment" or Swallow's reading the same newspaper item on page 172 that the reader has already read on page 166 disturb the reader far more than they comfort him, providing as they do additional evidence of the duplicity of "this duplex chronicle" (7).

Changing Places is "duplex," then, in a multiplicity of ways: in terms of its language, plot, structure, and of course characterization, with Zapp and Swallow "mirror[ing] each other's experiences in certain respects" and "exert[ing] a reciprocal influence on each other's destinies" (8).[4] And the novel is duplex in the additional sense that it duplicates, or parodies, the international novel of James (and Bradbury), the epistolary novel, and the other literary and subliterary forms already mentioned. In fact, the very word "duplex," as Lodge defines it, is itself duplex, meaning "twofold," but also referring "in the jargon of electrical telegraphy to 'systems' in which messages are sent simultaneously in opposite directions" (7–8). This second part of Lodge's definition applies clearly and readily to the ways in which Zapp and Swallow influence each other's destinies, but it applies equally well, if less overtly, I believe, to the way in which *Changing Places* dialogizes two novelistic traditions and two narrative styles. "When I read most American novelists," Lodge commented in 1970, shortly after completing his fourth novel, *Out of the Shelter*, and shortly before beginning his fifth, *Changing Places*, "they seem to be

4. "I tend to balance things against each other; my novels tend towards binary structures—with, for example, opposite characters—and they very much leave the reader to make up his own mind" (Interview with Haffenden 152).

rather battering me over the head, flexing their verbal muscles, and so on. All the linguistic energy going on is designed to impress you and works for a very powerful rhetoric. The English writer, though, is trying to get you into a conversation and starting to work on you rhetorically without your knowing it" (quoted in Honan, "Symposium" 205). This is what Joyce does in *Dubliners* and in *Portrait*; it is what Lodge sought to do in *Out of the Shelter*, but he failed, at least to the extent that the novel attracted few readers and still fewer reviewers and so, beginning no "conversation," necessarily ended in monologue. But *Changing Places* is different. Written in part about and in even larger part in the wake of his "fairly euphoric" year at Berkeley, and dedicated to a number of West Coast friends, including Leonard Michaels, *Changing Places* reflects essentially the same concerns and ambivalence as he later voiced in an essay entitled "Where It's At: The Poetry of Psychobabble" (*Working with Structuralism* 188–196) in which he points to the way in which the absurdities of West Coast language reflect the absurdities of West Coast life (or "lifestyle"). But even as he points to these absurdities, Lodge acknowledges the appealing and liberating vitality of that language and that life. In *Changing Places*, Lodge does more than simply acknowledge that vitality; he converts it into effective narrative art.

Zapp embodies this appealing verbal energy, and it is for this reason (along with his physical bulk) that he appears as vividly and strongly in the novel as Swallow, who receives a good deal more of the author's, and therefore the reader's, attention. Although (as I pointed out earlier) Zapp scorns Lodge's critical style, he nonetheless shares many of Lodge's own critical beliefs—beliefs that for all his verbal energy Zapp tends to reduce to monologue: "In Morris Zapp's view, the root of all critical error was a naive confusion of literature with life. Life was transparent, literature opaque. Life was an open, literature a closed system. . . . Life was what it appeared to be about. . . . Literature was never what it appeared to be about, though in the case of the novel considerable ingenuity and perception were needed to crack the code of realistic illusion" (47–48). The hard and fast opposition between life and literature that Zapp propounds is at odds with the structuralist and postmodernist view that a similar grammar underlies both and that human behavior can generally be understood, or read, as literature and interpreted according to the conventions of literary criticism. At the very least, the novel draws parallels between the two. Hilary tells Zapp that their affair has been "just an episode" (233), Zapp considers taking the offer of the chairmanship at Rummidge as a way to resolve the directionless plot his life has become (234), and Swallow experiences firsthand the way in which art impinges upon life. "I was sitting at my desk reading *Lycidas* when Wily Smith burst into my room and shut the door behind him, leaning against it with closed eyes, just like a film" (132). Eventually, Swallow goes much further when he proclaims not only that art has overtaken life but that film has overtaken prose fiction, which has become as anachronistic and impotent a form as Swallow once was a husband, lover, and academic. "All I'm saying," Swallow says in Lodge's filmscript "Ending,"

is that there is a generation gap, and I think it revolves around this public/private thing. Our generation—we subscribe to the old liberal doctrine of the inviolate self. It's the great tradition of realistic fiction, it's what novels are all about. The private life in the foreground, history a distant rumble of gunfire, somewhere offstage. . . . Well, the novel is dying, and us with it. No wonder I could never get anything out of my novel-writing class at Euphoric State. It's an unnatural medium for their experience. Those kids (gestures at [television] *screen* [showing live coverage of a student demonstration]) are living a film, not a novel. (250)

Even up-to-date Zapp objects to Swallow's death-of-the novel scenario, as well he should, and not just because he exists solely as a character in an outmoded form. (The reader may similarly object or else face the consequences of realizing that he has just wasted however long it took him to read the last 250 pages.) Swallow's fashionable view implies a crude literary evolutionism that not only is at odds with what Lodge has written concerning the literary continuum within which the novelist must necessarily operate but reflects as well one of the tenets of Beamish's *How-To-Write-A-Novel* approach to fiction writing: "life . . . goes forwards, not backwards" (186). Swallow and Beamish are wrong, however, for life and art are not simple and linear but duplex—doubled and doubling. Far from evidencing the used-upness of the genre, novels such as *Changing Places* and *The History Man* suggest that the novelist at the crossroads can resolve his dilemma. He can build his hesitancy and difficulty in the face of Swallow's (and Scholes's) challenge into the work itself and in this way create what Lodge calls "the problematic novel." Or he can exploit the very aspect of life and literature with which film has thus far not been much concerned, namely language, in all its manifestations. *Changing Places* renews, or replenishes, the novel by continuing to incorporate into itself other forms and other languages—absorbing, exploiting, and adapting them, in a deliberately self-conscious fashion. Lodge's novel mediates between life and art, between the liberal tradition and postmodern innovation, narrative drive and verbal texture, verbal muscle and quiet conversation.

Whether the novel's "Ending" helps to accomplish this aim has been a matter of some debate. James Gindin, for example, has complained that "the novel cannot accommodate its own ending," because "the switch to another art form appears as only a flippant rejection of the interesting and intractable material the novel itself generated and an evasion of its own comic terms" ("Risks" 157). I can hardly deny Gindin his complaint, but neither can I agree with it. The filmscript ending represents not any flippancy or literary flinching on Lodge's part but instead, as Malcolm Bradbury has pointed out, yet another stage in the author's "steady renegotiation of his position" that has been going on throughout *Changing Places* ("Donswapping" 65). The title, therefore, may be said to refer as much to the author as to the major characters. The six chapter titles—all of them participles—imply a similar interest in open-ended process over even the kind of consistency and relative closure that Gindin demands. "We cannot, of course, be denied an end," Frank Kermode has written; "it is one of the great charms of books that they have to end. But unless we are extremely naive, as some apocalyptic sects still are, we do not ask that they progress towards that end precisely as we have been given to believe. In fact, we should expect only the most trivial work to conform to pre-existent types" (23–24). Much to the credit of its author, *Changing Places* conforms neither to the campus novel tradition nor to the tradition of the new, of those postmodernist fictions of excess that it resembles in conception if not in execution. (I am thinking here, at one extreme, of the aleatory novels of Marc Saporta and B. S. Johnson and, at the other, of Barth's most baroque narrative orchestrations.) Lodge cannot disguise "the tell-tale compression of the pages" (251) as his novel draws to its inevitable conclusion, but he can imitate the form of the film (or the filmscript: "Philip shrugs. The camera stops, freezing him in mid-gesture" [251]), and in doing so he can (re)negotiate a tentative compromise, or truce, between the two forms. The novel cannot help but telegraph its end; film, on the other hand, need not: "The film is going along, just as life goes along, people are behaving, doing things, drinking, talking, and we're watching them, and at any point the director chooses, without warning, without anything being resolved, or explained, or wound up, it can just . . . end" (251). Lodge's novels of exhaustion and replenishment do not turn in upon themselves but instead spiral out into the "real world" that literary realism—heightened and not—once sought to imitate and explain but that has become, like the novel, "problematic," and happily so. Thus does the reader come to see *Changing Places* from his "privileged narrative altitude" much as Zapp, in his one visionary moment, comes to see Rummidge from the city's newly opened elevated expressway. "Seen from this perspective, it looked as though the seeds of a whole twentieth-century city had been planted under the ground a long time ago and were now beginning to shoot up into the light, bursting through the caked, exhausted topsoil of Victorian architecture. Morris found it an oddly stirring sight, for the city that was springing up was unmistakably American in style . . . and he had the strange feeling of having stumbled upon a new American frontier in the most unexpected place" (210).

10

How Far Can You Go?:
How Far Has Lodge Gone?

CHANGING PLACES AND *The British Museum Is Falling Down* are comic novels. *How Far Can You Go?*, on the other hand, at best "smiles" (74). Yet despite important differences in treatment and tone *How Far Can You Go?* is in its serious way no less playful a novel than, for example, *The British Museum*, the book to which it serves as a kind of sequel, or companion piece. What Lodge does in *How Far Can You Go?* is not only to look again and less optimistically (or less naively) at the birth control issue and its effects on the lives of Catholics but to extend much further and much more seriously the analogy between art and life that plays so comic a role in *The British Museum*. Having tested the postmodern position in *Changing Places*, Lodge seems even more determined, in his role as liberal novelist, to put his renegotiated aesthetic to use in the service of something other than its own workings. The result is his strongest and most compelling work, a novel in which he cultivates an artful simplicity in order to undermine the power of whatever is static and singular, in a word, monological.

Three general areas in which Lodge undermines the seeming simplicity of his own novel are time, characterization, and narrative language. Seen from one perspective, *How Far Can You Go?* is Lodge's most straightforward novel, following as it does an extended but simple chronological line. It may be said to be even more clearly focused, chronologically speaking, than *The British Museum*. While the action in the earlier novel may be limited to a single day in the life of Adam Appleby, the reader's sense of time in that work is as befogged as the main character's as a result of Lodge's working his *Ulysses*-like stylizations on them both. *How Far Can You Go?*, on the other hand, covers a lengthy but clearly defined chronological period, beginning in 1952 with a Thursday morning St. Valentine's Day mass and ending in 1978 with the deaths of Pope Paul VI and Pope John Paul I, the installation of a successor, John Paul II, and Lodge's—or his authorial narrator's—writing of the novel's seventh and final chapter. The postmodern author of *How Far Can You Go?* appears to be even busier than the linear God of Genesis, though not too busy to include numerous temporal markers to assist the reader (as catechumen) through this deceptively straight and narrow, yet in its own way duplex, chronicle.

One of the ways in which Lodge undermines the novel's chronological continuity is by doubling it, mixing and matching two temporal schemes: the fictive and the historical. "In the same year that Masters and Johnson published the results of their sex research," one sentence begins, and, later in that same paragraph, "in the spring of that year, 1966, at Duquesne University, Pennsylvania, and a little later at Notre Dame University, Indiana, small groups of Catholics began to experiment with 'Pentecostal' prayer meetings" (102). Lodge's purpose here seems only partly to authenticate his fiction in order to create, as Dreiser, Norris, Zola, and other realists did, a fictional world that would correspond as closely as possible to the author's and reader's "real world." For one thing, Lodge's use of such realistic details seems in its effect on the reader to be less naturalistic than excessive. To return to the already quoted paragraph—"In the same year that Masters and Johnson published the results of their sex research, England won the World Cup at football, which millions saw as the bestowal of a special grace on the nation; John Lennon boasted that the Beatles were more popular than Jesus Christ and, to the disappointment of many, was not struck dead by a thunderbolt; Evelyn Waugh died, shortly after attending a Latin mass celebrated in private by an old Jesuit friend"—Lodge continues on and on for some 160 words more, providing similar historical information. While this excessiveness recalls to some degree the technique Robert Coover uses so effectively in *The Public Burning*, the result in Lodge's case seems much closer to what E. L. Doctorow achieves in *Ragtime*. Doctorow juxtaposes fiction and history (or alternately, the private and the public) in order to give the former its due in a world largely given over to the latter. Or, to put all this in a slightly different, more Bradburyian way, Lodge and Doctorow seem intent on saving the individual self from being engulfed by the sands of history. Consequently, even as Lodge places his characters in a detailed, historically verifiable world, he strives to blur the very focus he has established, writing, for example, "in the same year" or "at the same time" or "in October of that year," even though he has not identified the year for the past ten, twenty, or thirty pages. The reader's sense of time becomes, like that of the characters, at once specific and yet vague and confused, an ambiguous present, a pathless narrative wood. Of course, the reader here does enjoy a certain privileged position, though not nearly as privileged as he would like to assume. His relative omniscience parallels the characters' own retrospection and will generally prove just as limited, as becomes evident in a passage such as this one: " 'whereas I,' [Michael] said one weekend in February 1975, recalling his honeymoon in 1958, 'was legally married' " (62). The conflation of two temporal periods (the years 1958 and 1972, of course, as well as historical and narrative time) results in a slight confusion that Lodge's clear and notably simple prose style serves to disguise but not entirely to dispel. In another passage, Adrian, thinking about the Profumo scandal that was then (1963) rocking England,

. . . did not admit, even to himself, that he was deeply fascinated by the shameless self-possession of the call-girls, Christine Keeler and Mandy Rice-Davies, when interviewed about their sex-lives on TV and in the press. They spoke as if there was no such thing as sin in the world. At this time Adrian and Dorothy were abstaining totally and indefinitely from sexual intercourse, since Dorothy's womb was in bad shape following two babies and a miscarriage in quick succession. (At about the same time, President Kennedy was confiding to his friend Ben Bradlee, later editor of the *Washington Post*, that if he didn't have a woman every three days or so, he got a bad headache; and by woman the President didn't mean Mrs Kennedy. But Adrian only read about that many years later in a newspaper excerpt from Mr Bradlee's memoirs.) (76–77)

What Adrian, or for that matter the reader (and, as we shall see, the author, too), can know at any given time is limited. Even if he can jump ahead in time and in this way gain a privileged historical perspective, or "narrative altitude," Lodge's method only proves that even this wider perspective must necessarily be limited in its own turn and in its own way. Moreover, as has been pointed out in previous chapters, it is this sense of limits—personal, epistemological, aesthetic, and moral—that lies at the heart of Lodge's vision and writing.

Similar to his handling of time in *How Far Can You Go?* is Lodge's handling of his major characters, all ten of them (plus a number of spouses added as the narrative progresses). Of course, to speak of ten "major" characters in so short a novel (243 less-than-densely-printed pages) poses an interesting question about their status as characters. (All but one are referred to by first name only; the exception, Father Brierly, eventually leaves the priesthood and thereafter becomes sim-

ply and democratically "Austin.") "One of the possible weaknesses of the book," Lodge has said, "which is an almost inevitable result of dealing with a homogeneous social group, is that
the characters are likely to be confused with each other in the
reader's mind" (Interview with Haffenden 154). There may
be more at work, or at risk, here than Lodge's remark at first
seems to suggest, for while Angela, Dennis, Michael, Miles,
Polly, Edward, Adrian, Ruth, Violet, and Austin are certainly
not the "rounded" characters of conventional fiction, neither
are they the depthless, merely nominal caricatures of many
postmodernist works, as Barthelme's Kevin, Edward, Hubert,
Henry, Clem, Dan, and Bill surely are. Although it is true that
none is the protagonist of the novel, each "is the hero of his
own sequence" (Barthes 59). Moreover, Lodge's, and/or his
authorial narrator's, attitude towards the members of this homogeneous group and towards the group itself is double. It is
at once comically detached, even at times condescending, and
yet sympathetically close. Young and Catholic, and therefore
sexually and theologically naive, they stumble towards sixties
liberation about a decade late, and it is this gap between their
fictional lives and the reader's experience that generates much
of the novel's humor. Miriam, for example, bravely questions
the doctrine of the Immaculate Conception, and "Michael
himself was uneasy about the Assumption" (58). Part of
Lodge's achievement in *How Far Can You Go?* stems from his
ability to deride such concerns (from his historically privileged
narrative position) without merely dismissing the people who
have them. The characters possess a certain hold on the reader's imagination and sympathy and so do not exist "merely as
excuses for the novelist to dramatize recent history," as Paul
Theroux has charged. Theroux is at least partly right if *How
Far Can You Go?* is chiefly or solely a novel of character, but
he is surely wrong if it is something else (just what remains to
be defined, but not, I believe, a realistic novel or a historical
fiction or a novel of ideas).

Theroux's complaint reflects that myopic readiness on the part of many reviewers and more than a few critics to judge a contemporary work not on its own merits but instead according to outmoded criteria that, while they do not help us understand novels such as *How Far Can You Go?* any better, do help to explain Theroux's impatience with passages such as the long historical digression (if that indeed is what it is) on pages 113–121. This "digression" not only comprises considerably more than half of the novel's fourth chapter (pages 113–127); it includes, halfway through, a narrative aside to the reader: a digression within a digression, an intrusion within an intrusion. "Patience," the narrator adds parenthetically, "the story will resume shortly" (115). Such counsel invites the Therouxian reader to distinguish between "story" and digression as if the two were somehow separable rather than integral and complementary parts of the same dialogic whole. Consider the following passages from Lodge's long duplex digression. Late in its first half we read: "Thus it came about that the first important test of the unity of the Catholic Church after Vatican II . . . was a great debate about—not, say, the nature of Christ and the meaning of his teaching in the light of modern knowledge—but about the precise conditions under which a man was permitted to introduce his penis and ejaculate his semen into the vagina of his lawfully wedded wife, a question on which Jesus Christ himself had left no recorded opinion" (115). The passage suggests, even if it nowhere asserts, the authorial narrator's belief that the entire birth control debate was itself a theological digression insofar as it involved a drifting away from Christ's own teachings into a realm that is at best speculative and at worst merely fictive. The passage further implies sympathy with liberal Catholics who viewed the Church's prohibition on birth control as an imposition of the Church's power in an area where it had no real authority. Late in the digression's second half, the authorial narrator makes a quite different point, as if in an effort to revise and refine what he reported earlier: "The crisis in the Church over birth control was not, therefore, the absurd diversion from more important matters that it first appeared to many observers [including, of course, Lodge's own readers], for it compelled thoughtful Catholics to re-examine and redefine their views on fundamental issues . . ." (120). And, steadily renegotiating his position, speaking in one tone of voice but from various points of view, the authorial narrator concludes with a warning quite at odds with the flippancy of a line such as "a question on which Christ himself had left no recorded opinion": "Let copulation thrive, by all means; but man cannot live by orgasms alone. . . . The good news about sexual satisfaction has little to offer those who are crippled, chronically sick, mad, ugly, impotent—or old, which all of us will be in due course, unless we are dead already. Death, after all, is the overwhelming question to which sex provides no answer, only an occasional brief respite from thinking about it" (121). At this point, after a Melvillean "but enough of this philosophizing," the authorial narrator returns us to the pleasures of his text, his "story." But the reader's pleasure in this "story" is offset by his confusion. "Story" and "aside" appear to have changed places. The "story" which forms a fictive alternative to a troubling reality has become the digression, the "occasional brief respite" from that "philosophizing" about death which no longer seems quite so digressive.

The juxtaposition of the passages (and views) quoted above reflects Lodge's overall narrative method, which is evident as well in the multiplicity of major, but in a sense nearly nameless, characters, each with his or her own life, plot, and voice. Thomas Pynchon renders Benny Profane's endless yo-yoing; Lodge provides us with something less startling but no less effective. He offers endless oppositions, qualifications, and coordinations (including coordinated plots) designed to undermine, however subtly, the novel's deceptively simple catechetical style and structure (the titular question, the chapter

title answers: how it was, how they lost their virginities, etc.).
How Far Can You Go? is, to borrow Lodge's own metaphor for
growing-up Catholic, a game of Snakes and Ladders in which
the reader moves ahead—"on the whole, the disappearance
of Hell was a great relief "—only to lose ground in the next
chapter, paragraph, sentence, or clause—"though it brought
new problems" (113). The problem for the reader is not simply
a matter of deciding where to place interpretive stress,
whether on this or that character or chapter or passage, but
instead of learning to remain open to all the conflicting possibilities, all the heterogeneous voices. This is precisely what
Lodge teaches the reader to do even at the microlevel of the
individual sentence, such as, "I did say this wasn't a comic
novel, exactly" (112), in which what is affirmed (I did say) is a
negation (this wasn't a comic novel) that is in its turn qualified
(exactly). To return to Theroux for a moment: his criticism of
Lodge's novel derives from precisely the kind of presumptu-
ousness that *How Far You Can Go?* works against. Having a
little too confidently identified the author's aim and voice,
Theroux has no trouble identifying the novel's failings,
Lodge's literary sins.

But the novel that Lodge has described as being at once
"serious and rather drab," "comic and exuberant" resists easy
definition (Interview with Haffenden 153).[1] It is a novel that
appears to advocate change within the Catholic Church and
that at the same time uses comedy to undermine the authority—the monological seriousness—of those characters in the

---

1. In this same interview, Lodge characterizes himself as "by nature
. . . a compromiser . . . looking to reconcile apparently opposed
positions" (157). The emphasis should, however, be on the looking
rather than on the reconciling, for Lodge is, as he has admitted,
"by temperament tentative, sceptical, ironic"; this temperament is
reflected in the "texture" of his fiction and "comes across in the
novels [or so Lodge hopes] more as honest doubt than as evasiveness" (152).

novel who advocate the liberal course. The leader of Catholics for an Open Church—COC—takes pride when the Automobile Club bestows legitimacy on their group in the form of a road sign for their Paschal Festival. And the Lodge who devised the decrowning acronym COC is not above having a fifty-year-old spinster deliver one of the novel's funniest, most trenchant, and most self-consciously dialogical lines: " 'With Bede teaching situation ethics in the Theology Department, it's hardly surprising the young people should decide it's all right to sleep with each other—always providing, of course, that it's a serious interpersonal relationship based on genuine trust and a non-exploitative giving of oneself to another' " (197). Sympathetic towards the liberalizing of the Church's attitude towards sex and birth control, Lodge nonetheless seems to raise the same question that a Bradbury character raises in his story, "A Goodbye to Evadne Winterbottom," namely "what else [is there] one can do with sex besides have it" (*Who Do You* 3). What the characters (especially Michael, his sexual imagination fueled by D. H. Lawrence and others) want is a satisfying sexual life, but what they discover is just how elusive that satisfaction can be as the longed-for goal of frequent sex turns into yet another numbing routine. At every turn of the narrative screw, Lodge undermines the logic of both the old morality and the new (and, one might add, of the old novel and the new fiction as well). He does so less out of "moral ambivalence," as A. N. Wilson contends, than the need to evoke a necessary and healthy indecidability. Recounting the Catholic Church's debate on birth control, for example, Lodge constructs a five-page daisy chain of thus's, however's, but in fact's, this's, if's, for example's, why's, therefore's, or's, as long as's, and (of course) on the contrary's to make his dialogical point. Into this moral, logical, and narrative labyrinth (the threads are by no means separable), Lodge inserts his array of characters who, though poorly prepared to do so, must nevertheless struggle on (as does the reader), in search of precisely that static wholeness and closure which the novel resists in a variety of ways.

At times, the novel resists wholeness by flaunting it in the form of obviously makeshift transitions that call into question the very seamless continuity they pretend to serve. At other times, Lodge pretends to permit a character in the novel to direct the course of the narrative. At the very end of Chapter 5, for example, "Polly decided to make death the subject of her next article, and cheered up immediately" (157), and Chapter 6, though not about Polly's article per se, is about "how they dealt with love and death." More pervasively, Lodge disrupts the narrative continuity by repeatedly breaking off a single character's story and then picking it up again some pages later (usually in the next chapter). This kind of disruption occurs so frequently as to take on a rhythm and continuity of its own. Even this newly formed continuity is disrupted, though, by Lodge's adoption of the intrusive Barthian authorial narrator who alludes to Lodge's *Language of Fiction*, who explains that Tessa was "classically ripe for having an affair" and in some other novel "might well have had one" (154), who outlines Gerard Genette's structuralist theory of narrative frequency and then applies it to sexual relations, who explains the novel's symbolism, thus effectively undermining it, who acknowledges that "the omniscience of novelists has its limits" (114), and who repeatedly foregrounds his own indecisiveness and artifice in a novel that for many reads more like a documentary than as a piece of either the New Fiction or the New Journalism. The particular "authorial mode of address" used in the novel, Lodge has noted, serves a double purpose. On the one hand, it is used "to convey basic information about Catholicism to a largely secular audience." On the other, it serves "to foreground the quaint obsolescence of the system of belief described"—and, one might add, the quaint obsolescence of a narrative mode based on such a system of belief. Used in this fashion Lodge's narrative strategy contributes to that "sense of provisionality," including "the provisionality of writing," that he sought to evoke in this work (*Write On* 156). As Patricia Waugh has pointed out, in stepping into his own narrative, Lodge "reverses the effect of heightened sensibility and authority usually attributed to the convention, and expresses some of the doubts and concerns expressed thematically, in the text, about sexuality and finally about the Catholic Church itself" (74). For the Catholic doctrine of papal infallibility, Lodge substitutes the postmodern doctrine of authorial fallibility, a doctrine that, contrary to the claims of Christopher Lasch in *The Culture of Narcissism* and Gerald Graff in *Literature Against Itself*, proves not to evidence an evasion of responsibility on the author's (in this case Lodge's) part but instead constitutes a complex and necessary moral act. Let me clarify this point. The fallible narrator is not synonymous with the unreliable narrator. The unreliable narrator (Jonathan Browne, for example, in *Ginger, You're Barmy*) *does not* speak with authority; the fallible narrator *cannot*. The unreliable narrator's discourse may be measured against an implied standard of "truthful discourse." In the case of the fallible narrator no such standard exists; thus there can be no appeal to an ultimate truth, a final authority. Lodge's narrator is, moreover, not only fallible; he is elusive (as textually elusive as he is intertextually allusive). "The more prominent the author is," Lodge had noted, "the more he becomes a rhetorical trope, and the more difficult it is to identify that voice with me" (Interview with Haffenden 153).[2] We can go a bit further and say that not only does

2. Although in this same interview Lodge claims that "the reader is indeed in a position to identify the voice-over [in the novel's concluding chapter] as the narrative voice, and those speeches do represent my own view as authorial narrator about the whole issue I've raised" (155), it is worth recalling at this point Barthes' warning: "Who speaks is not who writes and who writes is not who is" (283). In one of the notes he made shortly before his death, Bakhtin made a similar point concerning "the problem of the

Lodge's own voice elude the reader, replaced as it is by that of the fallible narrator, but his fallible narrator's voice eludes the reader as well. Consider the case of Polly, also a writer. Having had her Ann Landers-like column appear pseudony-mously for some time, Polly is now permitted to publish it under her own name (that is to say, under her married name, one that will probably change again after her divorce, men-tioned at novel's end). Interestingly, Polly writes "in a subtly ironic style that undermined [her 'radical and progressive ideas'] even as it expressed them, an effect which perfectly suited the paper's readership, mostly middle-class profession-als and their wives, with leftish views and bad consciences about their affluent life-styles" (156). This is, of course, also a fairly accurate description of Lodge's own audience and more disconcertingly of his narrator's (and his own) subtly ironic style of expression and concealment, right down to the final stylized word (or words), "life-styles." The difficulty arises when the reader attempts to ascertain just how far this irony— Polly's of course, but also the authorial narrator's and Lodge's—extends. In one of the novel's many authorial intru-sions (for want of a better word), the authorial narrator— here assuming a certain authority—comments on the death of Angela and Dennis's young daughter: "Adrian and Dorothy had not followed this and had to have it explained to them, as will you, gentle reader. . . . I have avoided a direct presentation

image of the author. The primary (not created) and secondary author (the image of the author created by the primary author). . . . The primary author cannot be an image. . . . When we try to imagine the primary author figuratively, we ourselves are creating his image, i.e., we ourselves become the primary author of the image. The creating image (i.e., the primary author) can never enter into any image he has created. The word of the primary author cannot be *his own* word. . . . Therefore the primary author clothes himself in *silence*. But the silence can assume various forms of expression" ("Extracts" 181).

of this incident because frankly I find it too painful to contemplate. Of course, Dennis and Angela and Anne are fictional characters, they cannot bleed or weep, but they stand here for all the real people to whom such disasters happen without apparent reason or justice. One does not kill off characters lightly, I assure you, even ones like Anne, evoked solely for that purpose" (125). The passage is unsettling for two reasons, which, as will soon be made clear, are not quite so unrelated as they might at first seem. One is that the passage serves as a perfect illustration of what Genette calls a narrative metalepsis in which, as in the line "Virgil has Dido die," the author is said to *cause* the events he presumably otherwise only and innocently *narrates*. Genette expands the term to include "any intrusion by the extradiegetic narrator or narratee into the diegetic universe (or by diegetic characters into a metadiegetic universe, etc.), or the inverse" (234–235). Additionally, the passage unsettles the reader's equanimity less in terms of *what* is said (which, after all, evidences the narrator's sympathy and humanity) than of *how* the authorial narrator *may* be saying what he says, his sympathetic tongue perhaps in his postmodern cheek. As in the case of nearly all of Barthelme's fictions, Lodge's use of an elusive fallible narrator, though not quite so extreme, nonetheless requires that the reader remain on the alert. He must constantly be prepared to renegotiate his position in relation not only to a narrator who is not to be confused with the author (even though the text often seems to invite such identification), but to a narrator who is himself elusive and multiple, no less so than in certain postmodernist texts where the practice is more clearly foregrounded than it is in Lodge's pseudorealistic novel where it must vie with a compelling and certainly "realistic" subject matter and style. Speaking of all serious fiction of the postmodern period, from the seemingly conventional to the programmatically innovative, Lodge has recently concluded that "what we see happening . . . is a revival of diegesis [of telling]: not smoothly dovetailed with

mimesis [showing] as in the classic realist text, and not subordi-
nated to mimesis as in the modernist text, but foregrounded
against mimesis. The stream of consciousness has turned into
a stream of narrative" ("Mimesis and Diegesis" 108).

Far from having "no scruples about interjecting his authorial voice"—or, more accurately, his pseudo-authorial voice—
into the novel, as one reviewer has cheerfully claimed (Sullivan), Lodge is keenly aware not only of what he is doing
but of its implications as he draws upon Genette's exhaustive
analysis of narrative "voice." In his *Figures* series, Genette
analyzes voice according to time and level of narration, presence or absence of the narrator from the story he narrates,
and the variety of functions open to the narrator (telling,
commenting, narrating his own part in the story he is telling,
presenting the narrative situation itself, explaining or justify-
ing what is told). More importantly, Genette defines narrating
not as a single mode of discourse but instead as a set, or field,
of possibilities, all of which are available to the narrator in a
given text. Narrating, then, forms

a shifting but sacred frontier [or "boundary"] between two worlds,
the world in which one tells, the world of which one tells. Whence
the uneasiness Borges so well put his finger on: "Such inversions
suggest that if the characters in a story can be readers or spectators,
then we, their readers or spectators, can be fictitious." The most
troubling thing about metalepsis indeed lies in this unacceptable and
insistent hypothesis, that the extradiegetic is perhaps always diegetic,
and that the narrator and the narratees—you and I—perhaps belong
to some narrative. (Genette 236)

This destabilizing of the narrator's relationship to the narration—"the disturbing intervention of the narrative source—
of the narrating in the narrative" (Genette 211)[3]—results in

3. Genette's remarks concerning *Recherche du temps perdu* as a
   distinctly modern work are appropriate here: "If the *Recherche
   du temps perdu* is experienced by everyone as being 'not completely

the reader's experience of "pronominal vertigo" (246) and parallels and intensifies the destabilizing of the discourse within the narrative brought about by various dialogic means, including what Bakhtin calls stylization. Stylization involves imitation without any accompanying parodic—or ironic—intent, as in the following line. Lodge's narrator not only speaks about Miles, a homosexual Cambridge don, but in Miles's voice as well: "Cambridge . . . became hideous to him, a claustrophobic little place, crammed with vain, complacent, ruthless people" (138). At times, however, the line separating stylization from parody cannot be quite as clearly drawn as Bakhtin would like to assume, and the reader may well wonder if there is not some irony in the echo. For example, after attending an innovative church service, Michael and Miriam "both agreed that the mass was the most meaningful liturgical event they had ever participated in" (124). Lodge has, of course, used stylization before, largely in imitation of Joyce, but what distinguishes the usage in *How Far Can You Go?* is that all the voices— whether reported, quoted, stylized, or parodied—are, as Lodge has said of the characters themselves, "of more or less equal importance" (Interview with Haffenden 155). Each of them is, as the authorial narrator likes to say, "in [this or] that sense right" (79). This play of democratically dialogized voices stands not for truth but for the process of discovering truth. It stands therefore in opposition to monologism of all kinds, whether that of the Catholic Church, moving confidently and dismayingly from "one state of certainty to another" (105), as

a novel any more' and as the work which, at its level, concludes the history of the genre (of the genres) and, along with some others, inaugurates the limitless and indefinite space of modern *literature*, the cause is obviously—and this time too despite the 'author's intentions' and through the effect of a movement all the more irresistible because involuntary—this invasion of the story by the commentary, of the novel by the essay, of the narrative by its own discourse" (259).

one papal spokesman puts it, or that of the liberals, claiming to find in their innovative beliefs "the essential meaning" of this or that religious matter. However, in *How Far Can You Go?* "essential meanings" are not actually supplanted by existential acts and/or postmodern performance. Rather, each is brought into contact with and made to coexist with all others.

As Lodge has appropriately pointed out, *How Far Can You Go?* "doesn't really take up a clear position on the question the title raises, it explores the question" (Interview with Haffenden 152). It is in fact not only the answer that is multiple and finally elusive but the very question itself. Its meaning metamorphoses throughout the novel. It includes the adolescent Catholic's uncertainty about what is and what is not a sexual sin (accompanied by the priest's seemingly confident yet evasive reply: conscience will tell you). And it extends to the question of just how far liturgical and theological reform can go before it goes "too far" for Catholicism as such to survive (which itself begs the question: what is "Catholicism as such"?), and it encompasses—not finally, but as well—the not unrelated question of how far the novelist can go before the novel as such, or its audience, disappears. Although in outward respects quite unlike such decidedly radical texts and *ficciones* as those written by Beckett and Borges, *How Far Can You Go?* serves as a perfect example of what Lodge in *The Modes of Modern Writing* calls the postmodern fiction of "permutation." Such works attempt to explore the entire range of narrative possibilities, either, as in Borges, by proliferating them, in which case the effect is one of liberation, or, as in Beckett, by reducing them to just two, in which case the effect is one of closure and exhaustion (230–231).

As a permutation fiction, *How Far Can You Go?* tends towards liberation of a special and certainly qualified kind. Against the multiplicity of characters, plots, voices, and narratives (novelistic and historical, mimetic and diegetic), Lodge posits the repetition of certain lines, situations, and of course the question that serves as both the novel's title and refrain. The question of moral and aesthetic responsibility is what cannot be escaped, for the issue is not to go *As Far As You Can Go*, as the title of Julian Mitchell's 1963 novel has it, but to ask *How Far Can You Go?* Contraception, Lodge writes, "was the issue on which many lay Catholics first attained moral autonomy" (118), but moral autonomy has in this novel its own dark side: moral uncertainty. The artist in the twentieth century finds himself in a similar position, possessing more freedom than ever before but uncertain how to proceed and unable to go back to the simple pleasures of "the marquis left his house at five o'clock." That *How Far Can You Go?* has been called a "putative novel" nicely sums up Lodge's postmodern dilemma (review of *Souls and Bodies, Publishers Weekly*). In this case the dilemma takes on special significance to the extent that Lodge agrees with his narrator that "in matters of belief (as of literary convention) it is a nice question how far you can go in this process without throwing out something vital" (143). Even as he demystifies Catholicism and the Anglo-Catholic liberal novel, casting out the monological demon, Lodge seeks to discover what is essential—"vital." This "essence" is not a particular belief but an open-ended need to believe, and in part this need entails accepting fallibility and indeterminacy as articles of faith.

Having written an M.A. thesis entitled "Catholic Fiction Since the Oxford Movement: Its Literary Form and Religious Content," Lodge has since come to feel that it is no longer possible to talk about a sharply defined Catholic novel, "partly because Catholicism itself has become a more confused—and confusing—faith" ("David Lodge Interviewed" 109). To his credit, Lodge neither abandons the Catholic novel nor nostalgically attempts to perpetuate a dead form. Rather, he seeks to revitalize, or resurrect, the Catholic novel by renegotiating the terms upon which it, and the faith on which it depends, can be made viable in a postmodern, postChristian age. As

Austin, the whilom priest, sounding here a good deal like the novelist at the crossroads, says towards the close of the novel, "I think you could say that the crisis in the Church today is a crisis of language" (234). The novel's concluding chapter recalls the filmscript "Ending" of *Changing Places*, but in *How Far Can You Go?* Lodge goes much further. Of the chapter's fifteen pages, all but four are devoted to the BBC special, "Easter with the New Catholics," edited and produced by Polly's husband, Jeremy Elton. The reader comes to know the COC Paschal Festival in decidedly mediated form, through the eyes as it were of the formulaic Elton Special which, as a documentary, presents its subject "objectively" but which, as an edited version, simultaneously distorts it. Lodge's depiction of the crisis of language and mediation does not stop here, however, for the Elton Special he offers the reader is itself mediated, taking the form of the "polished transcript" (228) Michael prepares from a videotape. And even this professionally prepared, ostensibly objective transcript turns out to be contaminated (and thus in turn contaminates the reader's reading of the special). The transcript not only records Elton's record of the Paschal Festival (and his editorial biases), it reflects Michael's technical expertise and the pride he takes in his skills. Moreover, it is impossible to read the transcript without assigning to it the same value Michael does as "a kind of coda to everything that had happened to them in matters of belief" (228). And finally, it reflects the incompleteness of his knowledge in that he is unable to identify one of the voices-over he hears. The presumptuous and no less ignorant reader will very likely identify the voice as that of the author, Lodge, and accept it as a coda to the transcript/Elton Special/Paschal Festival, an interpretive trinity that most readers will probably not trouble to distinguish. The transcript concludes with a freeze frame (or rather Michael's words, "freeze frame"), and at this point the transcript "Ends." Lodge then appends one of those Austen-to-Thackeray conclusions in which the characters' later lives are all tidily disposed of—the early realists' version of that still earlier fairy tale ending, "and they all lived happily ever after." But to this ending to the transcript's ending to the special's ending to the festival's ending, Lodge appends yet another, catenating conclusions as if they were dramatic climaxes (or sexual, to borrow the analogy propounded by Barthes and Derrida which Lodge will use in his next novel, *Small World*). In this way Lodge keeps death, or the death of the novel, or the death of this novel anyway, playfully at bay just a little longer. Having exhausted his stock of characters, Lodge inserts himself into the narrative. He inserts, that is, the fictive and entirely nameless authorial narrator that has always been one of the novel's characters. In Genette's terms, the extradiegetic narrator inserts himself into the diegetic universe, much to the reader's dismay *and* delight. The authorial narrator's *envoi* to the reader not only bridges the gap between past and present, narrative time and historical time, but the time of the narration and the time of the narrating. In fact, it propels the reader beyond present time into a future at once real and fictive, the blankness of the as yet unwritten page. Lodge's tactic strongly yet playfully implies a possible resurrection. It suggests that there is life after death—after the death of the Catholic novel.

I teach English literature at a redbrick university and write novels in my spare time, slowly, and hustled by history.

While I was writing this last chapter, Pope Paul VI died and Pope John Paul I was elected. Before I could type it up, Pope John Paul I had died and been succeeded by John Paul II, the first non-Italian pope for four hundred and fifty years: a Pole, a poet, a philosopher, a linguist, an athlete, a man of the people, a man of destiny, dramatically chosen, instantly popular—but theologically conservative. A changing Church acclaims a Pope who evidently thinks that change has gone far enough. What will happen now? All bets are void, the future is uncertain, but it will be interesting to watch. Reader, farewell! (243–244)

11

A Small [Carnivalized] *World*

How Far Can You Go? illustrates particularly well that distinctly modern narrative movement in which, as Genette has pointed out, there is a gradual decrease in "the temporal (and spatial) interval that . . . separate[s] the reported action from the narrating act . . . until it is finally reduced to zero." At that point "the narrative has reached the *here* and the *now*, the story has overtaken the narrating" (227). Having accomplished this merging of past and present, of story and telling, Lodge turns in *Small World* to something more ambitious in its narrative breadth though perhaps less far-reaching in its implications. What he achieves is the kind of dialogic intersection of narratives that Bakhtin discovered in Dostoevsky's exemplary novels: "In Dostoevsky's world," Bakhtin writes, "all people and all things must know one another and know about one another, must enter into contact, come together face to face and *begin to talk* with one another. Everything must be reflected in everything else, all things must illuminate one another dialogically. Therefore all things that are disunified and distant must be brought together at a single spatial and temporal 'point'. And what is necessary for this is carnival *freedom* and carnival's

artistic conception of space and time" (*Problems* 177). One
of the novel's three epigraphs, appropriately the one from
Finnegans Wake—"Hush! Caution! Echoland!"—alerts the
reader to at least one aspect of the novel's carnival freedom,
its richly allusive intertextual texture: the novel as a vast but
not obtrusively erudite literary recycling project, a way of
looking back in order to move ahead. Yeats, Synge, Eliot,
Poe, the Brothers Grimm, Barthes, Derrida, Foucault, Ariosto,
Chaucer, Shakespeare, Amis, Terry Southern, Wolfgang Iser,
George Steiner, Jessie Weston, and a host of other writers and
critics make appearances of one kind or another, including
Bradbury.[1] Lodge is, in fact, not above plundering and recycling his own works and literary reception: the Zapps, the
Swallows, and several other characters from *Changing Places*,
a charter flight to Majorca from *Ginger, You're Barmy*, and
"the mystery of the disappearing review copies" of *The British
Museum Is Falling Down* ("Introduction," *British Museum* 9).

Small World is a novel in which *Troilus and Creseyde* and
absence and presence exist side by side. It is a campus novel
for an age of "the global campus," for "a civilization of light-
weight luggage [and] permanent disjunctions" in which "everybody seems to be departing or returning from somewhere"
(271). Consequently, a diagram of the novel's plot would more
closely resemble an airline route map than Freytag's pyramid.
Instead of a linearly and hierarchically developed plot, we find
a bewildering number of narrative lines of more or less equal
significance that intersect at both the mimetic and diegetic

1. The phrase "meeters and greeters" from *Rates of Exchange*; "I'm
John Winthrop—fly me" ("I'm Jane Austen—fly me") from "Dangerous Pilgrimages." In "Second Countries," Bradbury refers to
"the travelling scholar . . . journeying to some mythic destiny"
(15). A more immediate "source" for the use of the grail legend
in *Small World* is "the somewhat preposterous but very enjoyable
film, *Excalibur*," which Lodge viewed around the time he began
writing the novel (*Write On* 72).

levels. One character, for example, reads a novel written by a character from one of the other narrative lines whom she will meet later when their narratives momentarily converge. Thus, we have a double intersection, both, however, on the mimetic level. But when we read "Philip and Hilary Swallow are copulating as quietly, and almost as furtively, as if they were stretched out on the rear seats of a jumbo jet" (95), after having just read about Howard Ringbaum's narratively earlier but chronologically coterminous attempt to seduce his wife during their transatlantic flight, we experience the intersection of the two plots on the *diegetic* level. The *events* of the first story affect, or manifest themselves in, the *telling* of the second. As the reader comes to understand, the numerous mimetic plots (and perhaps the diegetic plot too) not only intersect but echo and double one another as well. Each contributes to the same general plot of desire—sexual, professional, and narrative— that underlies each of the novel's many and varied quests, Lodge's comic variations on a once serious theme. Even as the novel moves slowly towards this general intersection, fully figured in the final chapter, it provides delays and frustrations aplenty and at all narrative levels, from the segmenting and intercutting techniques perfected in *How Far Can You Go?* to the 194-word delay between a character's prefatory remark, " 'There's something I must ask you,' " and the actual statement of the question. What we have here is not the suspense of narrative interruptus but its parody (127–128).

The overall structure of the novel works in a similar but more relentless way to overthrow monological continuity by creating a carnival atmosphere. *Small World* is divided into five parts, with parts I, II, III, and V further divided into two chapters each and part IV into three chapters. Parts I, III, and IV are of virtually equal length (about eighty pages each), II is somewhat shorter (sixty-seven pages), and V considerably shorter (twenty-five pages). All of this relative regularity is, however, quite deceptive in terms of the way in which the reader actually experiences Lodge's text. Part I begins as many novels and epics do, *"in media res,* followed by an expository return to an earlier time" (Genette 36). (With *Small World* this entails returning to the events of the previous evening.) From here the novel moves slowly and in more or less linear fashion through the first section of the first part (I. One). All fifty-five pages are set at the University Teachers of English Language and Literature conference being held at the University of Rummidge, and they focus on Persse McGarrigle's pursuit of an unregistered "freelance" conferee named Angelica Pabst. The next section, I. Two, begins simply enough with the word "meanwhile," which at once serves to place the reader clearly in narrative time and to mark the beginning of the end of narrative linearity, supplanted by a simultaneity of plots. Having moved ahead, the narrative stops, loops back, and, in a sense, begins again, covering some of the same time period from a different focal point. First Lodge treats Zapp and Hilary, bringing their lives up to date since *Changing Places.* Then, having Hilary exit, he has Swallow enter to tell his story within Lodge's story, Swallow's leisurely, decidedly old-fashioned tale of a brief love affair some years ago with a woman named Joy, whom he believes dead. I. Two begins the narrative doubling; II. One begins the narrative deluge. Covering just a four-hour period, from 5:00 to 9:00 a.m. (Greenwich Mean Time), this section deals with no fewer than seventeen more or less major characters, in twelve different settings from London to Chicago to Australia, and various cars, planes, and phone lines in between: thirty-one subsections in less than thirty pages, the longest two and one-half pages, the shortest one and one-half lines. The narrative intercutting is greater here than anywhere else in the novel, as is the reader's sense of narrative vertigo as Lodge yo-yo's back and forth between not only time zones but narrative zones as well. The pace slackens a bit in II. Two (fifteen subsections in thirty pages) as Lodge's chronicle of the same day continues, and again in III. One (seventeen subsections in forty pages). Insofar as the action here is limited (relatively speaking) to just four or five main lines, it is possible to discern a degree of linear development based, however, on the narrative's own peculiar logic of improbable coincidences. In III. Two the narrative pace again slackens and the focus narrows still further. Although there are fifteen sections in just thirty-eight pages, the first five sections all deal with Persse's continuing and still unsuccessful pursuit of Angelica and the next ten sections, in complementary fashion, with the reunion of Swallow and his Joy. There is some narrative backsliding in IV. One (twenty pages, six sections, the first of which Lodge easily could have divided into five), but IV. Two (four sections in twenty pages) is devoted solely to Persse, whose adventures here, as elsewhere in the novel, take on an antic linearity. Retreating from the ever-elusive Angelica (whom he has come to mistake for her sister, a porn star), Persse goes to Innisfree where, instead of Yeats's peace and solitude, he discovers his cousin Bernadette's seducer. This discovery leads him to search for Bernadette, a search which in turn leads him back to his pursuit of Angelica, which in its turn leads the reader to IV. Three (fifteen sections in forty pages). Here Persse's nonstop narrative flights to Los Angeles, Honolulu, Tokyo, and Seoul alternate with the again complementary narrative of Zapp's captivity (he is being held hostage by a gang of leftists who mistakenly believe he is still married to the now wealthy Desiree Boyd, whom they again mistakenly believe will pay a huge ransom for Zapp's release). Into this duplex chronicle of Persse and Zapp, Lodge folds, or intercuts, two additional ongoing narratives: Rodney Wainwright's still unsuccessful efforts to complete a paper for Zapp's Jerusalem conference on the Future of Criticism and Robin Dempsey's further conversations with Joseph Weizenbaum's well-known computer program, "Eliza." V. One brings nearly all of the principal characters together at the annual, end-of-the-calendar-year, middle-of-the-academic-year MLA conference, and V. Two, less than two pages long, completes the novel and the year (it's 31 December) on a typically Lodgean note of incompletion and expectancy. We find the hapless but always hopeful Persse about to embark on yet another quest, or alternately, on another episode in a seemingly endless cycle of romances within Lodge's cycle of romances within the larger literary history of romance.

As even this brief summary makes clear, *Small World* is a decidedly carnivalesque novel that develops its own time standard, its own geography (based on the location of academic conferences from Rummidge to Chicago to Jerusalem), and its own set of permutational possibilities. All are held together by the numerous characters' varied quests: for Angelica, for the perfect conference, for an original idea, for lost relatives, for the ultimate academic appointment (the UNESCO Chair of Literary Studies), and finally (because it does not appear until the novel's last page) for Cheryl Summerbee. The carnivalesque atmosphere extends further, however, beyond the narrative multiplication and intersection of people, settings, and times to the convergence in one novel of various literary forms and styles. *Small World* is a novel at the crossroads by a novelist at the crossroads. It comprises a narrative conference of echoes, allusions, stylizations, parodies, parallel stories, inserted tales, and, in general, recyclings of material culled from a host of sources. Early in the novel Persse attends a performance of a pantomime version of *Puss in Boots* that includes Robin Hood, duets, a slapstick comic interlude, and "as a finale to the first act, a spectacular song and dance number for the whole company, entitled, 'Caturday Night Fever,' in which Puss in Boots triumphed in a Royal Disco Dancing competition at the Palace" (35). And later, in a similar vein, we learn that Desiree Boyd, Zapp's ex-wife, is currently working on "a book combining fiction and non-fiction—fantasy, criticism, confession and speculation" (86). Desiree's book is yet another carnivalization within Lodge's larger carnivalization. The latter in-cludes not only pantomimes and works-in-progress but bawdy songs, conference papers, Zapp's Barthesian lecture on "Tex-tuality as Striptease," student essay exams, Swallow's story of Joy (in its oral version, with commentary and digression by Zapp), letters, tape-recorded messages, poems (including one earth-, or snow-, poem), a dust-jacket biography, a computer read-out which takes the form of a psychiatrist-patient inter-view, a street-theater version of *The Waste Land*, and more. The reader's vertigo is similar to that which Persse experiences in Lausanne: "A babble of multi-lingual conversation rose from the tables and mingled with the remarks of the parading pedestrians, so that to Persse's ears, pricked for a possible greeting from Angelica, the effect was rather like that of twist-ing the tuning knob of a powerful radio set at random, picking up snatches of one foreign station after another" (261). The reality Persse experiences has more in common with John Cage's aleatory music, the Nighttown section of *Ulysses*, and slapstick comedy than with conventional Anglo-liberal fiction. It is an intertextual reality in which one finds not language but languages, not speech but ways of speaking—grist for Lodge's carnivalizing mill from which no one and nothing escapes decrowning.

Lodge's carnivalization operates at both the micro- and ma-cro-levels. There is, for example, the one-sentence stylization of the speech of Marxist poststructuralist Fulvia Morgana, author of an "essay on the stream-of-consciousness novel as an instrument of bourgeois hegemony (oppressing the working classes with books they couldn't understand)" (238). Others involve entire scenes. In one, novelist Ronald Frobisher ex-plains that although he has writer's block (as do most of the writers in this novel) and as a result cannot write fiction (" 'with fiction it's the narrative bits that give the writing its individuality' " [181]), he can write television scripts because they consist entirely of dialogue. Itself written in dialogue only, Lodge's scene mimics Frobisher's condition. In *Small World* stylization extends even to the level of the recurrent scene or situation. Those involving Swallow and Joy are rendered in the style of popular romance, including thirties' film romances (the waiting-in-the-railway-station-for-the-lover-to-arrive scene, for example), and of similarly melodramatic novels. "Here there was a hiatus in Joy's monologue while Philip once more fervently demonstrated how well-founded this [Joy's] intuition had been. Some time later she resumed" (220). The narrator's chaste summary here forms a narrative interruptus within a larger narrative interruptus (Swallow's story) within Lodge's novel of sexual, academic, and narrative frustrations.

In the line just quoted, Lodge's narrator uses the word "monologue" innocently, one might say; that is, he uses it without intending any Bakhtinian "sideward glance" at Bakhtin's dialogic theory. Yet even this presumably innocent usage has its own added significance insofar as monologues, and especially monologic views, abound in *Small World*. Homosexual critic Michel Tardieu's homosexual interpretation of *The Waste Land* is a case in point, as is the reading of the *Puss in Boots* pantomime as a version of the grail legend, according to Miss Sibyl Maiden, one of Jessie Weston's former students. In *Small World*, such monologues do not, in fact, *cannot*, exist on their own, for in the small but dialogically dense world of Lodge's novel nothing is without its decrowning double. This doubleness is not the means to some higher (thematic) end requiring the subordinating of certain plots to some one.[2] Rather, it is the end itself. Thesis

2. As Katerina Clark and Michael Holquist have pointed out, "One of the difficulties posed by Bakhtin is to avoid thinking from within an all-pervasive simultaneity without at the same time falling into the habit of reducing everything to a series of binary oppositions: not a dialectical either/or, but a dialogic both/and" (*Mikhail Bakhtin* 7).

and antithesis are brought together without any hope of—
and without any risk of—their being resolved in that synthesis of abstraction that led Bakhtin to carefully distinguish
dialogics from dialectics. We detect this dialogical doubling
in Zapp's comment, " 'in the Grail legend the hero cures
the king's sterility. In the Freudian version the old guy gets
wasted by his kids' " (42). (It is Zapp, not Lodge, who
resolves the play of ideas by judging the Freudian version
" 'more true to life.' ") And we see this doubling as well in
Lodge's choosing to write a novel that would be "highly
literary and yet in a curious way frivolous" (Interview with
Haffenden 163) at the same time, a novel drawn from such
diverse sources as Patricia Parker's scholarly study *Inescapable
Romance* and Brian Moynahan's quite different *Airport International*. It is "a novel about desire" but "not just about
sexual desire." "I conceived it," Lodge has noted, "as an
academic comedy of manners which would have a romance
plot underneath it, and in some ways the two elements are
incompatible. Satire is the antithesis of romance, because
romance is ultimately about the achievement of desire; satire
is saying that you won't get what you desire, you don't
deserve it" (Interview with Haffenden 159). *Small World* is,
therefore, neither romance nor satire but what results from
the dialogical convergence of the two. It is a work in which
"romance" is doubled and redoubled beyond all monological
definition and which consequently has as much to do with
Hawthorne's notions as with Weston's theories and Harle-
quin's publications. What *Small World* does, then, is to enact
within its own pages what Lodge feels any book worth
reading must do (though most books will, of course, do it
in a far less self-conscious fashion): "No book . . . has any
meaning on its own, in a vacuum. The meaning of a book
is in large part a product of its differences from and
similarities to other books. If a novel did not bear some
resemblance to other novels, we should not know how

to read it, and if it wasn't different from all other novels we shouldn't *want* to read it" (*Working with Structuralism* 3–4). It is precisely this endless play between convergence and divergence that, even more than the self-evident quest structure, unifies this, Lodge's most diverse novel. It is reflected in the work's semiotic layer—in the way, that is, the literal mimetic reality in the novel continually dissolves into an indeterminacy of signs and semiotic interpretation. At the very end of *Small World*, there is an airport flutterboard that recalls the one Petworth observes near the beginning of *Rates of Exchange*, whose meaning Bradbury's narrator glosses in the following way: "out of redundancy is coming word" (124). Reading *Small World* provides an analogous experience; out of its redundancy, multiplicity, and sheer excessiveness, come not the word but a plurality of words, possibilities, quests, transformations. "The meaning of signs," Umberto Eco has pointed out, "is not a mere matter of recognition (of a stable equivalence); it is a matter of interpretation" (*Semiotics* 43), though many of the characters in *Small World*, and perhaps many of its readers too, would like to believe otherwise. This tendency towards "endless semiosis" Lodge both indulges in and turns to his own novelistic advantage. He finds in the comic plurality of a sign's meaning a comic vitality as well as a viable alternative to monologic seriousness. We see this especially well in the long paragraph on page 236 in which Lodge chronicles the ways in which signs can go awry, turning every decoding, every reading, into a misreading. And it is evident too in the transformation of Persse's M.A. thesis (concerning Shakespeare's influence on Eliot) into, first, the more Borgesian subject of Eliot's influence on Shakespeare and, later yet, " 'the modern reception of Shakespeare and Co. being influenced by T.S. Eliot' " (156).[3]

3. "The fact is that every writer creates his own precursors. His work modifies our conception of the past, as it will modify the future" (Borges, "Kafka and His Precursors," *Labyrinths* 201).

Persse McGarrigle is especially prone to mistaking interpretation for recognition, the single meaning for the plurality of possible meanings. Persse is not the novel's protagonist because *Small World*, like *How Far Can You Go?*, does not have one. However, the novel does begin and end with him and does involve to a large but by no means overwhelming extent his particular desire. More importantly, his and Angelica's incompatibility and complementarity, like the intersection of their narrative lives and lines, recapitulate the novel's underlying dialogic principle and serve as the recurrent background against which the rest of Lodge's narrative plays itself out. Therefore, I have chosen to single them out for brief discussion here, less as the principal characters in *Small World* than as the most exemplary. As Bakhtin has explained, "the device of 'not understanding'—deliberate on the part of the author, simpleminded and naive on the part of the protagonists— always takes on great organizing potential when an exposure of vulgar conventionality is involved" (*Dialogic* 164), including, as in *Small World*, the exposure of academic pretentiousness. It is precisely this naivete which distinguishes Persse from most of the other characters. "A conference virgin" (18), he is a walking anachronism in contemporary literary circles in that he is completely ignorant of critical theory and incapable of putting abstraction over object, indeterminacy over moral valuation. He is, in short, " 'a hopeless romantic' " (39). And he is also representative of the further decline of the hero, from the divine figure of myth and the more-than-human hero of romance to the postmodern *eiron* of contemporary fiction whose sphere of action is for the most part confined to the sphere of reaction. But as in all things Lodge, Persse, though naive and unfamiliar with poststructuralist theory and lingo, is not as simple or as single as he first appears to be. McGarrigle may be "an old Irish name that means 'Son of Super-valour' " (9) but "Persse" is more ambiguous, a sign of indeterminate meaning, of plural roles: Grail legend's Percival, Greek myth's

Perseus, semiotics' Charles Saunders Peirce, Latin's per se and Joyce's Persse O'Reilly, who is perce-oreille, or earwig, and therefore one more manifestation of Humphrey Chimpden Earwicker, the protean hero of *Finnegans Wake*. As one of Joyce's voices says of Persse O'Reilly and therefore of HCE as well, "but I parse him Persse O'Reilly else he's called no name at all" (44). Persse McGarrigle's quest is similarly multiplied; his desire for Angelica becomes entwined with his search for his fallen cousin and his exposure to contemporary literary theory.

As befits her role as the elusive object of Persse's desire, Angelica is an even more complex, if a less present, or more "absent," figure in Lodge's novel. She is the Angelica of Milton's *Paradise Regained*, "the fairest of her sex," and too the damsel in distress from Ariosto's *Orlando Furioso*. Yet at the same time she is the Alcina (Circe) figure in that same work and its predecessor, *Orlando Innamorato*, and in her guise as A. L. Pabst (the name she has adopted for the scholarly publications she has yet to write) she serves as the novel's Anna Livia Plurabelle to Persse's Humphrey Chimpden Earwicker. Worse, at least for her pursuer, is the fact that she is doubled in yet another way, by her twin sister Lily (Pabst, also "Papps"— her professional name) whose face Persse mistakenly "recognizes" as Angelica's in a number of pornographic contexts. In a nineteenth century novel, Lily and Angelica would have played their predictable parts in the author's manichaean plot, a variation on the poetic dialogue between the body and the soul. In *Small World* they serve a different and much more self-consciously wrought purpose. Telling Persse of her and Angelica's sole distinguishing physical feature, a birthmark shaped like an inverted comma high up on Angelica's left and Lily's right thigh, Lily notes, " 'When we stand hip to hip in our bikinis, it looks like we're inside quotation marks' " (325). The image is entirely appropriate, for an intertextual quotation is precisely what the sisters are. They comprise a plurality of literary citations in a novel whose purpose is not (to borrow again from Eco) to fix the name of the rose but instead to discover the process of naming by which the rose comes to be known, and known always and only provisionally, partially. Indeed, as the novel progresses, Persse and the reader learn first that she is a foundling, then that she has a twin sister, then that her adoptive father has bestowed on her the contemporary equivalent of a magical charm, an airline travel pass, and later still that she is about to undergo yet another metamorphosis as the wife of Peter (not Persse) McGarrigle, and finally that while her real parents may not have been a royal virgin and a shower of gold, they are Miss Sibyl Maiden and Arthur Kingfisher, the fisher king of Lodge's academic Waste Land and the consort of his younger days.

Concerning her dissertation on romance literature from Heliodorus to Barbara Cartland, Angelica tells Persse, " 'I don't need any more data. What I need is a theory to explain it all' " (24). Persse is, as has already been noted, not especially disposed towards theory, less so certainly than Lodge whose four books of criticism demonstrate particularly well the practical applications of literary theory, of the symbiotic or dialogical relationship between the two. His criticism implies that theory's reason for being is to help explain and clarify, not to replace the individual text, not to engulf it in abstraction. The UNESCO Chair of Literary Studies, the prize that Zapp and the other world-class academics covet, entails a large salary but no specific duties and no place of residence; it is so much "a purely conceptual chair" that even as it confers prestige and an enormous salary on the chosen academic, it in fact renders the winner redundant; for the important question is not who will be chosen by the selection committee (a euphemism for Arthur Kingfisher) but "what kind of theory will be favoured" (234). Losing not their souls but their identities, the academics have successfully reduced themselves to the theories they propound: formalist, structuralist, reader-response, Marxist, deconstructionist, liberal-humanist. At the special MLA session devoted to "The Function of Criticism," Swallow, Zapp, Tardieu, von Turpitz, and Fulvia Morgana play the parts of latter-day Saracens and Christians battling for control of the global campus. At one extreme is Swallow, author of *Hazlitt and the Amateur Reader*, and at the other, Zapp, author of *Beyond Criticism*. In the middle is Lodge, an ear cocked to each side, tongue somehow in both cheeks. "I don't come down on either side but my feeling is that literary studies are in a somewhat demoralized state partly because of increasing specialization and the use of highly technical language. . . . [The major critics] are unintelligible to the general public. Those who are intelligible often have nothing valuable to say" (Interview with Billington).[4] What *Small World* accomplishes in its own narrative fashion is precisely what Lodge claims is missing from the current critical debate. It is a highly readable text that nonetheless does not shy away from matters pertaining to narrative theory, matters that are no longer apart from but that have become a part of the general contemporary culture. (Witness the following from a capsule *New Yorker* review of a recent stage version of *Singin' in the Rain:* "the absence of the incomparable Gene Kelly becomes a rueful presence."[5]) *Small World* is, then, a novel that is at once accessible to Swallow's brand of amateur reading and that demonstrates its preemptive awareness of and interest in Zapp's deconstructive

4. Lodge maintains that theory is indispensable to the study of literature. However, the primary value of literary theory, Lodge believes, is "serving the cause of 'better' reading of texts" (Lodge, "Literary Theory in the University" 435).

5. *New Yorker*, 28 April 1986: 4. In an essay first published in 1980, Lodge takes the opposite view, claiming that structuralism has not had any significant impact on the general culture whatsoever; however, in a postscript to the reprinting of this essay in *Write On*, Lodge says that the situation has changed, though he nonetheless still doubts that the general audience actually understands what is being discussed or, as in the *New Yorker* review, alluded to.

method. In its dialogical doubleness, the novel seems to raise significant questions not only about Swallow's naivete but about the poststructuralist fashion as well. Explaining why he himself has " 'lost faith in deconstruction,' " Zapp says that although every decoding is another encoding, " 'the deferral of meaning isn't infinite as far as the individual is concerned.' " Sounding a good deal like the authorial narrator in *How Far Can You Go?* (as well as Umberto Eco), Zapp discovers a flaw, or perhaps a dialogical loophole, in deconstructionist thinking. " 'Death is the one concept you can't deconstruct. Work back from there and you end up with the old idea of the autonomous self. I can die, therefore I am' " (328).

Lodge has acknowledged his special attraction to Bakhtin's "rather impressive theoretical case for the comic mode," which, Lodge contends, "performs a very valuable hygienic function: it makes sure that institutions are always subject to a kind of ridiculing criticism. . . . Comedy reasserts the body, and the collectiveness of the body is what really unites us rather than ideologies" (Interview with Haffenden 166–167). That Lodge should find Bakhtin's theoretical refutation of theory appealing is entirely consistent with the working of his own dialogical imagination. In *Small World* it is Persse who performs, naively and unselfconsciously, the decrowning act, posing to the MLA panel the following question: " 'What follows if everybody agrees with you?' " (319). It is a question which none of the panelists can answer, or even understand, but which the panel's chairperson, Arthur Kingfisher, glosses, or monologizes, in the following Derridean way: " 'You imply, of course, that what matters in the field of critical practice is not truth but difference. If everybody were convinced by your arguments, they would have to do the same as you and then there would be no satisfaction in doing it. To win is to lose the game. Am I right?' " (319). Whether Kingfisher's question is entirely rhetorical or not is impossible to say. What is clear is that Persse cannot validate Kingfisher's understanding of his,

Persse's, question and so, having only questions at his disposal, cannot provide him with the satisfaction and finality he, Kingfisher, desires. Instead, Persse can only ask that the dialogue be kept open, the question left unanswered though still debated. His simple question demystifies the critical debate, just as his accidentally removing von Turpitz's Dr. Strangelovelike black glove reveals as perfectly normal what the everpresent glove made the subject of much mystery and speculation: a merely human hand. Lodge performs a similar feat, demystifying the MLA convention by transforming it into a vast academic carnival, a Joycean omnium gatherum to which "Here Comes Everybody." Whereas the others prefer to distinguish the humanist goats from the structuralist and poststructuralist sheep (or vice versa), Lodge's carnivalization achieves a quite different aim. As Bakhtin has explained: "As opposed to the official feast, one might say that carnival celebrated temporary liberation from the prevailing truth and from the established order; it marked the suspension of all hierarchical rank, privileges, norms, and prohibitions. Carnival was the true feast of time, the feast of becoming, change, and renewal. It was hostile to all that was immortalized and completed" (*Rabelais* 10). Persse's demystification decrowns, liberates, and restores, curing those who are present of their various forms of impotence—sexual, literary, and intellectual. It helps bring about the renewals, rebirths, and reconciliations that proliferate in all of the novel's concluding pages except the final two. There the wish-fulfillment of romance finally comes up against the sobering irony of literary realism: the potentially endless form of the one meets the slice-of-life incompleteness of the other. Because his desire remains unrealized, Persse remains unsatisfied; but at the same time his dissatisfaction is the precondition that allows, or causes, him to continue his quest. He becomes Lodge's version of Beckett's pilgriming voice in the void, unable to go on but going on nonetheless. Persse may therefore (if only partly) be understood as the stubborn residue of liberalism's autonomous self in a postliberal, postmodern age, "small but beyond elimination," as John Hawkes says of *The Lime Twig*'s Michael Banks. In this sense, Persse recalls Bradbury's Petworth, or at least that part of Petworth that evoked, or that was evoked by, Katya Princip's folk hero, "Stupid." Stupid is her magic realist's version of the main character of the early Greek romances, who, although a stock type whose experiences do not change him in any significant way, is nonetheless, as Bakhtin has explained, "a *living human being* in whom . . . . there is always preserved . . . some precious kernel of folk humanity; one always senses a faith in the indestructible power of man in his struggle with nature and with all inhuman forces" (*Dialogic* 105). What Lodge does with Persse is at once to ironize and yet to endorse his position. Anachronistic yet hopeful, experienced yet still innocent, wise yet still naive, Persse functions, as does the novel itself, as a dialogical intersection of before and after, a harking back to a simple past that somehow manages to look ahead to an ongoing present. And a similar intersection occurs when Persse finds his glass being "refilled in an absentminded fashion by a shortish dark-haired man standing nearby with a bottle of champagne in his hand, talking to a tallish dark-haired man smoking a pipe. 'If I can have Eastern Europe,' the tallish man was saying in an English accent, 'you can have the rest of the world.' 'All right,' said the shortish man, 'but I daresay people will still get us mixed up' " (331–332). They undoubtedly will, for who else is "Brodge, the author of *Changing Westward*," but the dialogical intersection of two writers whose novels and criticism have enacted the process of doubling and decrowning, both within individual texts and between them.

Their sense of carnivalistic play must, however, be put in perspective. Lodge and Bradbury have consistently sided with caution over either excess or abandon, but a caution that has flirted with both in an effort to keep their own ailing enterprise afloat and at the crossroads and not yet engulfed by sand. One of the reasons that the novels of Bradbury and Lodge, as well as their criticism, are so important is that we live, in the eighties, in a literary age that seems to have witnessed, or at least experienced, the end of postmodernist experimentation and energy and that is often said to have lapsed into a period of stultifying and regressive realism: Ronald Reagan in the White House and Raymond Carver in Walden Books. I am not sure this is either a fair or an accurate assessment of Carver's fiction, but it is a widely held view that does apply all too well to much of what one finds praised in the pages of this week's *New York Times Book Review* and *Times Literary Supplement*. Moreover, it is a view against which we can with confidence place the work of Bradbury and Lodge, two writers who have continued to keep realism alive—not by any rearguard action, not by committing themselves to either a conservative aesthetic or conservative (or even reactionary) politics, but, instead, by steadily renegotiating the terms by which realism can continue to be made viable, by testing it against the innovations of the postmodern age. Theirs, then, has been a caution that has consistently sought to extend fiction's reach and vitality by moving, somewhat hesitantly it is true, and somewhat skeptically, towards an ever freer and broader and more self-conscious use of the novel's inherently dialogical means, towards a plurality of voices and forms, while stubbornly holding on to—and alternately searching for—whatever is essentially novelistic and essentially human. And these may very well be, as Bakhtin felt, one in the same.

Works Cited
Index

Works Cited

Amis, Martin. Rev. of *Rates of Exchange*. *Observer* 3 Apr. 1983: 29.

Bakhtin, Mikhail. *The Dialogic Imagination: Four Essays*. Trans. Caryl Emerson and Michael Holquist. Ed. Michael Holquist. Austin: U of Texas P, 1981.

—————. "Extracts from 'Notes' (1970-1971)." *Bakhtin: Essays and Dialogues on His Work*. Ed. Saul Morson. Chicago: U of Chicago P, 1986. 179–82.

—————. *Problems of Dostoevsky's Poetics*. Ed. and trans. Caryl Emerson. Minneapolis: U of Minnesota P, 1984.

—————. *Rabelais and His World*. Trans. Helene Iswolsky. Bloomington: Indiana UP, 1984.

Banks, J. R. "Back to Bradbury Lodge." *Critical Quarterly* 27.1 (1985): 79–81.

Barth, John. "The Literature of Exhaustion" (1967). Bradbury, *The Novel Today* 70–83.

—————. "The Literature of Replenishment." *Atlantic* Jan. 1980: 65–71.

Barthes, Roland. *A Barthes Reader*. Ed. Susan Sontag. New York: Hill & Wang, 1983.

Booth, Wayne. "Introduction." Bakhtin, *Problems of Dostoevsky's Poetics* xiii–xxvii.

Borges, Jorge Luis. *Labyrinths: Selected Stories & Other Writings*. Ed. Donald A. Yates and James E. Kirby. New York: New Directions, 1964.

Bradbury, Malcolm. *The After Dinner Game*. 1982. London: Arena, 1984.

―――. "An Age of Parody: Style in the Modern Arts." *Encounter* July 1980: 36–53.

―――. *All Dressed Up and Nowhere to Go*. 1982. London: Arena, 1986. Comprises *Phogey! How to Have Class in a Classless Society* (1960) and *All Dressed Up and Nowhere to Go* (1962).

―――. "Coming Out of the Fifties." *Twentieth Century Literature* 29 (1983): 178–189.

―――. *Cuts: A Very Short Novel*. London: Hutchinson, 1987.

―――. "Dangerous Pilgrimages: Transatlantic Images in Fiction." *Encounter* Dec. 1976: 56–67; Feb. 1977: 50–65; May 1977: 56–71.

―――. "A Dog Engulfed by Sand: Abstraction and Irony." *Encounter* Nov. 1978: 51–59; Jan. 1979: 36–42. See Bradbury, "Putting in the Person," below.

―――. "Donswapping." Rev. of *Changing Places*. *New Review* Feb. 1975: 65–66.

―――. *Eating People Is Wrong*. 1959. London: Secker & Warburg, 1976. With an "Introduction" by the author.

―――. "Foreword." Halio, *British Novelists* xi-xviii.

―――. ed. *Forster: A Collection of Critical Essays*. Englewood Cliffs: Prentice-Hall, 1966.

―――. *The History Man*. 1975. New York: Penguin, 1985.

―――. Interview with John Haffenden. Haffenden, John. *Novelists in Interview*. London: Methuen, 1985. 25–56.

―――. Interview with Christopher Bigsby. *The Radical Imagination and the Liberal Tradition: Interviews with English and American Novelists*. Ed. Heide Ziegler and Christopher Bigsby. London: Junction Books, 1982. 60–78.

―――. "An Interview with Malcolm Bradbury." With Richard Todd. *Dutch Quarterly Review of Anglo-American Letters* 11 (1982): 183–196.

―――. "The Language Novelists Use." Rev. of *Language of Fiction*. *Kenyon Review* 29 (1967): 122–136.

―――. "Lionel Trilling: End of the Journey." *New Statesman* 14 Nov. 1975: 619.

―――. *The Modern American Novel*. New York: Oxford UP, 1983.

―――. "Modernism/Postmodernism." *Innovation/Renovation: New Perspectives on the Humanities*. Ed. Ihab Hassan and Sally Hassan. Madison: U of Wisconsin P, 1983. 311–327.

―――. *No, Not Bloomsbury*. London: Deutsch, 1987.

―――. "One Man's America." *Author! Author! A Selection from "The Author," the Journal of the Society of Authors since 1890*. Ed. Richard Findlater. London: Faber and Faber, 1984.

————. *Possibilities: Essays on the State of the Novel.* New York: Oxford UP, 1973.

————. "Putting in the Person: Character and Abstraction in Current Writing and Painting." Bradbury and Palmer 181–208. Rpt. in *No, Not Bloomsbury* in revised form, under its original title, "A Dog Engulfed by Sand."

————. *Rates of Exchange.* New York: Knopf, 1983.

————. Rev. of *Mulligan Stew*, by Gilbert Sorrentino. *New York Times Book Review* 26 Aug. 1979: 9, 18.

————. Rev. of *The Stories of John Cheever*, by John Cheever. *New Statesman* 29 June 1979: 956–957.

————. Rev. of *Slow Homecoming*, by Peter Handke. *New York Times Book Review* 4 Aug. 1985: 11.

————. *Saul Bellow.* London: Methuen, 1982.

————. "Second Countries: The Expatriate Tradition in American Writing." *Yearbook of English Studies* 8 (1978): 15–39.

————. *The Social Context of Modern English Literature.* New York: Schocken, 1971.

————. "The State of Criticism Today." *Contemporary Criticism.* Ed. Malcolm Bradbury and David Palmer. London: Arnold, 1970. 11–38.

————. *Stepping Westward.* 1965. London: Secker & Warburg, 1983. With an "Introduction" by the author.

————. *What Is a Novel?* London: Arnold, 1969.

————. *Who Do You Think You Are?: Stories and Parodies.* Rev. ed. London: Arena, 1984. A 2nd revised edition was published in 1987.

Bradbury, Malcolm, ed. *Forster: A Collection of Critical Essays.* Englewood Cliffs: Prentice-Hall, 1966.

————. ed. *The Novel Today: Contemporary Writers on Modern Fiction.* London: Fontana, 1977.

Bradbury, Malcolm, and James McFarlane, eds. *Modernism: 1890–1930.* Hammondsworth: Penguin, 1976.

Bradbury, Malcolm, and David Palmer, eds. *The Contemporary English Novel.* New York: Holmes & Meier, 1979.

Bradbury, Malcolm, and Allan Rodway. *Two Poets.* Nottingham: Byron P, 1966.

Bradbury, Malcolm, and Howard Temperley, eds. *Introduction to American Studies.* London: Longman, 1981.

Burden, Robert. "The Novel Interrogates Itself." *Bradbury and Palmer* 133–155.

Burton, Robert S. "A Plurality of Voices: Malcolm Bradbury's *Rates of Exchange.*" *Critique* 28 (1987): 101–106.

Byatt, A. S. "People in Paper Houses: Attitudes to 'Realism' and 'Experiment' in English Postwar Fiction." Bradbury and Palmer 19–42.

Church, Michael. Rev. of *The History Man. Times Education Supplement* 25 Dec. 1977: 21.

Clark, Katerina, and Michael Holquist. *Mikhail Bakhtin.* Cambridge: Belknap-Harvard UP, 1984.

Culler, Jonathan. *The Pursuit of Signs: Semiotics, Literature, and Deconstruction.* Ithaca: Cornell UP, 1981.

Cunningham, Valentine. Rev. of *The History Man. New Statesman* 7 Nov. 1974: 528.

D'haen, Theo. "Fowles, Lodge and the 'Problematical Novel.' " *Dutch Quarterly Review of Anglo-American Letters* 10 (1980): 160–175.

Dickens, Charles. *Martin Chuzzlewit.* The Works of Charles Dickens. New York: Books, n.d.

Eco, Umberto. *The Role of the Reader: Explorations in the Semiotics of Texts.* Bloomington: Indiana UP, 1979.

———. *Semiotics and the Philosophy of Language.* Bloomington: Indiana UP, 1984.

Evans, Walter. "The English Short Story in the Seventies." *The English Short Story 1945–1980: A Critical History.* Ed. Dennis Vannatta. Boston: Twayne, 1985. 143-45.

Fletcher, John. "Iris Murdoch." Halio, *British Novelists* 546–561.

Friedman, Melvin J. "Malcolm Bradbury." Halio, *British Novelists* 108–116.

Gass, William. *Fiction & the Figures of Life.* Boston: Nonpareil Books, 1971.

Genette, Gerard. *Narrative Discourse: An Essay in Method.* Trans. Jane E. Lewin. Ithaca: Cornell Up, 1980.

Gindin, James. "Bradbury, Malcolm (Stanley)." Vinson, James, ed. *Contemporary Novelists.* 3rd ed. New York: St. Martin's P, 1982. 90–92.

———. "Taking Risks." *Granta* 3 (1980): 155–60.

Green, Martin. "Transatlantic Communications: Malcolm Bradbury's *Stepping Westward* (1966)." *Old Lines, New Forces: Essays on the Contemporary British Novel, 1960–1970.* Ed. Robert K. Morris. Rutherford: Farleigh Dickinson UP, 1976. 53–66.

Haffenden, John. *Novelists in Interview.* London: Methuen, 1985.

Halio, Jay L. "Rev. of *The History Man. Southern Review* 15 (1979): 706–707.

Halio, Jay L., ed. *British Novelists Since 1960*. Dictionary of Literary Biography 14. Detroit: Gale, 1983.

Hayman, Ronald. *The Novel Today 1967–1975*. Burnt Mill: Longman Group [1976].

Holquist, Michael. "Introduction." Bakhtin, *The Dialogic Imagination* xv–xxxiv.

Honan, Park. "David Lodge and the Cinematic Novel in England." *Novel* 5 (1972): 167–173.

Honan, Park, ed. "Realism, Reality and the Novel: A Symposium." *Novel* 2 (1969): 197–211.

Jackson, Dennis. "David Lodge." Halio, *British Novelists* 469–481.

Joyce, James. *Finnegans Wake*. 1939. New York: Penguin, 1978.

———. *A Portrait of the Artist as a Young Man*. 1916. New York: Viking, 1969.

Kakutani, Michiko. "Letter from London: Novelists Are News Again." *New York Times Book Review* 14 Aug. 1983: 3, 22–23.

Kermode, Frank. *The Sense of an Ending: Studies in the Theory of Fiction*. New York: Oxford UP, 1966.

Kristeva, Julia. *Desire in Language: A Semiotic Approach to Literature and Art*. Trans. Thomas Gora, et al. New York: Columbia UP, 1980.

Leitch, Vincent B. *Deconstructive Criticism: An Advanced Introduction*. New York: Columbia UP, 1983.

Lodge, David. *The British Museum Is Falling Down*. 1965. London: Secker & Warburg, 1981. With an "Introduction" by the author.

———. *Changing Places*. 1975. New York: Penguin, 1979.

———. "David Lodge Interviewed." With Bernard Bergonzi. *Month* Feb. 1970: 108–116.

———. *Evelyn Waugh*. New York: Columbia UP, 1971.

———. *Ginger, You're Barmy*. 3rd ed. London: Secker & Warburg, 1982. With an "Introduction" by the author. Originally published in 1962.

———. *How Far Can You Go?* London: Secker & Warburg, 1980.

———. *Language of Fiction*. 2nd ed. London: Routledge & Kegan Paul, 1984. Originally published in 1966.

———. "Leading Three Lives." Interview with Michael Billington. *New York Times Book Review* 17 Mar. 1985: 7.

———. "Literary Theory in the University: A Survey." *New Literary History* 14 (1983): 435.

———. "Mimesis and Diegesis in Modern Fiction." *Contemporary Approaches to Narrative*. Ed. Anthony Mortimer. Tubingen: Narr, 1984. 85–108.

216
Works Cited

———. *The Modes of Modern Writing: Metaphor, Metonymy, and the Typology of Modern Literature*. London: Arnold, 1977.

———. *The Novelist at the Crossroads and Other Essays on Fiction and Criticism*. London: Routledge & Kegan Paul, 1971.

———. *Out of the Shelter*. 2nd ed. London: Secker & Warburg, 1985. With an "Introduction" by the author. Originally published in 1970.

———. *The Picturegoers*. London: Macgibbon & Gee, 1960.

———. Rev. of *Roger's Version*, by John Updike. *New York Times Book Review* 31 Aug. 1986: 1, 19.

———. *Small World: An Academic Romance*. London: Secker & Warburg, 1984.

———. *Working with Structuralism: Essays and Reviews on Nineteenth- and Twentieth-Century Literature*. London: Routledge & Kegan Paul, 1981.

———. *Write On: Occasional Essays '65–'85*. London: Secker & Warburg, 1986.

Lodge, David, ed. *20th Century Literary Criticism: A Reader*. London: Longman, 1971.

McCaffery, Larry, ed. *Postmodern Fiction: A Bio-Bibliographical Guide*. New York: Greenwood, 1986.

McEwan, Neil. *The Survival of the Novel: British Fiction in the Later Twentieth Century*. Totowa: Barnes & Noble, 1981.

Malamud, Bernard. *A New Life*. 1961. New York: Pocket Books, 1973.

Martin, Jay. *Harvests of Change: American Literature 1865–1914*. Englewood Cliffs: Prentice-Hall, 1967.

Morgan, Edwin. Rev. of *Stepping Westward*. *New Statesman* 6 Aug. 1965: 191–92.

Morrison, Blake. Rev. of *Rates of Exchange*. *Times Literary Supplement* 8 Apr. 1983: 345.

New Yorker 28 Apr. 1986: 4.

Percy, Walker. *Conversations with Walker Percy*. Ed. Lewis A. Lawson and Victor A. Kramer. Jackson: UP of Mississippi, 1986.

Rabate, Jean-Michel. "La 'Fin du Roman' et Les Fins des Romans." *Etudes Anglaises* 36 (1983): 197–212.

Rev. of *Souls and Bodies* [American title of *How Far Can You Go?*]. *Publishers Weekly* 20 Nov. 1981: 44.

Scholes, Robert. *Structuralism in Literature: An Introduction*. New Haven: Yale UP, 1974.

Steiner, George. "Party Lines." Rev. of *The History Man*. *New Yorker* 3 May 1976: 130–132.

Stevenson, Randall. *The British Novel Since the Thirties: An Introduction.* London: Batsford, 1976.

Sullivan, Jack. Rev. of *Souls and Bodies* [American title of *How Far Can You Go?*]. *Washington Post Book World* 7 Feb. 1982: 4.

Theroux, Paul. Rev. of *Souls and Bodies* [American title of *How Far Can You Go?*]. *New York Times Book Review* 31 Jan. 1982: 3, 23.

Thiher, Allen. *Words in Reflection: Modern Language Theory and Postmodern Fiction.* Chicago: U of Chicago P, 1984.

Todd, Richard. "Malcolm Bradbury's *The History Man*: The Novelist as Reluctant Impresario." *Dutch Quarterly Review of Anglo-American Letters* 11 (1981): 162–182.

Todorov, Tzvetan. *Mikhail Bakhtin: The Dialogical Principle.* Trans. Wlad Godzick. Minneapolis: U of Minnesota P, 1984.

Tucker, Martin. Rev. of *Eating People Is Wrong. New Republic* 2 May 1960: 19–20.

Vinson, James, ed. *Contemporary Novelists.* 3rd ed. New York: St. Martin's P, 1982.

Waugh, Patricia. *Metafiction: The Theory and Practice of Self-Conscious Fiction.* London: Methuen, 1984.

Widdowson, Peter. "The Anti-History Men: Malcolm Bradbury and David Lodge." *Critical Quarterly* 26.4 (1984): 5–32.

Wilson, A. N. Rev. of *Ginger, You're Barmy. Spectator* 31 July 1982: 23–24.

Index